The Repercussions

The Repercussions

Catherine Hall

W F HOWES LTD

This large print edition published in 2015 by
W F Howes Ltd
Unit 4, Rearsby Business Park, Gaddesby Lane,
Rearsby, Leicester LE7 4YH

1 3 5 7 9 10 8 6 4 2

First published in the United Kingdom in 2014
by Alma Books Limited

A CIP catalogue record for this book is available
from the British Library

ISBN 978 1 47128 183 9

Typeset by Palimpsest Book Production Limited,
Falkirk, Stirlingshire

Printed and bound in Great Britain
by TJ International Ltd, Padstow, Cornwall

MIX
Paper from
responsible sources
FSC
www.fsc.org   FSC® C013056

For Sandra D.,
with love

One finds it in the midst of all this as hard to apply one's words as to endure one's thoughts. The war has used up words; they have weakened, they have deteriorated.

HENRY JAMES

If off the war you hope to live,
Take what you can. You'll also give.

BERTOLT BRECHT

CHAPTER 1

Susie, I think I'm in trouble.

I'm not in Kabul any more. I'm not in London either. I'm in Brighton.

Trouble or not, there's a comfort to being at the very end of England, on the coast, right where ground meets sea. I could find my exact location on a map in a second, and after all those times of having no idea where I was, stuck somewhere dark and lost and dangerous, that's a real relief.

I'm sitting in one of those old-fashioned wicker chairs – Lloyd Loom, I think they're called – on a balcony. Well, not quite a balcony: one of those covered-in terraces you get in seaside towns, like a greenhouse stuck to the wall, one floor up. A *gulkhana*, they'd call it in Afghanistan, a flower room for ladies to sit in and catch the winter sun, although that's a grand word for such a small space, just enough for a chair, and a little glass-topped table, and plants, lots of them, all over the place, hanging from the ceiling, in pots on every surface, climbing up the window frames. I could almost imagine I was in a jungle, although after everything that's happened it's probably better I don't.

I can see the mad, glittery mess of the pier, lighting up the water, bouncing its reflection off jet-black sea.

Wait, I'm going to open the window, I want to smell sea air, even though it's freezing cold outside. There, it's flooding in, as if the tide's pushing it into the flat. I can hear the waves breaking, steady and soothing, calm.

I need a bit of soothing. I feel strange tonight, like I always do when I get back, caught between different worlds. This morning, high up in the mountains, I heard the call to prayer as I packed my bags. Now it's banging music and shouts from kids out on the town.

My bags are in the corner, where I dumped them when I got here. I haven't unpacked yet. It used to drive you crazy – didn't it? – the way I'd come back home and leave my stuff in the corner for weeks, just pulling things out as I needed them. Presents too, though, always, for you – I was good at those, at least.

I know there's not much point in remembering. I know we can't go back to what we were. But I wish I could crawl into bed and put my arms around you and know that I was home.

I'm not at home, though, wherever that might be. Do you remember Edith, my ancient, fabulous great-aunt? This is her flat, right on the Brighton seafront. Or rather, it used to be – now it's mine. She left it to me when she died, two weeks ago today. I hadn't known she had cancer, hadn't noticed anything wrong the last time I saw her, back in March. I'm still kicking myself for that. When the phone call came, I was still in Afghanistan. I couldn't even make it back for the funeral – too much was going on. Bad stuff, this time, Suze, really bad, which meant I couldn't leave.

I loved Edith. She gave me my first camera, when I was eight, to take pictures of the animals at London Zoo. She'd tell me stories about the elephants she'd seen in India as a girl, all dressed up in ceremonial colours, with paintings on their foreheads and howdahs on their backs. I'd lick my ice cream slowly, fascinated, watching her bracelets jingle as she talked.

It's strange to be in the flat without her. It suited her so well. Each piece of Meissen china, the Persian rug on the floor, the jade vase on the sandalwood table – each of them has a story, and there, in the middle of them all, perched in her armchair, was always Edith, ready to tell me those stories over coffee served in tiny espresso cups she'd bought in Rome in 1968, from a shop just off the Via Condotti.

She smoked two cigarettes a day, one after lunch and one with her first whisky of the evening, which she called her *chota peg*, in honour of her years in India. I'm doing the same now, in honour of her. I've poured myself some duty-free Johnnie Walker and lit up a Marlboro.

To Edith: may she be as extraordinary in the next life as she was in this.

The booze and fags aren't working like they normally do. My mind's churning, turning things over. Usually I switch on the radio when I get somewhere new, to get a feel for what's happening. Edith's old wireless is on the sideboard, marked with stickers for Radio 4 and the World Service, but I'm leaving it off. I don't want to know what's going on in the world, at least not for now.

There's always an element of having to sort my head out when I get back from a job, but this feels different. Afghanistan isn't the worst place I've been to . . . no, forget that – comparing wars is pointless. What I mean is, the violence wasn't there in front of me. War in Sierra Leone or the Congo is manic; in Afghanistan it's more like a chronic depression. I wasn't dodging snipers or facing stoned kids with wild eyes holding AK-47s. There weren't piles of bodies rotting under the sun or bombs going off all through the night. But under the surface there was a sense of things simmering, a dirty, dangerous soup that could boil over at any point and create a scalding mess.

It did boil over. It did create a mess, one that's not cleared up. I can't stop thinking about it. I can't get it out of my head.

I've been looking for distractions, poking about, trying to stop myself from thinking about it all.

There's an old wooden box on one of the book-shelves, rough-looking, out of place among the ornate china and fine silver. I'm intrigued. I don't remember it from before. Perhaps Edith left it out for me on purpose.

I'm going to open it, Suze. Let's see what's inside.

There. Done. It smells musty, dry, of old paper and ink.

A manila envelope has fallen out, stuffed with photographs, faded black and white. I'm laying them out on the hearthrug.

A group portrait: formal, men standing in front of an Indian palace, all filigree and carved columns, domes and minarets. The men are in uniforms and turbans, their long beards neatly trimmed. They stare out at the camera with fixed expressions. They have injuries: legs in plaster, arms in slings. Some have no legs or arms at all, just bandaged stumps.

A hospital ward: long rows of tightly tucked beds, each with a soldier sitting up in it, dressed in white pyjamas and a turban to match the sheets.

An operating theatre: a gurney in the centre under a ceiling light, a washstand, instruments laid out neatly, bottles of disinfectant on a side table. Seven staff, dressed in surgical scrubs. All white, except for one who looks as if he's Indian, like the patients. All male, apart from one woman: a nurse.

At the bottom of this one is a description:

Pavilion Hospital, Brighton 1915.

There's something else in the box – a small book, leather-bound, its pages filled with cramped black writing.

There's a little prickle of excitement I always get when I come across a story. I'm feeling it now.

CHAPTER 2

1st December 1914

It is with great pleasure that I begin this diary, which is to be my record of this war. I do not pretend it to be anything more than that: I speak only for myself, to put down in writing my impressions and experiences so that in years to come I can look back and remember.

It is no accident that I am starting now: at last, I have good reason to write. Tomorrow I am to take up a position at the Royal Pavilion. One might ask why nurses should be needed at a destination for day-trippers. The answer is that it is no longer that: the Pavilion has become a hospital.

I found out from Hugo; his scout troop helped last week to clear things out so it could fit in the beds. He came home full of news. Apparently it was the King himself who told the Mayor to turn it into a military hospital. For me the thrilling thing is this: the patients will be Indian – soldiers who've been fighting for us at the Front.

7

This was the announcement in the *Gazette*, which I cut out to keep:

> Valiant soldiers of our great Indian dependency, after fighting so nobly for their King-Emperor, are now to be cared for in a Royal Palace in the greatest of British watering places. It is like a chapter out of a wonderful romance. It will appeal to the world as a thing almost incredible. It will give the Brighton Pavilion a name it has never had before. Generations of Brightonians yet unborn will marvel in reading of these days.

Of course, I thought of Robert immediately. If I am to marry a man whose whole life is the Indian Army, what better way to understand it than to nurse its soldiers? Perhaps some of them will even be from his regiment, which came here all the way from Bombay just last month. And so, as soon as I heard the news, I rushed down to Matron and asked if my name could be put forward. She was somewhat hesitant at first, and said that there'd been a terrible commotion about it all, but eventually, after some persuasion, she said that, if Mamma and Papa agreed, she would recommend me for a position. When I asked, Mamma looked anxious, and said she hoped the patients wouldn't be in too awful a state, and Papa grunted and shuffled his newspaper, and said he was proud of me for following in his footsteps.

I'm not, of course, since he is a surgeon and I am just a nurse, but I was glad all the same.

I've decided not to tell Robert yet. I'm going to wait until his next leave. We never seem to be able to say what we really mean in our letters, and he's not much of a writer, so I feel silly sending pages and pages. I will wait until he comes back, when I'll be settled at the Pavilion, and can show him what I'm doing, instead of trying to explain it in words.

CHAPTER 3

What were they doing here, those soldiers, so far away from home, fighting in a war that had nothing to do with them? I guess that's not so unusual. Poor men are always available for hire – I've seen enough ten-dollar Taliban to know that. I wonder what they thought about being put in a king's palace to recuperate. How strange it must have seemed to them, although perhaps no stranger than the trenches at the Front.

I'm feeling strange too, can't stop thinking about Kabul. This morning I decided to go for a walk to try to clear my head. I pulled on a pair of old jeans and my big boots, wrapped up warm in a scarf and gloves and took myself off to the beach. The cold wind, fresh and salty, hit me like a slap. I crunched over the pebbles, glad of the lack of sand, glad of many things, of not needing to ask permission to be there, of not being stared at by curious eyes, of being able to walk without thinking and not be scared of being blown up.

I smoked as I walked, like always, thinking of you. Do you remember how I used to say it wasn't an addiction, that in the places I work it's practically a requirement? Cigarettes are bribes when you want to pass a checkpoint. When the snipers have stopped and you're planning your next move, a fag fills the pause. Soldiers all want something to do while they wait for the next bit of action. For the five minutes that you're smoking together you're almost one of them.

You weren't having any of it. You said I was a filthy addict who didn't want to give up, and it was all excuses, and they would kill me in the end. You were right of course, but it was hard to care. You don't think much about your long-term future in a war zone.

I wasn't thinking of my future on the beach, either. I was thinking of the past, of when you took me to Madrid to see Goya at the Prado because – you said – he knew more about war than any other painter. We walked along cool corridors, a soft May breeze coming through the open windows. We'd spent the morning in bed between crisp sheets, drinking coffee and feeding each other oranges. I could smell the juice of them still on your skin.

You took me first to see *The Third of May 1808*. I stood and looked at the enormous canvas, a firing squad focused on a man, brilliantly lit. He faced it on his knees, his hands raised like Christ on the cross. At his feet a pile of corpses, to his side a group of other captives, panicking, knowing what was going to come next. The look on their faces was one I recognized too well.

11

'If I'd photographed that,' I said, 'I'd have had to question being so close, in case they were acting up for the cameras.'

You said nothing, just nodded, and took me to his Black Paintings, the ones he painted straight onto the walls of his house just after the Napoleonic Wars, when he was pretty much a recluse. He was scared of going insane, and when I saw those fourteen pictures, the people eating their children, beating each other with cudgels, a decapitation, a witches' Sabbath, all in tones of black and sludgy brown, I saw why.

'Don't go crazy like that,' you whispered in my ear.

'No,' I said. 'I won't.'

Standing at the water's edge, thinking, smoking, I looked back up to the seafront. Kabul's brown, a thousand shades of desert dust. On my first trip there, I'd lie in bed, unable to sleep, listening to the crack and shatter of the air strikes, and I'd play our game in which we'd compete to think of all the words we knew for a colour.

Chocolate, khaki, mouse. Chestnut, hazel, beige. Ochre, copper, bronze.

Brighton's white (*chalk, cheese*), from the foam of the waves to the dirty seagulls and the peeling Regency townhouses – even, today, the sky. I walked right along the beach, all the way to the part reserved for nudists. An old man was sitting in a deckchair, naked except for a pair of flip-flops, shielded by a stripy windbreak flapping in the breeze. He caught my eye as I passed.

'Lovely day for it,' he said.

And suddenly it was a lovely day. I loved the man and his happy nakedness. When I got back to the flat, I turned on the gas fire full blast and stripped off all my clothes. I got out Elizabeth's diary, put on my sunglasses and sat on the chair in the *gulkhana* with my feet up on a Moroccan-leather pouffe, reading and grinning to myself and feeling the winter sun on my body, just because I could.

Perhaps it'll be all right, Suze. Perhaps I won't go crazy, like I promised you back in Madrid. Perhaps I'll be all right too.

CHAPTER 4

ELIZABETH WILLOUGHBY'S DIARY

5th December 1914

Our first patients are safely installed.
It looks very different to when I gave a nursing demonstration here just weeks ago. All the beautiful Persian carpets have been taken up and replaced with rather drab khaki linoleum. They have put boards up in the banqueting and music rooms to protect the wallpaper, and taken down the curtains. It's much more practical, I suppose, but I do miss the fantastical dragons and those life-sized Chinese figures, who looked as if they were going for a moonlit walk across the walls.

The kitchen has become an operating theatre. Not, it seems, that I'll have much to do with that. When we reported for duty, Colonel MacLeod, our commanding officer, said that all medical treatment is to be carried out by British doctors and surgeons from the Indian Medical Service, assisted by some Indian doctors and a few Indian medical students who were studying here when the war began.

He didn't mention the Queen's Nurses. After a while, I could contain myself no longer and put up my hand to ask. The Colonel frowned, and said that it had been decided that no nursing was to be carried out by Englishwomen. I waited for him to explain why not, but he simply nodded, as if that settled it. I was not bold enough to ask again, but while he went on speaking of hospital protocol I couldn't stop thinking about it, and so afterwards I followed him to his office.

I told him that I was terribly sorry, but that I didn't understand what he had said, since nursing was, after all, what we have been trained to do. He looked at me from under his great white eyebrows and said that it would be improper. When I asked why, he harrumphed a bit, and then said that I must understand that India is one of our colonies and therefore its subjects are under our command.

I said I didn't know how that changed things, at which point he harrumphed again and said that in India, Englishwomen never nursed the native population, because it wouldn't do to be so 'intimately involved', and so the Queen's Nurses would act in a supervisory capacity only, working with the orderlies to 'maintain the highest standards'.

He then said very firmly that if I was not happy with this state of affairs he would rather I told him now before the patients arrived.

'I . . . no, I am happy,' I said.

It wasn't true of course. I left quickly, feeling rather cross. It really is a bit of a blow. I cannot see what would be so improper about it: as Papa always says, we are all the same on an operating table. If it weren't for Robert, I would be tempted to go off to one of the other hospitals, where I could be properly useful, but I do so want to learn about his world, and so I have decided to bite my lip and make the best of it.

This morning, I went up to the station to collect our patients from the hospital train. It was a dreary day, with rain streaming down since dawn, the streets all churned up with mud, and I felt sorry that this would be their first impression of the place, although I suppose for those poor men anything would be better than where they have just come from.

A crowd of well-wishers huddled under umbrellas outside the station entrance. When the first stretcher-bearers emerged there was a moment of silence, unplanned but observed by everyone, a mark of respect for the soldiers' bravery and for what they have suffered. Then came cheers and applause, which I was pleased about, because they are such a long way from home, and it is so terribly important to make them feel welcome.

The men were in an awful state. More than half of them had to be carried on stretchers, the others limping along on crutches, or staggering with their arms around their comrades. They looked exhausted, as if they were at the end of a very long journey, which of course was the case: an interminable voyage across the Indian Ocean, then up to fight in the trenches in northern France; out again, once wounded, to the field hospitals, and then put on a train and then a boat to cross the Channel, then another train to Brighton, right at the end of the line.

It was an odd sight; they looked so very – well – foreign. Before today, the only Indian I had ever seen was Mowgli in the picture book I had as a girl, but here were a good two dozen of them, slowly making their way along the windswept platform. The first thing I noticed were lots of rather grand moustaches, and beards, long and black, and dark eyes under neatly wound turbans. Some of the men were very tall, and elegant in the way that they held themselves, despite their injuries; others were small, without moustaches or beards, and looked awfully young.

We took them back in motor ambulances to the Pavilion, where the grandeur of their surroundings made them seem all the more ragged. I can now say in all truthfulness that I have seen the famous mud of the Western Front: pale, sticky clots that clung to their uniforms and boots, which were hanging off them in tatters. They smelt of old sweat and damp, their fingers filthy, nails encrusted and long. Seeing them scratch, I suspected lice. The sweepers had been heating water since dawn for their baths, and I can only imagine the relief they must have felt when they got into them. Their uniforms were taken to the back of the building and burnt.

After that there was a flurry of dressings and making them as comfortable as we could, then we got them into bed, at which point a hush fell over the Pavilion, as if all of us, patients and staff, were taking a moment to rest.

I stood in the music room, staring up at its extraordinary chandeliers that look like enormous, upturned flowers, with painted Chinese figures in each pane of glass. They glitter and sparkle quite magically, hanging from a ceiling made of thousands of leaves of gold. I should think it will be rather wonderful for the patients to lie in bed and look up at them.

One of the Indian doctors had seen me looking. 'They're lotuses,' he said.

'Really?' I said.

'Yes, they're very important to us.'

'Us?'

He gave a little cough. 'Indians.'

'Ah.'

'They represent purity and honour.'

'Lovely,' I said. 'Do you—'

Just then, one of the men let out a terrible moan, and I ran to him. When I looked up again, the doctor had gone.

★　★　★

I couldn't bear it if Robert ended up like those men. On my way home, I went to the seafront and stood at the railings, looking out over the Channel towards France, towards him, less than a hundred miles away. A strong wind was blowing straight off the sea, and I leant into it, breathing in the salty damp. Suddenly it hit me, carried on the wind: a far-off rumble, followed by an explosion, and I realized that I was hearing the guns of the battleground. I listened again to the terrible, crunching sound and shuddered, because I knew that any of those explosions could be the one that put an end to his life.

CHAPTER 5

I'm feeling slightly ridiculous, Suze. Seems like I spoke too soon about being all right. This morning was glorious, so clear I could almost see France from my window. People were smiling as they walked along the seafront; kids played on the miniature-golf course, dogs chased sticks on the beach, a shoal of canoeists bobbed about on the waves. Even the birds were having a good time, circling high in the sky, cawing loudly as if they were joining in. I knew I had to go out – there was nothing left of the food I grabbed from the shop at the airport and I was hungry, properly hungry for the first time in weeks. All I had to do was put on my coat and walk out of the door, but I couldn't.

And you know why not? Because I was scared.

I know it doesn't make sense – Josephine Sinclair, award-winning war photographer, unable to leave the house? I've spent the last fifteen years going to the worst places on earth, places where to be afraid is to stay alive, where fear is the only reaction that makes sense. When I'm there, I can take it. I've run past snipers, bent double, trying not to get hit. I've slept in trenches next to soldiers not knowing if we'll make it through the night. I've walked along roads stuffed with mines, step after cautious step, praying to God or whatever higher power might be out there that I don't disturb one. Each time I deal with the fear, manage it so I can function. But today – a perfectly lovely day in Brighton – I couldn't do it.

I tried to be logical, to weigh up the risks, go through scenarios, reassure myself that they weren't going to happen, to remember what I'd learnt on all those courses the bureau sent me on – Security Training, Reporting in Hostile Areas, Captive Situations. The problem was that they were all about reacting to real life, when there was truly something to be scared of. No one ever told me what to do when it's all in your head.

It took me an hour to talk myself down, to get myself out, and when I closed the door behind me, I was still on hyper-alert, my senses pricked. I stayed close to the houses, moving slowly, looking as far ahead as I could, staying prepared, assessing the risks. There weren't any, of course. Brighton was going about its business, seagulls shrieking, cars revving, people walking along the pavements. Dogs pulled on their leads, sniffing round lamp-posts, straining to get into well-kept gardens in the middle of squares. It's nice, this part of Brighton, Kemptown, away from the city centre, towards the marina. Within five minutes I'd passed a little bookshop, a couple of pubs, a fancy bakery and a posh-looking deli.

St James's Street was shabbier, lined with cut-price off-licences, charity shops, a bookmaker's, a place to cash pay-day cheques. The narrow streets that led down to the seafront were lined with old-fashioned B&Bs – signs saying 'Rooms Available' propped up in windows lined with net curtains. It was eleven in the morning, check-out time, and guests were stumbling out, blinking in the sunshine.

The supermarket was at the end of St James's. I'd made a mental note of its location when I first arrived in the taxi. Force of habit, Suze, mapping new terrain.

In a war zone, food's fuel, a functional thing. When you're on the front line, it's usually cold and portable, something you can stash in a pocket to bring out when you need it. Muesli bars, Ready-to-Eat Meals, bits of processed cheese. It matters a lot and not at all – when there are food shortages you'll take what you can get, but a nugget of something good is prized beyond anything else: a tiny piece of chocolate found in the corner of a rucksack pocket, the bag of nuts you'd forgotten you bought at Heathrow.

Do you remember how I'd always go to the supermarket when I got back? I'd wake early, too wired to sleep, so we'd get up and have breakfast, then you'd go to your studio and I'd take myself off to look at the reassuring stacks of fruit and vegetables. Bright packets, all within their sell-by dates, tempting snacks. The best thing of all would be that I could get my hands on it without any sort of human contact, just push my trolley around and put in the food, with no haggling, no conversation apart from saying hi to the person at the till. I know it's cool these days to go to small shops, farmer's markets, to know your shopkeeper by name, but when I'm back from a trip all I want is anonymity, no connections.

I went in and got a basket, and started to walk around, picking up apples, some pears, a punnet of grapes, a cucumber, watercress. I wanted fresh things, salad that I could eat without wondering if I'd get ill from it. As I lingered near the cheese counter, trying to decide between some Brie and a nice-looking Wensleydale, I began to feel better. I'd get myself a lovely dinner, I thought, something healthy washed down with water instead of whisky.

Pasta, tomatoes, mozzarella; a little basil plant to put in the *gulkhana*. I hummed to myself as I put them in the basket, sniffed at the smell of baking bread. I added a chocolate tart, took a bottle of orange juice from the shelf.

It was all going well until I caught sight of the meat counter, with its slabs of flesh lying bloody and cold, marbled beef, ribs sticking out of a rack of lamb. Slick liver, bulging kidneys, eviscerated organs. I stopped humming, my breath coming out instead in little pants.

Suddenly there were too many people in the shop, too much colour on the shelves, too much light, too much of everything. An announcement came over the tannoy, something about a spillage in Aisle 4, and I dropped my basket, putting my hands over my ears, remembering men shouting into loudspeakers, giving orders, making threats.

Leaving my basket, I ran out of the door, looking for somewhere to hide. The street was busy with people coming out of their offices for lunch. I leant against the wall next to the shop, my heart hammering, trying to hold myself up, knowing I was about to be sick.

I told myself to calm down, that nothing bad was going to happen, that I was on a normal street in a normal English town. I tried to breathe slowly, counting up to ten as I exhaled.

A gang of girls came out of a side street, wearing headbands with horns, gauzy fairy wings, tight T-shirts with *Caz's Last Fling* printed on the back. Caz was all in pink with an L-plate on her chest. They looked like a flock of drunken butterflies, their wings flapping in the breeze, and I turned away, panicked, not wanting to attract their attention.

One of them noticed me anyway. 'Are you OK?' she asked, and I nodded, just wanting her to move away.

'Well, if you're sure,' she said.

As they passed, I began to retch. I'm not usually sick in public, not any more. I've trained myself not to give in to it, no matter what I see. I've learnt how to hold my camera up in front of me and just take the photograph, how to hold it all in until I'm by myself, in my hotel room, or a bathroom, anywhere with a lock on the door. Humiliated, I made my way back along St James's, slowly, my belly empty and aching. The panic had gone now, replaced with a dull ache in my head. I went back to the posh deli near the flat and bought bread and soup, a pint of milk, some coffee. Back inside, when I'd closed the door, I stood for a moment listening to the silence, glad to be alone.

CHAPTER 6

ELIZABETH WILLOUGHBY'S DIARY

15th December 1914

Goodness, I'm exhausted. I find myself almost falling asleep as I write this in bed, propped up against my pillows, balancing my diary on my knees.

The next batch (what a horrid word to describe human beings, as if they were a postal delivery, but I am too tired to think of another one) of patients has arrived, more than three hundred of them, even more battered than the ones before. Some of them were wearing tropical uniforms: to think it, in December! Others did not even have boots, their feet so badly swollen that they wore sandals fashioned out of a simple sole and strips of linen. We wrapped them immediately in blankets and got them to the Pavilion as fast as we could.

Another crowd turned out to meet them at the station, on yet another drab afternoon. The Indians really do seem to have captured people's imaginations. The Brighton ladies in particular find them captivating. Every day they wait in crowds at the openings to the Pavilion grounds, trying to catch a glimpse of the 'Dusky Warriors', as the *Gazette* has named them. I say ladies, but I don't think that's how Colonel MacLeod thinks of them. Today he gave orders that all openings should be boarded up and wooden screens put around the railings so that no one could see in. Some of them climbed up anyway and perched on top of the fence, peering in, as if the patients were exotic creatures at the zoo.

The men seem not to mind terribly much. They leave the Pavilion only to pray. The Sikhs go to their temple, which is a tent in the grounds, and the Mohammedans go to theirs, outside the Dome, next door. Five times a day, those of them who are capable go to the tent and repeat their special rituals. It must be terribly cold, but out they go, and never complain a bit.

I like to listen to the Mohammedan chants, which I find rather beautiful. This morning, the doctor from the other day, the one who told me about the lotuses, approached as I was standing outside the entrance to their tent.

'What are they saying?' I asked.

'*Allahu-akbar*. It means God is Great.'

'Aren't you going to join in?'

'I'm Hindu.'

Feeling rather embarrassed, I apologized. I always seem to get these things wrong. It is so difficult to know who is who, and I am aware that it is so terribly important. Everything here is divided, from the wards for patients from different tribes or castes, to the kitchens – all nine of them – the lavatories, the bathrooms, even the cutlery and the plumbing system and the water taps! It really is awfully complicated and difficult to remember, no matter how many times one is told.

A flicker of a smile passed over his lips, and I wondered if he thought me ignorant.

'Everyone's gone to an enormous effort,' I said, feeling rather defensive. 'To get it right, I mean. Not to offend anyone.'

'Indeed.'

'My name is Nurse Willoughby, by the way,' I said in a rush. 'Elizabeth Willoughby.'

'And I am Hari Mitra. Almost a doctor, but not quite.'

The patients' afflictions are many and varied, some caused by gunshots and shells, others simply by being stuck for so long in winter trenches. There is a horrible condition called 'trench foot', brought on by standing in cold water and mud, which begins as chilblains, then the feet pucker like after a long bath, the skin starts to rot and feeling is lost in the toes. Eventually the entire foot goes numb and it is impossible to walk. Many of our patients had amputations before they came to us, losing a foot or even the lower leg, right up to the knee.

There are still plenty of operations to be done. This afternoon it was the turn of a man called Mohan Ram, who had terrible wounds to his abdomen and chest. The same piece of shell passed through them both, perforating his intestines. The French surgeons had managed to save his life, but now the wound was infected. A terrible smell seeped through his bandages, the stink of dead and rotting flesh.

Major Williams, our officer in charge, stood by his bed, speaking to him in Hindustani. Both of them seemed to be getting rather cross. Mr Mitra was standing by, and told me that Major Williams was trying to persuade Mohan Ram to let us explore the wound under anaesthetic so it could be properly drained and dressed, but that Mohan Ram had a different way of seeing things: he believed we should let fate take its course, and if it was time for him to die, then so be it. After a moment he added that Mohan Ram was probably also frightened of being cut open, as he came from a tiny village in the Himalayas and did not under-stand how modern medicine worked.

The argument went on for some time. Eventually, Major Williams turned to Mr Mitra and asked him if there was anything he could do to change Mohan Ram's mind.

Mr Mitra thought for a moment, then moved close to Mohan Ram. Bending down, he spoke to him, his voice low. Mohan Ram frowned and then replied. Mr Mitra said something else. There was

29

a pause, and then Mohan Ram gave a little sideways shake of his head.

After that there was a flurry of activity as the orderlies came to wheel him into theatre. I turned to Mr Mitra, impressed.

'How did you manage to persuade him?'

'*Izzat.*'

'*Izzat?*'

It was hard to explain, he said. The best translation he could think of was 'honour', but it meant much more than that: reputation, saving face, prestige. It was one of the main reasons that the men had agreed to fight for Britain, just as important as the money they were paid for it, because it was glorious to die in battle. If one fought in a way that increased one's *izzat*, he said, one would be spoken of and remembered after one's death.

The other side of it, though, was that if one behaved in a way that damaged one's *izzat*, through desertion, or cowardice, or disloyalty, it brought terrible disgrace. He had simply pointed out to Mohan Ram that his fear of surgery would do just that, and so Mohan Ram had changed his mind, because to be seen to lose *izzat* in the eyes of someone else is already to have lost it, and Mr Mitra just thinking that he had done so was enough.

I would have liked to have asked Mr Mitra more about it, but we had arrived at the operating theatre. I decided to go in to observe.

Major Williams shook his head when the bandages came off.

'I thought the Boer War was bad enough,' he said quietly. 'These multiple wounds are dreadful. This shelling is a whole new way of causing damage, and I don't like it – I don't like it at all.'

I looked at the patient, lying on the operating table, and the surgical instruments, laid out neatly on a cloth, and I had a terrible vision of the theatre when it was the Pavilion kitchen: of whole pigs lying on the table ready to be roasted on the spit, or joints of beef waiting to be carved up. I swallowed hard to steady myself and waited for the first incision.

Major Williams cleaned out the wounds, which had gone horribly septic. We covered them with some of the new dressings made of sphagnum. It seemed such an odd combination: an Indian patient lying in the kitchen of an English king, wounded in France and stuffed with Scottish moss. Suddenly the world seemed very small.

CHAPTER 7

I'm all messed up, Suze. Not like Elizabeth's patients – I'm not missing limbs, or suffering from gangrene – but in my head. I'm trying not to let it take hold. I can't let myself get lost in things that happened in Kabul: I know that's a slippery slope. I don't like being unable to function, it's not me.

Last night I realized I hadn't spoken to anyone since I got here, apart from the man in the deli. Not good. I decided to look for a bar and have a drink and find someone to chat to.

There were plenty of places to choose from. Brighton's not like the cities I usually end up in, where you pick out your bags from a pile on the ground at the airport and take your own padlock for the hotel bedroom door. It's packed with everything you need for a happy holiday. In the daytime, the seafront's crammed with people down for the day from London, walking on the beach, playing on the pier. Couples of every sort smile and kiss, taking snaps of themselves with their phones. Late afternoon there's a lull, when the dirty weekenders go back to their hotels and the Londoners catch the train home. Later at night it comes alive all over again.

I made a bit of an effort before I went out, used the last of Edith's sandalwood oil in the bath, shaved my legs, did my hair. Not for anyone else's benefit, just mine. It had been a long time since I'd bothered, and it was nice to make the effort. Smelling of the bath oil, I felt pretty good as I wandered through Kemptown, a million times better than on my crazy stumble to the super-market. As I walked I looked into windows, at people eating dinner, watching television, getting ready to go out. I spied a naked chest in an attic room, a man throwing poses in front of a mirror. It was a still night, with no wind, and sash windows were thrown open in the tall Georgian terraces, music blasting, voices spilling, excited at the thought of the night to come. The tang of sea air mingled with the sweet whiff of spliffs escaping from balconies.

Brighton was revving up for Friday night – hen nights, stag dos, groups of lads in pressed shirts and tidy hair eyeing up girls in heels and tiny dresses next to students in jeans. Gay boys packed the terraces of the seafront bars, even now, in the autumn chill, smoking, flirting, on the pull.

I decided to avoid the bars on the seafront. I wanted somewhere quieter, where the flashiest cocktail was a gin-and-tonic, not something pink and fizzy with a sparkler sticking out the side. In the end I chose a place I heard about years ago, on the Old Steine, where once upon a time fishermen spread out their nets to dry, now the main road into town.

The Marlborough Pub – a townhouse with bay-fronted windows – looked nice from the outside. There were two doors to choose from, and for a moment I hesitated, feeling that little surge of nerves and possibility that I still get when I go to a gay bar on my own. But then I told myself not to be silly and picked the one to the right.

It was busy inside, hot and loud from voices competing with the music from the DJ booth in the window. Most of the girls were young, dressed in an unofficial uniform of jeans and sleeveless vests. They crowded at the bar, around the pool table, drinking pints of lager, slamming tequila shots.

One of the pool players had an elaborate tattoo that spread over her shoulders and down her arms. Do you remember how you used to joke that I was the only lesbian in London without one? I could never do it. I loved those little swallows flying in formation over your back, but they were the exception. To me, tattoos mean troops: snarling dogs, bullets and bombs, rifles, naked women, Bible passages, skulls and crossbones, the Grim Reaper, crucifixes, women's names. *Infidel* scrawled across the young chest of a British soldier in Afghanistan.

Did you know that Islam forbids tattoos? When I was in Iraq with a platoon of marines, young blokes in their early twenties, there was a running battle between them and their superiors, who were trying to get them to limit their tattoos to places where they couldn't be seen. They failed, of course: those guys didn't care, they flaunted them, trying to provoke a reaction, like the teenagers they almost still were.

I didn't want to think about soldiers. Spotting a door at the end of the bar, I pushed my way to it and stepped through into the other room.

It couldn't have been more different – quiet, no music, with just a few couples sitting in cosy booths. There was carpet on the floor, a cheese plant in the corner and a fish tank behind the bar. Not what you'd call cool, perhaps, but I liked it.

I ordered a gin-and-tonic and perched on a stool at the bar. The barmaid was friendly, flirty even, but when I took out a cigarette she shook her head and said:

'Mm-mm, not in here.'

I'd forgotten about the smoking ban. I'm used to drinking in places where the air's thick with smoke, the kind of places where a ban like that would never be tolerated. Neither would a bar full of women, come to think of it – not this sort, anyway. I remembered a hotel bar in Kigali, Rwanda. The ceiling fans were broken, the tables sticky with beer. Cats prowled, looking for scraps to eat. We'd been out all day, staring at the bodies and the devastation, and we were tired and drinking to forget. The bar was filled with the usual suspects:

arms dealers, aid workers, mercenaries, journalists. A very drunk man came up and put his hand on my bum. His breath smelt of whisky, his skin flushed and eyes bloodshot from drink and years of looking into the African sun.

'How much?' His accent was hard to place: South African perhaps, Belgian, Dutch.

'What?'

'You know,' he said, touching my bum again.

I kept my voice steady. 'I'm not a whore.'

He lifted an eyebrow. 'Then why are you here?'

'I'm a photographer, a journalist.'

He laughed, a high, mad cackle.

'Worse, girlie, worse.'

I've spent so many nights in places like that: hotel bars with no windows, so you don't know what time it is; bars next to swimming pools emptied by drought or war; bars in bad parts of town, where you hear the rumbles of disturbance coming closer; bars behind iron grilles, where only foreigners or the elite can get away with drinking alcohol. It was good to sit with my gin-and-tonic and be sure no man was going to try his luck. I drank it quickly, liking the head rush that came with it. I was ordering another when a girl came through the door. She sat on the barstool next to mine, looked at me and smiled.

'Wow, it's busy in there,' she said, nodding to the other side of the bar.

She was tall, like you, with dark hair, shiny and long. I put my hand up to the back of my neck, feeling the uneven line. Do you remember when I called you from Congo to tell you I'd cut off all my hair? I'd been to a hospital where I'd spent the whole day taking photographs of little girls as young as six who'd been raped with bottles, old ladies assaulted by a dozen militia and left for dead. All of them looking back at my camera with empty eyes. Back in my hotel room, I took my nail scissors and chopped my hair off in clumps, not bothering to look in the mirror. Afterwards I picked it all up and put it in one of those airport bags for toiletries, suddenly scared of witchcraft. That was the effect that Congo had on me: it screwed me up for months.

My hair's still short. It's easier that way. Better not to look good in a war zone. But when that woman began to talk to me, my hand went up to my hair, almost without me realizing. It's been so long since I've been chatted up that I didn't even know if that was what she was doing, or if she was just being friendly.

The conversation didn't last long, because I soon began to feel sick again, like at the supermarket. I held on to the bar, gulping, trying to swallow it down. My heart was thumping, and not because of her.

'I'm Florence,' said the girl.

'I'm Jo,' I said, and then jumped off my barstool and ran outside, because I knew I was going to throw up. Pushing past the group of girls smoking outside, I puked onto the pavement.

I wondered what was happening, how I'd lost control for the second time in a week. When I felt the hand on my shoulder I flinched.

'It's me,' said Florence. 'Are you OK?'

I knew how it looked, as if I couldn't hold my drink.

'Yes,' I said, then got to my feet and stumbled off in the direction of the seafront.

She called something after me, but I kept going, past the Pavilion, all lit up by moonlight, past the chippy on the corner, belting out rancid fumes, past the clubs, the karaoke bars, the drunks, the bus shelter, right along the promenade until I made it home.

CHAPTER 8

ELIZABETH WILLOUGHBY'S DIARY

25th December 1914

Today was Christmas Day, but I had volunteered to work: there didn't seem much cause for celebration, not with Robert so far away and in such danger. On my way to the Pavilion, I stood for a moment on the seafront. It was a clear day, very cold and very still, with no trace of wind and, thankfully, no sound of guns. The tide pushed little ruffles of foam up onto the deserted beach. I thought of families sitting down to breakfast, opening stockings, the smiles on children's faces, and I looked out over the sea and said a prayer that Robert would come back safe and well, and that one day we would have a family of our own.

Christmas means little to our patients, of course, but they seemed delighted with their royal gifts. Queen Mary had sent a little tin of sweetmeats, postcards and cigarettes to each of them, which were closely examined and exclaimed over with great pleasure, then put carefully with their other belongings in the pack store: trophies from the Front, horrid things like German helmets or fragments of shells.

Nurse Clarkson had brought in some mince pies, and we had a jolly time, sharing them over afternoon tea. Someone had the idea of singing to the patients, and we formed an impromptu choir, performing a carol to each ward. We were decidedly amateur, but the men seemed to like it, some of them even tapping out time on the side of their beds.

All in all, it was a pleasant day, a welcome lull, apart from one upsetting episode involving a Gurkha from Nepal. Lal Bahadur Thapa is a very small man, a boy, even, who looks no older than fourteen. His features are different to the other men: they are almost Chinese, as if he had stepped down from the paintings on the panels of the music room and slid between the starched sheets of his bed.

We have kept a special eye on him ever since he arrived last week in a terrible state, his legs shattered by shellfire. His notes say that he was blown over by the blast, then half buried by debris, and not rescued for hours. In France he had a double amputation. His wounds had become gangrenous, and he had been terribly nervous and couldn't bear the thought of being moved. Apparently the orderlies spoke to him in his own language, trying to calm him down, but he went on screaming all the way into theatre. When he came to us, his legs bandaged, cut off at the thigh, he looked like a tortured child, tiny and shocked.

Usually he lies hunched in his bed, his body barely disturbing the bedclothes, simply staring into the distance, hardly seeming to blink. His hands are the only parts of him to move, twitching all the time. But this afternoon, just after the carols, his twitching quickened, until it was something like a flutter, his hands and arms flapping, slow at first, then faster, like a bird trying to take flight. He began to make strange, strangled noises, as if he wanted to speak but could not.

The other patients were showing signs of upset, too, shifting in their beds. Some of them covered their heads with their pillows to block out the noise. Others began to twitch as well, shouting for help.

Suddenly, Lal Bahadur let out a wild, terrible shriek, like an animal in pain. Calling to an orderly to fetch Colonel MacLeod, I ran to him and held his shoulders, talking to him gently, trying to break the spell, but by the time the Colonel had arrived he was convulsing, his little body jerking and twisting about. He was surprisingly strong: it took three orderlies to hold him down while they gave him a sedative, then he went limp, flopping back against the pillows.

Afterwards, in his office, Colonel MacLeod demanded an explanation. I began to describe how Lal Bahadur had seemed to go off into another world, but he said that wasn't what he had meant. Giving me a stern look, he asked why I had gone to him. I knew the rules, he said: I wasn't there to nurse the patients.

When I protested that it was impossible to see someone in such pain and not try to help as a matter of common decency, he said that it wasn't my place, and that if I would not abide by the rules he would be forced to ask me to leave.

A knock came at the door.

'Sir.' It was Mr Mitra, who launched into an explanation of what had happened, saying that my help had been 'vital'. I have never been called 'vital' before. I smiled to myself, feeling rather pleased. Colonel MacLeod asked what it had to do with him.

'As a doctor, I—'

A flush of anger had risen up Colonel MacLeod's neck. I looked at it, thinking how calm Mr Mitra was in comparison, how he showed no reaction as the Colonel reminded him that he was still not qualified.

'The matter we are discussing is not simply a medical one,' the Colonel said huffily. 'It is to do with something else entirely.'

When another knock came at the door, I thought that the Colonel might lose his temper, his neck growing a deeper shade of crimson.

A nervous-looking orderly stammered that there was another emergency. As the Colonel rushed out of the room, Mr Mitra and I exchanged glances.

'Thank you,' I said.

'I don't think I was much help.'

'You probably haven't done yourself much good stepping in for me like that.'

He shrugged. 'You're probably right: I never do.'

For a moment I hesitated, thinking of hospital protocol, then decided to ignore it.

'I think,' I said, 'that you should call me Elizabeth.'

He gave a little bow. 'Then I am Hari.'

There was a pause as I wondered what to say next. Then, remembering that he was still in training, I asked him where he had been studying before the war. When he said Keble College, Oxford, I was delighted and told him that Robert had been at Balliol. When he was back from leave I would introduce them. They have Oxford in common, and Robert was born in India. Perhaps they could be friends.

'Perhaps,' he said.

I wanted to keep talking. 'And what made you come to England?' I asked.

He shrugged, and said that when he was a boy he had read Shakespeare and Milton, Thomas Hardy, George Eliot. He had been inspired by those books. He had wanted to come and see for himself.

Just like me and India, I thought. I had something in common with him too. 'And is it how you imagined it to be?'

'Since I've been here,' he said, 'I've realized that England's not the place I read about in books.'

I felt oddly disappointed.

43

'So why did you come here, to the Pavilion?'

'Oxford is a strange and wonderful place,' he said, making a little grimace. 'But as soon as I arrived there I started to think of India again. When I heard that the Pavilion needed doctors, I felt a strange affiliation to my country. I decided to come to Brighton to help.'

The more I see of Hari Mitra, the more intrigued I am. He seems like a man who has stories, if I can prise them out of him. I think that I should like to try.

CHAPTER 9

When I first got into this game, I loved the thought of being free, but the flip-side of freedom is loneliness. Writing it down for you, trying to describe it in words, was important. I wanted you to know – really know – about the things that happened away from the photos in the papers, the bits I didn't capture with my camera, the stories behind the shots.

I loved getting your stories too, especially the emails – much more than the rushed calls on a borrowed satellite phone, the sporadic texts when I had reception – getting to my inbox and finding something from you, a reassurance that there was something else out there, away from the madness, something normal and human and sane.

That was one of the worst things about the breakup, not having you there while I tried to make sense of it all in my head. That's what I need to do now, Suze. I need to tell you what's been going on, like I used to, to explain what happened in Kabul. I'm not expecting an answer, I know it's too late for that, but you're still the only one who might get it, the only one who might understand.

Do you remember my first trip to Afghanistan, back in 2001? It was a few weeks after 9/11, when we'd sat together on the sofa and stared at the television in horror as the Twin Towers collapsed. The Americans were about to start bombing the city, and I was desperate to cover it. I packed my bags, kissed you goodbye and left pretty much straight away.

I never told you much about that trip. You were too angry with me, first for leaving, then for staying away so long. I saw the paintings you did while I was gone, the anger in them, the hurt and the loneliness. That was when you slept with someone else, your first affair, and that was what filled our conversations in the weeks that came after, not where I'd just been.

That trip was where it all started to go wrong, the stuff between you and me. That's where I have to begin.

I knew I'd never be allowed directly into Kabul, so I went the long way round, via Moscow and Tajikistan, then a helicopter to Khoja Bahauddin, seat of the Northern Alliance, a bleak Afghan desert town the colour of mud, houses rising seamlessly up from the ground, their walls moulded out of the same dull earth, camels and donkeys carrying firewood – no electricity, no sewerage, no running water, no paved roads. I found myself a driver and an interpreter. My friend Tim, a reporter from the *Washington Post*, hitched a ride, and ' together we drove in an old Russian jeep through the Hindu Kush, across tumbling rivers, dusty foothills, desert plains, past soldiers kneeling to pray, the curve of their backs mirrored by the shape of the mountains behind them. We went through villages whose inhabitants went barefoot in the freezing cold, and stayed at filthy guest houses where we ate greasy goat and naan bread, then wrapped ourselves in anything we could find to sleep as best we could. The landscape was extraordinary: enormous walls of rock towering above us, streaked with torrents of water that splashed to an ending out of sight far below.

It took us a week to get to the Shomali Plains, a no-man's-land, a buffer zone between the Northern Alliance and the Taliban – a desolate, windy place, dotted with houses riddled with bullet holes, wrecked tanks and burnt-out jeeps. Bodies lay at angles in the dust, legs twisted, heads thrown back. Plastic sandals lay scattered along the road, next to pieces of clothing and dark splashes of blood.

We made our way to the top of a hill and suddenly Kabul was below us, a vast spread of low houses broken up here and there by Soviet-style blocks of flats. The setting was magnificent: a city surrounded by a ring of mountains and more mountains behind them, tipped with white. The sun was disappearing over the horizon, drenching the mountains in a soft pink glow. Lights were being switched on, the first sign of electricity I'd seen since I'd arrived, little twinkles dotting the hillsides.

I wondered what we'd find when we got into the city. My mental image of Kabul came from news reports and a handful of faded photographs. Edith had visited in '68, on an epic trip in a Land Rover from London to Calcutta. In her photographs, women in dresses rode on buses and children slid down brightly coloured slides in playgrounds. The news reports from when the Taliban were in control had been very different: women reduced to silent blue forms; that secret footage of one of them publicly executed in Kabul's football stadium, brought in on the back of a truck and forced to kneel, then shot in the head as her seven children watched and wept.

Now the city was in ruins. We drove past block after block of houses without roofs or walls, gaping holes where windows once had been. Façades were pocked with bullet holes, walls punctured by tank shells. Joists and girders stuck out at crazy angles, holding up what little there was left. Filigree balconies hung, cracked, off the front of once gracious houses. Rubble lay in mounds. As evening fell, smoke began to fill the air, as families cooked or huddled close to fires to stay warm.

'It's like Dresden,' said Tim. 'Or Hiroshima. Fuck, Jo, what have we done?'

Mahmoud, our interpreter, coughed. 'It wasn't the Americans,' he said quietly. 'It's been like this for years. It was the Taliban, and before them it was the civil war, it was the mujahidin. It wasn't outsiders. We did this to ourselves.'

★   ★   ★

The Intercontinental Hotel was a white, rather ugly building high up on a ridge in the middle of the city, packed with journalists fighting for rooms. We'd poured in as fast as we could persuade anyone to bring us, the only species on earth to run towards trouble instead of away. I'd managed to blag a bed in a room with Molly, a CNN correspondent I'd been with in Sierra Leone. As usual, she had a bottle of gin on the go. We mixed it with some cans of sour lemonade and sat, wrapped in our sleeping bags, drinking it from chipped glasses.

'What kept you?' she asked, with a smile.

It was only three days since the Taliban had collapsed. Molly had been one of the first journalists to get to Kabul, sneaking across the border with Pakistan.

'It was pretty crazy,' she said. 'The road was packed with Taliban, lines and lines of those white Toyotas that bin Laden paid for, all filled up with wives and children, and baggage piled up right to the back of the trunk. It reminded me of the highway out of New York on Labor Day.'

All I wanted to do was to get drunk with her and gossip, but after the first gin she stood up and went over to the table in the corner, ran a lipstick over her mouth and pulled a brush through her hair.

'I have to give a broadcast,' she said. 'From the roof. Come and watch if you like.'

The roof was full of correspondents, cameras and satellite dishes, powered by a row of generators, one for each news corporation. For the first time I was working freelance – no contract, no deadline, no boss. To have any chance of competing, I knew I had to find myself someone to help me, and fast: a translator, a fixer, someone I could work with, someone I could trust, the person who would make all the difference to what kind of shots I'd be able to get.

Early the next morning, avoiding the offers from the group of men outside the hotel gates, I took a taxi to the bazaar. The city looked even worse than the night before, the bright sunlight making everything seem more tattered. Children with orange hair from malnutrition played in open gutters; stray dogs ran about sniffing for food. Men sat by the side of the road with things for sale spread in front of them – a pile of mismatched sandals, spare parts for cars, scrap metal.

I bent to look closer at a collection of what looked like human bones. The vendor's face suggested nothing unusual, they might as well have been vegetables or flowers.

A voice said softly in English, 'Yes, that's right, they're vertebrae. And look, there's a fibula too.'

I turned to see a man, youngish, in his twenties, his chin blotched and covered with bits of cotton wool.

He saw me looking and smiled. 'I got rid of my beard this morning,' he said. 'The barber was a little out of practice. My name is Faisal. *Salaam alaikum.*'

'*Walaikum salaam*. I'm Jo.'

'The Taliban banned us from trading in many things. Bones were one of the few that they didn't.'

'Why would anyone want to buy them?'

'To send to factories in Pakistan. They make them into buttons and soap.'

'Where did they get them?'

He laughed. 'The bombs made the earth shake so badly that the graves spat out their bones. You don't have to dig hard to get them. Little children usually do it. Their hands are small, so they're good for the job.'

He noticed my expression. 'You know, people didn't have much choice.'

'And how about you?' I asked.

'When the Taliban came, I was at university, studying medicine. I've always wanted to be a doctor. It's my dream. So while they were here, I kept on studying, at home.'

'And now?'

'I'm waiting for the university to open again.'

'I'm here to take photographs,' I said. 'I'm looking for someone to work with me, to translate, show me around, tell me where is good to go. Would you be interested?'

He thought for a moment, then nodded. 'Yes,' he said. 'It would be my pleasure.'

Faisal took me through narrow walkways, past deserted compounds with cracked flowerpots fallen onto their sides and birdcages that hung

51

empty. We walked for hours, as if he were reclaiming his city's streets, pointing out barbers shaving off more customers' beards, crowds of men outside a cinema waiting for an afternoon show, hordes of teenage boys staring at postcards of Bollywood stars pinned up for sale. As we made our way down a street full of fruit stalls, he stopped.

'Can you hear that?' he asked.

The faint sound of tinny pop drifted down the street.

'That makes me very happy,' he said. 'It's the first music I've heard for five years.'

On the way back to the Intercontinental I took a picture of a man pushing his bicycle, an enormous bunch of balloons tied to the handlebars, bobbing as he bumped over the potholes. They glowed in the winter sunlight, hopeful snatches of colour in the dust.

Kabul was at such an altitude that just walking down the street was enough to make me dizzy. Over the next few weeks it grew so cold that it hurt to breathe. My nose was constantly running, my lips sore and cracked. I moved with Molly and the rest of the CNN crew to Wazir Akbar Khan, a posh part of the city to the north. I'd been desperate to leave the Intercontinental. There were too many of my own sort there, too many journalists and photographers and camera crews.

It had become – like the Holiday Inn in Sarajevo,

or the American Colony in Jerusalem – a little community, full of intrigue, gossip and sex. It was, as it always is, the buzz of the front line, the aphrodisiac effect of danger and distance from home, from normality from everything that might, in real life, make you think twice. I didn't get involved – I never did, despite your fears and the arguments we had about it all. Even if I'd wanted to, war reporting's a pretty straight sport.

But let's not get into that particular discussion. I settled into a routine, walking the streets with Faisal, looking for subjects. At first I photographed a lot of burqas, trying to figure them out, trying to capture what they meant. Aesthetically, they worked beautifully, pale blue against beige dust, but I began to feel uneasy at reducing them to a colour palette.

When I said so to Faisal, he laughed.

'Come to my house. I have five sisters. Ask them.'

Faisal's sisters were very different to the ghostly blue creatures on the street – beautifully dressed in silk shalwar kameezes, their faces expertly made up. They were quiet at first, then bolder, firing off questions, with Faisal translating.

'Where do you come from?'

'London.'

'How old are you?

'Thirty.'

'Are you married?'

'No.'

They looked at me pityingly, whispering amongst

53

themselves. I wondered what they thought of me, scruffy from weeks of travel and not particularly clean.

After a minute or two, Sushila, the eldest sister, went over to a box in the corner. She rummaged in it for a minute, then took out a little bag.

'The Taliban banned us from painting our nails,' she said. 'So we kept our nail polish hidden. But now it is allowed. If we paint yours you'll have more chance of finding a husband.'

You'd have laughed at my face, but I could hardly turn them down. I nodded and smiled and tried to look enthusiastic. They told me off for not looking after my hands properly, and tutted over my nails being so short. Their hands had smooth skin and long nails, all painted the same shade of bright red.

By the time they'd finished, so were mine. I smiled and nodded, and thanked them very much.

We huddled around the old *bukhari* stove, which gave off a cosy smell of burning sawdust.

'Will you tell me about burqas?' I asked. 'I want to know what it's like to wear one.'

They brought them down from their hooks. I was surprised at how different they were from each other. I'd assumed they were all exactly the same.

When I said so, the sisters laughed.

'No, no,' said Sushila. 'Sometimes the material is fine, sometimes rough, and the embroidery around the top comes in lots of designs. Look, this one has flowers, but this one is very plain.'

'But they're always blue, right?' I said.

'No,' said Leila, the second sister. 'Sometimes they're white.'

'But only if you're rich,' said Sushila. 'They're hard to keep clean, so you have to be able to afford more than one, and have someone to do your laundry.'

They made me try one on, lifting it carefully, then arranging it until the top part fitted closely around my head. They spread the material out around me and stood back. I was immediately conscious of the weight of it. Faisal's house was already warm from the *bukhari*: now I felt hot and almost unable to breathe.

'Walk around a bit,' said Leila.

Slowly, feeling my way, I walked across the room. It was difficult to see out, my vision restricted to the little mesh. I could only look straight ahead, unless I turned my head.

'Stop,' said Leila. 'There's the mirror.'

I stared at myself, transformed into one of the blue shapes I'd seen making their way slowly along the streets.

Leila laughed. 'She's feeling it.'

'What?' I said.

'The same thing we all felt when we first put one on. Like you don't know who you are.'

I watched the blue shape nod. 'Yes. That's it,' it said, in my voice. 'I don't.'

CHAPTER 10

ELIZABETH WILLOUGHBY'S DIARY

5th January 1915

A letter from Robert!

France, 28th December 1914

Dear Elizabeth,

I hope you had a very happy Christmas. Mine was uneventful, which was the best we could have hoped for, although the most extraordinary thing happened: a ceasefire, of all things, a truce of sorts. Unofficial, of course. Apparently, some of our Tommies and the enemy exchanged carols and greetings, and on Christmas Day itself they met in no-man's-land to play football. I know that this will be reported in the newspapers, despite our best efforts to the contrary, so I am not giving anything away by telling you.

My boys didn't have much to do with it. Christmas is just another day to them, although the night before, my orderly pointed over to the German trenches, where I saw a line of tiny trees lit with candles.

'Like Diwali,' he said.

Have I ever told you about Diwali, the Hindu festival of lights? I used to love it as a boy in Calcutta. The whole city glows; they put lamps everywhere – in the houses, on the streets – to bring prosperity and luck.

We could certainly use some luck. It's been particularly ghastly these past few weeks, as the weather has got even worse. The men are in bad shape, and morale has been awfully low.

I have no words to describe the mud: a miserable, stinking quagmire that slops everywhere and holds onto one's boots like some awful creature of the deep. Two days ago, I found three of my sepoys sitting in it almost to their armpits, huddled together, moaning in their sleep. I woke them and got them out, and found a man for each one to rub them warm and put them somewhere dry outside the trench for a few hours, until the morning mist had cleared, at which point I had no choice but to order them back in again, which felt all wrong.

But there is some good news in the midst of all this gloom. My leave has been confirmed: a week, beginning on 1st February. I'll visit mother and father in Aldershot, and then I'd very much like to come to see you. These last two months have passed very slowly and very quickly at the same time, if that makes any sense at all.

I hope that you are well.

Love,

Robert

Poor, poor Robert. I find it hard to imagine what life has been like in those trenches, although I have some small idea from the state of our patients. I am so much looking forward to seeing him again and having a proper conversation. I didn't get his letter until this evening; the newspapers have already done as he predicted, and published photographs of the truce. After everything one has read in those very papers about the Hun assaulting nuns and mutilating children, it is odd to see German soldiers standing next to ordinary Tommies singing carols. Apart from their uniforms, they look almost exactly the same.

CHAPTER 11

It's Guy Fawkes Night, Suze. I haven't changed. The curtains are closed and I'm wearing earplugs to block out the noise. Those flashes and bangs, that horrible whistle as the fireworks begin to fall will always remind me of mortar attacks. Do you remember that New Year's Eve display on Primrose Hill, when I dropped to the ground with my hands over my ears? I couldn't help myself: it was a reflex action.

I'm not going to make a fool of myself again. Better to stay in and get on with my story.

Afghanistan: May 2011. Ten years after that first trip. I wasn't going to the front line. You can't, now, unless you're embedded with the troops, and I didn't want to do that again, to take photos through the filter of what the army allows. It's always been the things I'm not supposed to see that interest me, the things they'd rather keep hidden.

I'd be confined to Kabul, but that was fine with me. For the first time, I was doing something against my journalistic instincts, away from the main story. If I'd wanted to be in the thick of things, I'd have gone to Egypt, Libya, Syria with everyone else, racing to get the story, to catch the news as fast as it happened. Afghanistan's a long war, a tired war, a drawn-out war, a war that follows on from thirty years of other wars. Osama's gone, and so is most of the press. The world's moved on, even if the troops remain and the Taliban are back, making strongholds, gaining strength, regrouping, waiting for the foreigners to leave.

The freelancing hadn't really worked out that first time, as you know. I was too inexperienced, couldn't quite compete. It costs a lot to report from a conflict and I soon realized the benefits of life insurance, satellite communications, help at the other end of the phone. So I went back to a proper job, to calls from the bureau chief, to jumping on planes to dreadful places to take photos of the terrible things that happened in them, sending them back to my editor, hoping that no one else had got there first.

A decade on I'd had enough. There was a moment in Iraq, when I was taking photos of rockets in the night sky, and I suddenly realized I didn't want to be there. The world doesn't need another picture of a burnt-out tank in a desert. Or at least, not from me. I wanted to change the way I did things, to take control, to choose where I went and what I did. In the past, not so very long ago, when Elizabeth was alive, men used to go off to battlegrounds and fight it out. It's not so neat and tidy any more. War's the little kid still holding on to his mother's hand after her head's been cut off with a machete. It's the father laying his dead child down to be buried by a bulldozer before disease begins to spread. It's refugee camps, starvation, cholera.

There's more to Afghanistan than conflict, but that conflict's linked to everything else, to the war widows begging outside expat restaurants, the little boys forced to work instead of going to school, the heroin addicts who can't see any other way out. Those are the things I decided to photograph, the bits outside the news, not extreme enough to make it into the papers, but miserable enough for the people who have to live them. I wasn't quite sure what I'd find in Kabul, but I knew there'd be stories to tell.

I caught a plane to Dubai, then another to Kabul, flying for hours over red-ridged mountains, peaks of snow and shadowed valleys, hard, secretive terrain, making me think of the men who've hidden there on and off for decades, waiting to outwit their enemies. When the mountains turned into flat, unforgiving plains, I knew we'd almost made it. Soon, the dusty earth was criss-crossed with the straight lines of a brown grid, dotted with little spots of greenery. As the plane descended I saw houses within the squares of the grid, each huddled within the walls of its own compound.

Hangars painted the colour of sand, a mass of military planes and helicopters, then the runway, the landing crunch.

Here we go again, I thought, and covered my hair with a scarf.

Airports in war zones are misleading, the last scraps of normality almost clinging to them, a no-man's-land between the fighting and the rest of the world, where the right papers can still get the right people to the right places. A place where there are queues and rules, neat rows of seats, adverts for Coca-Cola. As soon as you step outside, though, you hit reality. At Kabul International Airport the arrivals hall was almost deserted, with just a few grim-faced private security guards waiting to pick up embassy passengers. As soon as I stepped outside, my rucksack on my back, camera bags on the front, I was hit by a wave of hard, dry heat. They don't let cars near the airport for fear of suicide bombers, and so the taxis were a long walk across the car park. Every step of the way I felt watched. Finally I made it, found a cab, told the driver where I wanted to go and settled myself in for the ride into town.

I was ready for big changes in Kabul, but there was one thing about it that was exactly the same: the smell of shit. The first time I was there, I'd thought that the air would be fresh at such a high altitude, but it wasn't then and it wasn't now. As I drove from the airport I could see ditches full of human waste drying in the sun, ready for the wind to lift into the air and swirl around the city.

It was much busier than it had been in 2001 – more traffic, more people on the streets. The city was spreading up into the hills, clusters of mud-brick houses that looked as if they'd been thrown onto the mountainsides next to blank, flat-fronted buildings surrounded by walls topped with spikes – the homes of warlords.

There were still plenty of pitted walls and metal rods sticking out of blasted cement. Children played among the ruins of abandoned blocks of flats. But there was a lot of new construction too. As we bumped along the potholed road, we passed endless plate-glass buildings, shiny and enormous.

'Wedding halls,' said the driver.

Outside them stood a bizarre collection of palm trees, pyramids, a replica of the Eiffel Tower stretching high into the sky. On the top of the buildings were neon signs in Dari and English – fancy names like Sham-e Paris or Kabul Dubai. Stretch limousines, garlanded with flowers, slid up to park outside. It looked more like Las Vegas than Kabul.

Dusk was falling, flocks of birds wheeling and swooping in the sky. As it grew darker, more lights came on in the hills, and wood smoke began to hang in the air.

The taxi drew up outside the guest house that

Faisal had found for me in the north of the city. In my room, I dumped my bags on the floor and looked around. It was pretty standard: a single bed, a desk, a rickety wardrobe, all made of cheap wood. A plastic bucket for laundry. Dirty white walls, a thin blue carpet. There was, at least for the moment, internet access. I switched on my laptop and got myself online.

Faisal and I met the next day at a *chaikhana* in the old city, on the first floor of an ancient building, sleepy fans rippling the air. As usual, I was the only woman in the place, my foreignness making me an honorary man. He was on the balcony, waiting. He looked very well, prosperous and smart.

When he saw me he smiled.

'Jo,' he said. 'I am so pleased to see you.'

I wanted to fling my arms around him and give him a hug, but I knew that even shaking hands would make him uncomfortable, so I just smiled.

'I'm very happy to see you too, Faisal,' I said.

'Are you well?'

'I'm very well.'

'And your family?'

Faisal knows I don't have any family. It was his way of asking if I was married. I never quite knew what Faisal thought of that side of my life. Unlike his sisters he was far too polite to say.

We ordered tea.

'Your children, Faisal, how are they?'

He dug in his pocket and brought out pictures of a boy and a girl, aged about six and eight.

'They're beautiful.'

'You must meet them, and my wife, Sonia.'

'Of course.'

I thought of Leila and Shushila, giggling as they painted my nails. 'How are your sisters?'

He hesitated, then said, 'They are OK.'

'I'd love to see them too.'

'Perhaps.'

Faisal had achieved what he'd wanted – qualified as a doctor, and a good one at that. He'd become a consultant at one of Kabul's hospitals and so was too busy to help me again, but I'd emailed him to ask if he knew anyone who could. He'd been a bit stumped at first when I'd said I'd prefer a woman, but now he had a suggestion.

'Her name is Rashida. She's the daughter of one of my colleagues, who's also a very good friend. She's just graduated in journalism and is looking for work. It would be good experience for her and I think she would be useful to you.'

'Great!'

He hesitated.

'What?'

'You know she won't be able to do all the things a man can do. You'll need to be accompanied by someone if you want to go to certain places.'

'It's fine,' I said. 'We can take a driver – we'll need one anyway. And I'll figure out the rest.'

'I know!' he said, with a smile.

'So when can I meet her?'

'Let's try tomorrow afternoon. I'll find out if she's available. There's a place called the Flower Street Café. I go there sometimes with my European colleagues.'

'I know Flower Street,' I said, remembering the stalls selling dusty bouquets of plastic roses.

'Actually, it's not there. It's in Qala-e Fatullah, near the guest house. They will give you directions. Let's meet there at three.'

The next day I went to the café, down a dusty, empty street. The guest house had insisted on a taxi, which in the end I was pleased about, because the blank concrete walls didn't suggest any café to me. When we stopped outside a metal door, I sat for a moment wondering if we were in the right place, then saw a hand-painted sign.

I got out of the taxi and knocked on the door. A peephole slid open and a security guard looked out at me.

'Flower Street Café?' I asked.

He grunted, and let me in. I stepped into a little courtyard where another stern-looking security guard stood, a Kalashnikov slung over his shoulder. He pointed to my bag.

'You have gun?'

I shook my head and opened the bag, nervous about my camera equipment, but after a quick check he nodded and I went through another door.

A tiny path led to a garden, with roses and a

patch of lawn with tables placed around it under cheerful red umbrellas. At the far end was a gazebo wound about with grapevines, where people sat, deep in conversation or typing on laptops. I couldn't see Faisal so I wandered into the house. It was even busier than the garden, filled with more expats at work, frowning down at screens, phones next to them, cups of coffee to hand.

Returning to the garden, I picked a table in the shade and ordered a mango smoothie from the friendly waiter. A few minutes later, Faisal arrived.

'This is Rashida,' he said. 'And this is her brother Ahmed.'

Ahmed had clearly come to suss me out. I decided the best strategy was charm.

'Hello,' I said. 'It's great to meet you.'

He just nodded, but Rashida smiled. 'I'm very pleased to meet you too.'

There was a pause while the waiter came to take their orders, then we got down to business.

'Rashida, Faisal told me that you're looking for work. I'd love it if you could help me,' I said, making sure I looked at Ahmed as well as her.

'What would she be doing?' asked Ahmed. 'What do you hope to photograph?'

'I want to look at what the war means to ordinary people.'

He looked sceptical.

'I don't want to photograph ISAF forces,' I said. 'And I'm not looking for Taliban.'

Both he and Rashida looked rather startled.

'Really,' I said, quickly. 'I just want to talk to people and take their pictures. Faisal will tell you, I'm always very careful. I don't take unnecessary risks.'

Faisal nodded. 'She doesn't.'

'Rashida, do you think you can help me? Would you be interested?'

She and her brother exchanged glances, then she nodded. 'Yes, please.'

CHAPTER 12

7th January 1915

A photographer came to visit today. His pictures will be made into postcards to be given to the patients to post home to their families and sold in town. I find it rather strange to imagine them next to pictures of the Aquarium and the Palace Pier, but I suppose there is no accounting for taste!

Mr Fry was a small, dapper man, accompanied by an assistant, Mr Cartwright, whose job seemed to be to carry the large amount of equipment while Mr Fry made sure each portrait was exactly how he wanted it.

We had taken a great deal of trouble over the preparations: orders had come from the very top to make a good impression, and so the patients were dressed up, beds smoothed, flowers picked and well arranged, but Mr Fry began to fuss about, getting us to move the beds a fraction of an inch here and there, then back again, saying that his

69

photographs must reflect the fact that the Pavilion is a military hospital, and thus have what he called 'perfect lines'.

I was anxious about moving the beds with the patients still in them, but remembering Colonel MacLeod's instructions to make a good impression, I directed the orderlies to do as he said. Once they were in position, Mr Fry looked at them for a long time, squinting, his head cocked, then turned to me and asked if I could smooth the blankets, as they were a little creased.

Although slightly indignant at his suggestion that the beds might be anything less than perfect, I began to do as he said.

Hari was suddenly at my side.

'You're not meant to do things like that,' he muttered. 'Remember?'

'Oh,' I whispered, startled. 'Yes. Of course.'

As the orderly worked his way along the row of beds, patting down the covers and making them smooth, I turned to Hari and whispered my thanks. The ghost of a smile flitted over his lips and he gave a little shrug of acknowledgement.

In the meantime Mr Fry had turned his attention to how we should compose ourselves. The patients were to sit up straight in bed, their hands crossed above their blankets, looking straight ahead, not at the camera, which Mr Cartwright was patiently positioning towards the other end of the room. Mr Fry carefully picked out six staff and ushered us into position next to the patients' beds.

It was a fresh day, but not cold, and so some of the patients were persuaded to pose in groups in the gardens: Sikhs together, then the Gurkhas, Dogras and Pathans. I was reminded of school, as Mr Fry posed them as if for one of those ghastly end-of-term photographs, some sitting in front, the others standing behind, and thought of Miss Hewitt chivvying us into position as we shivered with our lacrosse sticks, the wind blowing in gusts off the sea.

I had not expected to be included in the pictures of the operating theatre, as usually I have so little to do with it, but Mr Fry wanted a woman to make it look less austere. I stood between the British doctors and Hari and tried to look as if I belonged.

When Mr Fry had finished, I turned to Hari, who had been as awkward in front of the cameras as me, and confessed that I was pleased it was over, and that I had found it hard not to feel self-conscious.

'My worry is what they'll be used for,' he said.

I asked what he meant, and he said his guess was that the postcards would be used for recruitment. When the patients sent the postcards back to their families everyone in India would think how marvellous the hospital was, and be grateful and send more sons to fight.

I thought about it for a moment. 'Well, our hospital is rather good. And we do need more men at the Front.'

71

'I have a theory,' he said. 'Do you remember our conversation about the efforts being made not to offend the men and keeping everything separate?'

I nodded.

'And have you heard of the Indian Mutiny?'

I nodded again. Robert's grandfather died in the Siege of Delhi; he told me all about it.

'And do you know that it was started by a rumour that the cartridges to be used by the East India Company Army were greased by pig or cow fat?'

I said yes, eager to show off my knowledge. 'The sepoys had to bite them to release the gunpowder, and that was offensive to Mohammedans and Hindus alike.'

Looking somewhat surprised that I knew about it, he said his theory was that the British had learnt from their mistakes: now they knew that they had to get these things right. With thousands of Indian soldiers at the Front, the last thing they wanted was another mutiny. What they did want was more men, to carry on with their campaign, and so it was vital to show that good care was being taken of the Indians already here.

'They're not making postcards of the other hospitals, are they? They chose the Pavilion because it looks so impressive.'

Perhaps Hari was right: that nothing is as simple as it seems, and everything good is done for other reasons, but I was not so sure.

'I nurse the men because I want to make them

well again, I want to make a difference. Isn't that what everyone wants, really, in the end?'

He stood very still for a moment, thinking, then smiled. 'Of course: that's why I'm here too.'

I smiled back, relieved. I don't know why, but somehow I want Hari Mitra to think well of me.

He was looking at me rather oddly, as if he was trying to puzzle something out, then said something strange. 'I'm not . . . not always very good at . . .'

'At what?'

'I mean, I don't always see the best in a situation, in people. It's a fault I have, I know.'

I was surprised at the intimacy of his confession.

'You . . . you're the first person since . . .'

He broke off, then took a breath, as if he were about to say something else, but then turned and quickly made his exit. I was left there, standing, unsure as to what had just happened, and what he had meant to say. I am still wondering now.

CHAPTER 13

In the first few days that we worked together, Rashida seemed nervous, and I worried that I wasn't going to get what I needed. I didn't want to push her, but perhaps Faisal's fears about employing a woman had been right. She was so unassuming that it was hard to see how she'd ever manage an interview.

'Are you sure you want to do this?' I asked. 'You seem uncomfortable.'

She shook her head. 'It's not that. I've been trying to understand what it is you want. What's your story? I don't want to get it wrong.'

'Don't worry about that,' I said. 'I don't know quite what it is yet. I'm trying to figure it out. I just want to talk to as many people as I can, and see as much of Kabul as possible.'

'OK,' she said. 'I'll make sure that's what we do.'

After that, Rashida took me all over the city. On the advice of other Westerners at the guest house, I hired Bazir, a driver with a firm called Kabul Cars. Against their advice, we didn't always use him, but walked the streets, too, rising at dawn to

74

see the city waking up, watching the bazaar open, vendors wrapped in blankets against the morning chill, frying food to sell to other early risers, smoke hanging in the air, the smell of fat mingling with baking bread and exhaust fumes from cars revving their engines in the cold. I got great shots of little boys running with long loaves back to their families, old men's turbans turned to gold in the early-morning light.

Once Rashida got started, I realized I'd underestimated her. We talked to popcorn sellers, taxi drivers, kite-flyers, blacksmiths, butchers and people outside cinemas waiting to go and see the latest Bollywood blockbuster. There was a quiet intelligence behind her unobtrusiveness, an awareness of when to let others speak. As a translator she was careful not to interrupt or impose her own opinions onto what people were trying to say.

I took to going to the Flower Street Café in the afternoons, after Rashida had gone home. I liked its sense of calm, a welcome respite from the vague tension I always felt on the streets. It also served the best coffee in Kabul and the waiters were happy to leave you for hours, seeming not to mind that the place was an unofficial office for international freelancers.

One Saturday morning, Rashida and I met there for brunch. The security guards were used to me by now.

'Gun?' said the chubby one, his moustache twitching with a smile.

'Not today.'

'You are sure?'

'Uh-huh.'

'Then please go in.'

The café was busy as usual, but we managed to get a table in the garden. I was happy to be there, and liked the fact that the waiter knew how I took my coffee.

'I'm going to have the Kabuli Breakfast,' I said.

'What's that?'

'Eggs, sunny or scrambled . . .'

'Sunny?'

'Sunny side up – because they look like little suns when they're fried.'

Rashida made a note in the little book she always carried with her.

'They come with onions and tomatoes. And naan, cheese and walnuts. I'm pretty hungry.'

She picked up the menu and studied it. 'I'll have a sandwich.'

While we waited for our food we looked through the photos I'd taken so far.

'I'm pleased with them,' I said. 'But have you noticed? Something's missing.'

Rashida frowned. 'I don't see—'

'There's no women in them. They're just not there. I'd like to speak to some ordinary women, the ones we see shopping in the bazaar.'

'I don't know,' Rashida said. 'I don't think they'd be happy talking to us, not there on the streets. Or having their photographs taken.'

The waiter brought our food and we began to eat. Two men were sitting at the table next to us, tucking into bacon sandwiches and chips and talking loudly. They looked like consultants, the sort who usually sat inside, tapping away on laptops at reports for the UN or ISAF.

'It's a lawless place,' one of them said. His accent sounded Italian.

'Yes, but isn't everywhere we work?' said his British friend.

'Afghanistan's different. The Afghans love war. They're instinctive fighters. I mean, they've been at it for what – thirty years? This time round, anyway. And there was plenty of it before, as well. It's not like Africa: no one's killing because they're drunk or high. Afghans always have a reason. They love war. They love violence. It's always on purpose, and they'll do it as brutally as they can.'

I glanced at Rashida, who was listening too, her face expressionless. An Apache helicopter passed overhead, casting a shadow over the lawn.

'There was that warlord, remember, who locked his enemies in shipping containers in the desert during the summer and let them roast to death. Can you imagine? Or what about the way the Taliban dealt with President Najibullah – castrated him, dragged him through the streets, strung him up?'

I knew the last thing Rashida would want was a scene, but I couldn't help myself. I leant over and tapped him on the shoulder.

'The Italians strung up Mussolini,' I said. 'That was pretty brutal.'

His face darkened, then he saw Rashida and had the grace to look ashamed.

'I don't think the Afghans love war,' I said. 'Why would they? Most people hate it. They want to get on and live their lives, just like anywhere else.'

Faisal put us in touch with a midwife who agreed to us joining her on a visit to a compound on the edge of town. She wanted to check up on a woman who had given birth a few days before.

'She wasn't allowed to go to hospital,' she said. 'It would have been better for her if she had. She nearly died.'

As we entered the compound, a gang of children ran towards us, laughing and pulling at our hands. They led us to the woman, who was lying on a carpet, covered with a blanket, the baby curled up next to her. The midwife knelt down and spoke quietly.

The other women gathered around, offering tea and snacks. I didn't want to get in the way of the midwife, so we moved over to the other side of the courtyard, where there was some shade. The women bustled about, making tea, sending out a boy to buy snacks. When the tea was ready, we settled down to talk.

'How many families live here?' I asked.

Rashida translated the question.

'We are four families,' one of the women said.

'But there are so many of you,' I said.

'We are nine wives.'

'And do you all get along?'

She shrugged. 'We spend our days together. We cook together, clean, do our laundry, look after our children.'

'What about the men? What do they do?'

They laughed, and started to discuss it, everyone pitching in with their opinion, loudly, talking over one another. Eventually one of the women said something that made the others laugh, louder than before. Rashida blushed and hesitated.

'What's the matter?' I asked. 'What did she say?'

Rashida shook her head. 'She is very uneducated.'

'Don't worry,' I said. 'Just tell me.'

There was a long pause. 'It's not nice language,' she said.

'It's all right,' I said. 'I've spent a lot of time with soldiers. I'm not easily shocked.'

'They beat us and they fuck us,' Rashida said. 'That's what they were saying. That's all.'

CHAPTER 14

9th January 1915

An exciting day for us all: a visit from the King and Queen Mary! The news that they were coming sent us into a frenzy of preparation, supervised by Colonel MacLeod himself. We rushed to make the Pavilion spick and span, washing linen, finding clean pyjamas for patients confined to bed, fresh uniforms for the others, and for each of them a spotless new white turban. We even managed to find some flowers for their bedside tables: snowdrops and a bit of early forsythia, which cheered things up no end.

The sweepers swept and polished and mopped. I do find it very difficult to see them scuttling close to the floor like crabs across a beach. They never look one in the eye, their heads are always bowed and the patients simply ignore them. When I tried to thank one of them for clearing up a particularly horrible mess of bloody bandages, Hari stopped me, saying that I would embarrass him.

I felt rather cross about that, but there was no time for arguments. The morning was a whirlwind of washing patients and changing dressings and serving breakfast, then more ritual washing, prayers, then straightening sheets and then ourselves. The patients tied their new turbans even more carefully than usual; moustaches were clipped, uniforms pressed and boots shined. They absolutely revere the King. Queen Mary's Christmas gift had been followed at New Year by a photograph of him, and I had been surprised at their reaction. They handled the photograph carefully, as if it were a valuable family portrait, some of them kissing it solemnly.

'He's the King-Emperor to them,' Hari had said. 'That's tremendously important. To be killed in battle in the service of the King would be a blessing, because it would end the cycle of death and reincarnation. You'd be sent directly to paradise.'

By the time the royal party arrived, just before noon, everyone was on tenterhooks. We knew they had arrived from the cheering from the crowds outside: we were all lined up in the vestibule, which looked splendid with a red carpet and a hundred potted ferns, making the Pavilion look wonderfully exotic.

I think I was not the only person to be nervous as they made their way towards us, but the King gave a kind speech, thanking the city of Brighton for the sacrifice it was making on behalf of the patients, which put everyone at their ease, and Queen Mary had a smile for everyone. They visited every ward, stopping at patients' bedsides and asking questions of the men, who were eager to answer. I had not realized that the King spoke Hindustani, and indeed there were moments when he faltered a little and had to be helped by the various officers and surgeons who stood close by, but it was marvellous to see the King-Emperor face-to-face with the patients, speaking their own language.

An official photographer followed them everywhere, at a respectful distance of course, recording everything with his camera. By the end of the day he must have taken more than thirty pictures of the King and Queen Mary, the staff and, of course, the men on the wards. I should be used to having my photograph taken after the other day, but I was still not sure quite how to pose, a little intimidated at the thought of becoming part of history.

At luncheon, the King and Queen tried some Indian food: a thick and delicious lentil soup called dhal, and flat chapatti bread with curried lamb. We cannot have beef or pork in the hospital: the cow is sacred to the Hindus and Mohammedans are forbidden to eat the flesh of pigs, so lamb is often on the menu. I was not included in the luncheon party, but word spread that Their Majesties rather took to it, commenting that the spices were very warming and suitable for the time of year.

They left in the early afternoon to visit York Place and the other Brighton hospitals, seen off by the medical and the administrative staff, plus some of the able-bodied patients. As their motor car drove off there came a spontaneous cheer. The visit, I think, had been rather a success.

CHAPTER 15

Coming out of my room at the guest house, I bumped into Orla, an Irish doctor who worked at one of the women's hospitals. I'd met her a few nights after I'd arrived, and liked her a lot. She reminded me a bit of Molly the CNN journalist – tall and dark with a wicked sense of humour and a penchant for drink.

'Jo!' she said. 'I was hoping to catch you. Want to come to a dinner party?'

'Sounds swish.'

'It won't be anything fancy, but Veronique's a pretty good cook.'

I'd had a long day walking the streets. 'I don't know – I'm pretty tired.'

'Come on,' she said, 'Thursday's party night!'

I'd been pretty solitary since I'd arrived, apart from hanging out with Rashida. 'Oh go on, then,' I said, deciding to have a bit of fun.

When we arrived, the flat was already full of young and pretty people, drinking up a storm. The vodka was premium-strength duty-free and went down nicely. By the time we sat down to dinner, I was feeling pretty good. Orla knew everyone, and introduced me to all of them – a couple of journalists, a film-maker, doctors, human-rights lawyers, UN staff.

'Wow,' I said. 'It's the entire expat population. Is there anyone who *isn't* here?'

She laughed. 'There's plenty of private-security contractors. And the military – but they're all kept on base. That's no bad thing: they're not exactly safe to be around. My office is on the Jalalabad Road, near the Americans at Camp Phoenix. Makes it the perfect place for suicide bombers.'

'Ah.'

'Yep. I try to get to the office early to beat the rush hour. You want to avoid getting stuck in a traffic jam, especially near an American convoy. I don't want to get blown up by the Taliban, and I don't want to get shot by one of the Yanks because they think my driver's a bomber either.'

'It's that bad?'

'Sometimes, it depends. You shouldn't hang around after Friday prayers, or after dark, or in certain areas, but usually I feel pretty safe. It's always the same, though. Nothing happens for a while, then something does, and you remember.' She took a swig of wine. 'If you really want to find out how things are around here, go online, read the blogs. There are some that are pretty personal, but others that are trying to show the rest of the world what things are really like, not what's in the papers. Some of the military ones are actually quite good, though they often get shut down by the authorities. I've got one – check it out. I call it *The Kabul Chronicles*.'

One of the UN guys, a strapping Swede called Henrik, tapped his knife against his glass. The party grew quiet.

'It's Thursday night,' he said, grinning. 'Another week in paradise!'

Laughter and groans.

'Sh! I can't think of a better way to celebrate than being here, and eating this wonderful pasta.'

He raised his glass, and everyone followed. 'To the chefs!'

'*Merci*,' said Veronique, our hostess. 'Silvia brought the pasta back from Italy.'

Silvia smiled. 'It's the *parmigiano* that makes it good. I almost got searched at the airport, it smelt so strong. It took their attention away from the wine, though. I managed to get six bottles in.'

'Bravo!' said the handsome man sitting next to her, kissing her cheek.

As people went back to their conversations, the girl sitting opposite leant in towards us. 'I was listening to what you were saying, Orla,' she said. 'Sure, we're all scared of suicide bombers – but I'd rather be blown up than kidnapped.'

'This is Elsa,' said Orla. 'Dutch. Medic.'

'That's got to be the worst thing,' said Elsa. 'Not knowing whether you're going to get out alive, putting your family through all that. They were bad enough when I told them I was coming to Kabul.'

'Exactly,' said Orla, lighting a cigarette.

'Who's doing the kidnapping?' I asked.

'Depends,' said Elsa. 'Sometimes they're just petty criminals trying to get some cash from the families or from someone else who wants the hostages. Or it could be some warlord wanting to make a point. They're the ones who really run things around here.'

'Are they Taliban?'

'Some are, some aren't. They've been known to kill foreigners for un-Islamic behaviour. But I've heard it's often because they want their recruits to get some experience in killing.'

'And un-Islamic behaviour means?'

Orla rolled her eyes. 'It covers quite a lot. We'd be in trouble tonight, put it that way.'

There was a pause.

'Anyway,' said Orla. 'Let's not think about that. I've had a rubbish week, and I want to forget all about it.'

'Hear, hear,' said Henrik, who had come to sit next to Orla. 'Me too.'

'Is it still the affair?' asked Elsa.

Orla stubbed out her cigarette and lit another one. 'Uh-huh.'

Henrik reached over and took one from her pack. 'What's the latest?'

She sighed. 'So. Jo, to bring you up to date. We have a bit of a situation where I work. Two of our Afghan staff are having an affair. They're both married. People mustn't find out.'

'What would happen if they did?'

'She'd probably pay with death. He probably wouldn't.'

'What?'

'Well,' she said. 'The honour of the family depends mostly on the behaviour of its female members, or on what happens to them. So if a female member is dishonoured, it needs to be sorted out. If a girl's raped, for example, the only way to restore honour is by the other family giving their girl to be raped in return. But if a woman behaves badly, it brings shame on the whole family. So that has to be dealt with too.'

'Bloody hell.'

'Right. And apart from it being a terrible situation for them, it's also really difficult for their managers. Now that they know, they're implicated. They have to sort it out.'

'*They* have to?'

'Absolutely. If they don't – if we don't – the hospital will be in big trouble.'

'So what are you going to do?'

'Well, their manager, Dr Khan, isn't going to report them. Personally, she finds the whole thing unspeakably vulgar. She disapproves of their behaviour completely. But she doesn't want to be responsible for whatever terrible punishment they'd get, especially not death. She's in an awful position. And so this afternoon we had a meeting. It went on for hours, but we finally came up with some kind of solution. We're going to sack him now, then her in a year's time. They'll know why, even if we don't say anything about it directly.'

'And they'll accept it?'

'It's better than the alternative.'

'And then no fingers can be pointed at you,' said Henrik. 'Not a bad solution. Or about as good as it could be, anyway.'

'It's really that serious?' I asked. 'For the hospital, I mean.'

'Listen,' said Orla. 'Dr Khan's husband goes to a mosque where the imam has preached that if your wife is working for an NGO, you should tell her to stop, that it isn't right, because it's promoting Western culture. The imam also says that if she won't stop, you can kill her. That's how much we're hated. Not by everyone, but enough. We promised a lot when we arrived, and most of it hasn't happened. There's great resentment. Something like this would have serious ramifications. They'd see it as us not respecting Afghan values. It'd cause a riot.'

'What about Dr Khan? Will she be OK?'

'Yes, I think so. Her husband's an educated man. He's pretty liberal, relatively speaking. But there you go. It's been really bad.' She poured the rest of the wine into our glasses. 'Which is why I'm going to get good and drunk.'

As the night went on, bottles emptied and the room filled with smoke. People danced to music from an iPod, others sat around the table, talking intensely. I joined in, swigging back the Italian wine, smoking my head off, nattering to whoever was next to me.

'Having a good time?' asked Elsa.

'Great,' I said, realizing that I meant it.

'You planning to stick around for long?'

'I don't know,' I said. 'Depends what I find to photograph. I might.'

'Look,' said Elsa, nodding in Orla and Henrik's direction. They were talking quietly, looking into each other's eyes. 'I wonder if tonight's the night? I hope so, he's a lovely guy.'

There was something in her tone that made me look at her. 'Elsa?'

'Yeah. Soon after I arrived. It didn't work out, but it was fun while it lasted. No big deal.' She took a drag of her cigarette. 'That's what Kabul's like.'

The doorbell rung. I looked at my watch. It was midnight. 'Are you expecting more people?' I asked, surprised.

Elsa giggled. 'That'll be Alki-Drop.'

'Who?'

'When you run out of booze, you call him up and he brings more wine.'

'Really? Here?'

'Yep. It's risky, especially for an Afghan, but he makes a lot of money. I guess he's raking it in while we're still here and he still can. It's not cheap, and it's pretty disgusting. But at this time of night, who cares?'

I had some of the wine. She was right: it was

rotten, especially after the Italian red, which was long gone, but I drank it anyway, listening to Silvia discuss her trip back to Rome with Elsa.

'You know, it was weird,' Silvia said. 'I was so desperate to get home, and just be able to walk down the street without feeling in danger, and hang out with my friends – but after a couple of days I was lonely.'

'I know,' said Elsa. 'I felt the same in Amsterdam. There wasn't this big group of people always around. People had their own lives, their jobs. I saw my friends maybe once for coffee or a drink, and that was all. I never thought I'd miss Kabul, but I was happy to be back.'

'It's the "Afghan bug",' said Orla, leaving a disappointed-looking Henrik on the other side of the table.

'What's that?' I asked.

'There's something about Afghanistan that keeps you coming back. Once it bites you, you're done for. You never get it out of your system. I tell myself I'm doing it out of the good of my heart, but the truth is, I need this job as much as my patients need me. I'd be rubbish doing a nine-to-five in Dublin, I'd die of boredom.'

She stood up, drained her wine and went to drag Henrik off to dance.

'The Afghan bug,' I said to myself. 'I like it.'

I've been thinking about what Elizabeth said about everyone wanting to make a difference. It's what

Orla was talking about, despite her bravado. It's what I always hoped for too. Photographing something makes it matter, makes it important. It's how those who aren't there understand a war. At least, that's what I always thought, but now I'm not so sure. People look at my pictures over their cornflakes, but then they flick to the horoscopes or gossip pages and they haven't understood much more than before. While I'm there taking the photograph, I'm not doing anything to make the situation any better. If I have any power to help, it's trying to prevent it the next time, and really, will that ever happen? That's what's bugging me, Suze, almost as much as the stuff that happened when I was away. I know the power of photographs to move. I also know their lack of power to make any difference at all.

CHAPTER 16

ELIZABETH WILLOUGHBY'S DIARY

8th February 1915

I have not written in this diary for some time, not because I have had nothing to report: quite the opposite, in fact, is true.

At last Robert came back on leave, as he promised. I was awfully nervous beforehand, wondering how he would have changed after everything he'd been through and whether he would think that I was any different. When he was back in India, up on the North-West Frontier, I worried terribly, but it was nothing compared to these past few months. Perhaps it's because all I know of the Frontier is what little Robert has told me, whereas this is all so very close. The *Gazette* prints its list of casualties twice a week, as well as pictures of the Front; never quite enough to show exactly what is happening, but sufficient to pique one's imagination. They are horrible photographs: blank, muddy wastelands with scorched trees, deserted villages. The descriptions printed alongside tell equally terrible stories.

But I'm straying from the point, which is Robert and me. While he was here, he invited me to dinner at the Grand Hotel, where he was lodged. I had only been there once before, for afternoon tea to celebrate Mamma's birthday. Then I looked at it with the eyes of a child; this time I walked through the revolving doors proud to be a fiancée. I will become a proper captain's wife in India, a memsahib, and everything that entails. The day before, Robert had been in the *Gazette*'s weekly list of Brighton's most important visitors. I clipped it out and put it in the little rosewood box on my dressing table, together with the announcement of our engagement and news of Robert's promotion to captain.

I had dressed with care, feeling anxious. Next to 'Lists of Visitors' was 'In Society Circles', with its descriptions of the ladies at the Grand:

> Mrs Tarling, whose husband Major Tarling is at the Front, wore a gown of tête de nègre velour with a wrap of natural musquash. Lady Dunn was charmingly dressed in dull-rose pink broché cloth with a kimono of moleskin, ornamented with ropes and tassels of silk of the same hue.

Mamma was wonderfully soothing and said that anything would seem lovely to Robert after the trenches. Hoping that she was right, I chose an evening gown from before the war, pale-blue chiffon over silk, adding the string of pearls that Grandmother gave me for my twenty-first birthday.

Papa escorted me to the lobby. He and Robert have always liked one another, and they greeted each other with real affection.

'Bring her back safely,' Papa said, and I blushed, but Robert said: 'Of course.'

He looked so handsome in his uniform, taller somehow, but it was still the same old Robert underneath. When Papa had gone, he smiled and held out his arm, and we went to the bar for a drink.

Sitting next to the fire and sipping my sherry, I knew that I was exactly where I wanted to be and with exactly the right person. It was stormy, the wind coming straight off the sea and rain battering against the windows, but I felt safe and snug. We said nothing for a while, content just to look at each other, then Robert fumbled in his pocket, bringing out a box, which he handed to me.

Inside was a pair of pearl earrings in a silver setting.

'Robert!' I said. 'They're beautiful!' Taking them out of the box, I put them on and turned my head from side to side so he could see them, feeling cool pearls brush against my cheeks.

Robert was looking at me, an odd expression on his face, and I was immediately anxious again, and asked if they suited me.

'Oh yes,' he said, and his voice was proud. 'They suit you perfectly.'

★   ★   ★

I waited until he had chosen the wine and we had ordered our dishes: consommé to start, then roast beef for him, Dover sole for me.

'I've heard,' I began, 'that the Indian Corps has had a hard time of it, that the men have suffered a lot.'

He gave me a curious look. I had heard of men getting shot on purpose, I told him, of sticking their hands out above the parapet until they were hit, or getting a friend to do it, just to get away from the Front.

Robert frowned and said that would be a court-martial offence and that if he found out that any of his men had done something like that he would have to report them immediately.

'But I've also heard,' I said, 'about a thing called *izzat*. Surely that would prevent them from doing such a thing.'

At that point he guessed something was up. Of course, he said, no decent soldier would indulge in that sort of behaviour, out of concern for *izzat* or honour, call it what one liked. But what he was interested in was how I suddenly seemed to know so much about the Indian Corps.

I flushed and said that I had taken on a job at the Pavilion.

He put down his knife and fork. 'I'm going there tomorrow,' he said. 'Some of my men are there.'

I had to confess that I had thought so, and that I'd been even more worried on his behalf after seeing the state that they were in. Feeling rather guilty, I explained how I had decided to wait to tell him because I hadn't wanted to bore him by going into every detail of my life in my letters.

'I'm never bored by your letters,' he said. 'Please, Elizabeth. They're like – I don't know – sunshine to me, when they arrive.'

He launched into a story about being at boarding school and living for his mother's letters, which of course were sporadic because the post from India was never reliable. Later, after he had met me, he'd had to rely on my letters getting to the North-West Frontier, and now, at the Front, letters were the only thing that reminded him of why he was fighting at all: that there were things and people worth preserving.

I was astonished at the passion in his voice and was instantly filled with regret. I promised to write more often, every day if he liked.

Taking my hand, he asked me to tell him about the Pavilion, and so I began, telling him all the little details I could think of, from how the patients are cared for to how excited the townspeople seem to be about their arrival, to how different it is to work in a military hospital. He sat back and listened, seeming interested in what I had to say, and I continued, glad to have something to tell him.

The mood changed, though, when I explained about not being able to do any proper nursing. I smiled as I said it, expecting him to agree how silly it was. Instead I was astonished when he nodded.

'The authorities are quite right,' he said. 'The

men might be patients to you, but they're still men with all the usual rotten desires of an ordinary Tommy.'

I rushed to defend them, saying that I had never felt the least bit threatened; on the contrary, they were always extremely polite, and they even put their hands together to say thank you each time their wounds were dressed.

He snorted. 'A quick salaam means nothing. It's something they do all the time.'

I didn't want a fight. Putting my hand over his, I said it was very sweet that he was so concerned for my honour, but that I was perfectly safe and had taken the post because I had thought that, when we are married and living in India, it would be helpful for me to understand a little about the people and their customs. I might even try to learn some Hindustani, I added, as an afterthought.

He shook his head and told me I wouldn't need it: that memsahibs barely come into contact with the people, especially the kind of uneducated men from the countryside who join the army. Our paths, he said, wouldn't cross, and the only Hindustani I would need would be to instruct the cook.

I wasn't about to give up.

'I still want to find out about India,' I said, 'and make you proud of me. Are you proud of me, Robert?'

He took my hands in his. 'Yes, my darling,' he said, 'I am.'

★　★　★

98

I do hope that when he comes to the Pavilion he will see it for what it is, and the men for what they are. He seemed so very cynical about it all, as if being at the Front has made him somehow rather unfeeling. I do not believe that Robert and the authorities are right to doubt the patients so. When this war is over and we are together in India, I will make him see that people are better than he gives them credit for.

CHAPTER 17

I'm slightly envious of Elizabeth and Robert. How certain they were of their future – or, at least, their intentions of one. They knew what they wanted after the war was over: a wedding, moving to India, children, setting up home. I was never any good at that. You'd try to bring things up, to talk about the future, and I'd dodge the conversation and say 'After this trip' or 'It depends'. It always depended on something else, something outside our own world that you couldn't argue against, something bigger – a political situation, an uprising, rebellion, war.

I remember the post you'd leave out for me, stacked in a pile on the table in the hall – bank statements, cheques from magazines, subscriptions, the occasional postcard. I dreaded that pile. I could last for weeks, months, in the midst of war, of rockets exploding, of violent mobs, and not be afraid, caught up in what was happening exactly there and then. Nothing else mattered. Real, everyday life seemed a long way away, and that was the way I liked it. Bills, dental appointments, bank statements, relationships – those were the things that scared me, the things that made me want to run away and hide.

When things got bad between us, I remember you screaming that my leading my kind of life depended on you – paying the bills, fixing the boiler, taking out the bin. I never cared about those things: they didn't seem to matter next to bodies with their hands chopped off or orphans crying out for dead parents – but you were right, someone had to sort them out, and it was always you, not me.

I want you to know that I loved being with you – I really did – especially those nights in our flat when we'd shut out everyone and everything else. It was as if nothing else existed, just us, cooking dinner, drinking wine, listening to the radio, making silly jokes.

I loved the feel of your body against mine too, later on, between the sheets, the softest skin I've ever known.

But it was always the same; in the morning I'd switch on the radio and hear what was happening in the rest of the world, and I'd know I had to go back, to follow the story as far as it went, right to the end. When the news came on, something would rise up inside me, a sort of buzzing, an excitement, and I'd know I'd go, and that you'd hate it, and we'd have our usual conversations about keeping safe and keeping in touch and keeping the faith between us – and then I'd leave.

I'm sorry. I know it's too late, but I am.

★　　★　　★

I thought of you today when I went for a run along the seafront. I needed to exercise – my trousers are getting tight from all this sitting around. I used to love it when we'd get up early and throw on exercise gear and set off, running down to the canal and along its banks, past the warehouses, the posh flats and the scruffy houseboats with their cheerful pots of flowers and logs stored in baskets on the roof. I always wanted to stop at that barge that sold books, and you'd never let me because we had to keep our heart rates up, keep on going along the towpath, under the bridges, past mothers with buggies, and cyclists trying not to run anyone over, and the odd fisherman casting off for fish that no one would ever want to eat. We'd go all the way to Broadway Market, then come up the steps and stretch, then flop in the café and have coffee and croissants and read the papers. It felt great.

You always laughed at my choice of running music, said my pop classics were cheesy. You were right, but they reminded me of times when everything was much simpler, when I first came to London and hung out in clubs where men took their shirts off and danced on podiums until dawn, the Pet Shop Boys telling us it was a sin, and us loving it all the more for that. We'd drink too much and take whatever we could get our hands on, and none of us would care, because we had no responsibilities and nothing to get up for.

Sometimes I miss those days, Suze. I miss them a lot.

It's all changed now. Things don't work unless I pay them some attention. Apart from the tightness in my trousers, my whole body feels weird. I think it's left over from Kabul. When you're somewhere like that, always having to be on your guard, you tense up without noticing it, you hold yourself as if you're about to be attacked. When you come back and start to let go again, it gets you in strange ways.

Another reason to go running, I guess. I thought about Kabul as I ran, as well as you, and about Rashida. One afternoon she took me to the Ka Farushi bazaar, deep in the old city behind the Pul-e Khishti mosque – a strange place: hideous, fascinating, beautiful. Bazir came with us, keeping close. For once there were no honking horns or revving engines, just a medley of birdsong, the alleys too narrow for anything more than a bike. Hundreds of small booths bristled with brightly coloured cages. Some were old style, made of curved wicker, others wire or plastic, bent into the shape of domes or Chinese pagodas. Most of them were empty, the birds themselves stacked in practical square cages: everything from canaries and finches to pigeons, parrots and turkeys, sitting next to more cages full of quivering rabbits. The air was thick with bird dust and the dry smell of guano.

'Who buys them?' I asked.

'It depends,' said Rashida. 'Some are for eating, like the chickens, some are for singing, like that one there, the . . . I don't know the name – we call them *bulbul*.'

'It's a nightingale, I think.'

'And some are for fighting. Like those ones.' She pointed to a cage.

'Partridges.'

'Or those ones, *bodhana*.'

'Really? Those tiny ones? I think they're quail. In the UK, we'd eat them.'

'Here we use them to fight. I've never seen them, but my brothers go to watch. They gamble.' She smiled. 'Sometimes they win, but usually not.'

The alleys were crowded with customers, merchants and children balancing enormous bags of chicken feathers on their heads.

'They're taking them to the cushion shops to use as stuffing,' Rashida said.

At the end of the market, dozens of doves were packed into cages, waiting to be released. Men with Kalashnikovs casually hung over their shoulders stood nearby, like on any other Kabul street. I thought of all the ceremonies I've been to, when the fighting's stopped and people are full of hope, and doves are released as a symbol of peace, and all the times that I've gone back to those places, the doves long gone, and any hope of peace as well.

'Let's go,' I said, suddenly feeling sad.

We left the bird market and walked towards the river.

'What was it like to work in Iraq?' Rashida

asked, as we picked our way along what passed for a pavement, trying to avoid hawkers, stray dogs and small boys carrying enormous loads.

'How did you know I was there?' I said, surprised.

She smiled. 'I'm a journalist, Jo-jan, I looked you up on the internet.'

I realized that I'd underestimated her again.

'You've worked in so many places. And your awards! It made me very proud to see them. You must be proud too, no?'

I thought about it, wondering how to explain. I'm a bit embarrassed about them, actually. Of course it's nice to get a bit of recognition, to know that someone's looking at your work, someone who knows what they're doing and who likes what they see, but I find the whole thing about awards ceremonies and cocktail parties a bit, well, I don't know what the word is – obscene's maybe too strong, but they've always seemed in rather poor taste. You used to tell me to get off my high horse and not be so self-righteous, that it meant people got to see the pictures, which is what I'd wanted – and of course you were right, but there was always a bit of me that felt it was odd.

We arrived at the river, a filthy trickle.

'Could we go to the Titanic Bazaar?' I asked.

Faisal had taken me there ten years before: to a jumble of stalls on the dusty river banks, a crazy burst of colour, golden onions heaped up high, piles of red pomegranates, spices, nuts and sweets. It wasn't like the other bazaars, with each section dedicated to one thing. The Titanic Bazaar had it all: hanging animal carcasses, baskets of skinned sheep heads next to aluminium pots and pans to cook them in, sacks of sugar, bowls of lentils and rice. Pots of red geraniums jostled with piles of batteries and mounds of nuts and herbs. Osama bin Laden's face stared out from packets of coconut balls, surrounded by a halo of cruise missiles and jets, next to heaps of sturdy beige women's underwear and beauty products, dirty packets neatly arranged: soap and hand cream, body lotion, tubes of make-up. Small boys stood by, selling toilet paper, a few sheets at a time.

Faisal had told me the market got its name from when the river, after being dry for years, suddenly filled and washed away all the stalls.

'And of course, from the film,' he had said. 'We all loved *Titanic*. When the Taliban banned movies, we risked everything to watch it. We got a video-tape from the market and borrowed a machine to play it. I remember bringing it home on my bicycle, hidden inside my jacket. I was so scared, but so excited. I watched it in secret with my friends. The Taliban had made us paint the windows black so the women couldn't be seen from outside, so we were safe. We watched it over and over again. Such a beautiful story.'

As I had stayed longer in Kabul I had realized that *Titanic* was everywhere. Celine Dion's voice echoed through the alleyways of the old town. Leonardo DiCaprio, arms wide, was on stickers stuck on bikes, on transfers ironed onto the seats of taxis, labels sewn onto the pockets of the shirts young men were starting to wear instead of traditional clothes. They cut their hair like his, and brushed their teeth with Titanic toothpaste. Kate Winslet was stencilled onto the walls of women's beauty parlours, where you could have your face dusted with Titanic powder, or your fingertips dyed with Titanic henna, or scent yourself with Titanic Making Love Ecstasy Perfume Body Spray. Faisal's sisters loved Kate Winslet's pale skin and blonde hair, and admired the way she shaped her eyebrows.

'The Titanic Bazaar?' said Rashida now. 'I'm sorry, I've never heard of it. Bazir? Do you know?'

He shook his head.

'Never mind,' I said. 'It must have closed down.'

I was still thinking of Faisal. Usually he would have been quick to invite me to his house. I wondered if the fact that I wasn't welcome any more was anything to do with him being married. When I got back to the guest house, I called him and said I wanted to pick his brains about how the city had changed. He asked me to dinner at his house, as I'd hoped.

CHAPTER 18

ELIZABETH WILLOUGHBY'S DIARY

10th February 1915

Robert came to visit every day of his leave. Two of his Pathans are here, one missing a leg, the other with terrible wounds to his head. It moved me to see him sitting with them, chatting quietly in Urdu. I could see how pleased they were to see him, and how they respected him. He was patient with them, staying for hours by their bedsides, never giving any indication of boredom or of wanting to leave. Every so often he would look up and catch my eye, and we would smile at each other.

The day before he left, we sat, glum, over afternoon tea, trying to cheer ourselves up with some rather aged seed cake.

'Is it true what they say about the Pathans,' I asked. 'That they're the best fighters of all, a true warrior race?'

Robert shrugged. 'There's a lot of old guff spouted about it. The Pathans are good fighters, but so are the Gurkhas and the Rajputs and the Sikhs. If one's invaded all the time, one becomes used to it, and up to the fight. The tribal territories where the Pathans come from, up on the frontier with Afghanistan, are wild. They're ruled by bullets and blood feuds, so they need to be good fighters to survive.'

'Are they good at taking orders?'

He snorted and said they were, up to a point, but they bore no allegiance to anyone. At the end of last year, when Turkey entered the war, they hadn't liked the thought of conflict with other Mohammedans, nor the prospect of fighting near their holy places, and so lots of them had deserted and ran off home. They were probably back, fighting the British on the North-West Frontier.

'It's not so odd,' he said. 'When one thinks about it: their forefathers probably fought against us in the first Anglo-Afghan war back in '39, and the second one too.'

Lighting a cigarette from the end of the one that he'd been smoking, he added that perhaps he was becoming used to war, like them, and that it was curious, but somehow he wanted to get back to the Front.

'I almost miss the place,' he said. 'Partly because every minute one remains alive one is really aware of it. Sometimes I feel quite reckless, somehow free.'

A sense of dejection overtook me, as if I were not enough for him.

'I'd rather you were careful,' I said, my voice sharper than I'd intended. 'I'd like to have someone to marry when this beastly war is over.'

He looked startled. 'I'm sorry,' he said. 'Of course you would. So would I.'

There was a pause, then Robert asked me, in an off-hand kind of way, if I would write often, because my letters were something to live for. That made me feel better, and I said that of course I would.

'It would be wonderful if you could manage to write a little more too,' I said. 'So that I can try to understand how things are. Sometimes it's as if you're back at school and worried about the masters reading them.'

He nodded, and said that he would try. He was pleased, he confessed, not to have to go through his men's letters. All the other officers must, apart from those in the Indian Corps, who are excused from it because of the language barrier. Instead the letters are sent away to be translated and a report is posted back once a week on how morale is bearing up.

It isn't great, apparently – morale, I mean. Robert said that it is the first time the men have fought outside Asia, and that it is terribly hard for them to adapt. A few weeks ago a wounded man wrote that he was 'like a man who, once burnt, is afraid of a glow-worm'. The phrase had stuck in Robert's mind, because it was such an Indian way of describing it. The man and his family knew what a glow-worm was, they would see them every night in their village, and so it would make sense to them. How could that same man possibly describe the trenches?

'An Indian Shakespeare would find it a challenge,' Robert said. 'Let alone someone who has to get the company clerk to write his letters.'

Did he think the men knew that their letters were censored, I asked, and he said that he was sure they did, and invented little tricks to get around it, just as he had at school. It hadn't been until he reached the fifth form that he had realized he hadn't explained the code to his mother, and so she had never known what he meant.

'It's no surprise that she never came to rescue me.'

He smiled as he said it, but for a moment he looked utterly lost. I thought of the little boy, aged four, being sent away from home, and felt terribly sad.

I went with him to the station, which was a mistake. As soon as we arrived I thought of the last time I was there, when the patients had arrived on the hospital train, reeling and limping along in their lice-infested uniforms. I hugged him close on the platform, breathing in the familiar smell of his hair oil, trying to imprint on my memory the feeling of his arms around me. As the train pulled away, I prayed he would come back to me whole.

CHAPTER 19

I woke today at seven to the sound of seagulls, and for a moment didn't know where I was. Outside, the weather was miserable, rain lashing hard against the terrace windows. I lay still for a while, letting my head sink back into the pillow, thinking over what to do. It was the kind of day for staying in bed, for reading Elizabeth's diary, drinking tea, but I was restless. It was too wet to go for a run, so I decided to visit the Pavilion.

Brighton was deserted, its pavements dark and slippery, salt wind whistling up through the side streets. The elegant houses of Kemptown were streaked with rain, their railings blotched with rust. The town was suddenly dismal, an out-of-season holiday destination, postcard corners curling in the damp, an empty chippy, a drab sex shop with a half-naked mannequin in the window. Cars splashed dirty water up from the road as they passed, the faces of their drivers set grim against the weather.

I stuck my hands in my pockets, put up my hood and trudged on. As I reached the Old Steine, I saw the domes and minarets, creamy white like the stucco of the seafront, next to roofs that looked like tents cast out of copper, green with verdigris. It's such an odd building, the Pavilion, a two-hundred-year-old oriental fantasy, a seaside stage set that makes me think of the Taj Mahal and the *Arabian Nights* and *Confessions of an English Opium Eater* and 'Kubla Khan' all in one go – a crazy mash-up of styles and forms, a flight of fancy, fabulous, eccentric, a little bit vulgar, a folly, as out of place in Brighton as that replica of the Eiffel Tower in Kabul.

I passed under an ornate arch, stopping to read the inscription:

> This gateway is the gift of India in commemoration of her sons who – stricken in the Great War – were tended in the Pavilion in 1914 and 1915.

Inside the Pavilion was decorated in lavish chinoiserie, another spice to the mix. A hundred bells hung in the long room that I went into first, dripping from the ceiling, interspersed with tasselled lanterns. Enormous Chinese figures looked down from a stained-glass window halfway up a staircase, complete with bamboo handrail.

I remembered Elizabeth saying that the walls had been covered up with khaki boards to protect them – and looking at them now, I could see why. They were gorgeous: crimson in the music room, overlaid with golden palm trees and pagodas, serpents winding around pillars and dragons breathing fire from the top of the curtain poles. The rest of it was just as extraordinary, the banqueting room set for a feast with silver and candles. *Trompe-l'œil* palm trees pointed their leaves down at the diners below; a chandelier dripped with strings of crystal beads.

Little boards in each room told the history of the place. It started off as a farmhouse bought by George, Prince of Wales – or Prinny, as his friends liked to call him – at the end of the eighteenth century. When his father went mad and he became Prince Regent, he got John Nash to transform it into an oriental palace and spent more and more time there, holding lavish parties and having a great old time. Later, Queen Victoria wasn't amused by the decadence of her naughty uncle and sold it back to Brighton. She preferred to spend her summer holidays on the Isle of Wight, which tells you all you need to know about the difference between them.

I decided not to go to the exhibition about the Pavilion being used as a hospital – I didn't want to ruin Elizabeth's story. The rain had stopped and so, instead, I decided to take a wander down the Steine. At the very end of it, the pier was open for business as usual, jutting out over the sea, its neon lights brave against the dark sky. It's as odd as the Pavilion, in its own way and like old Prinny and his entourage, the people on it are determined to enjoy themselves, to have a good time. On a whim – it seemed to be a day for whims – I decided to take a look.

Hardly anyone was on the wooden boardwalk except a few truant teenagers and an old lady with a shopping trolley eating a curled-up sandwich. Seagulls perched on the railings next to her, waiting, following every mouthful with bright black eyes. Despite its lack of customers, the pier was full of action and noise: lights flashing on the helter-skelter, a ghost train's creepy laughter, waltzers spinning, the rickety-racket of the roller-coaster, the turning of the carousel. Bumper cars crashed into one another, the tide rushed underneath, all to a background of tinny stadium rock.

I looked back at the beach, the hunched figures making their optimistic way over the pebbles, at what was left of the heroic West Pier, still resisting the sea's advances. The smell of chip fat and candyfloss was making me feel nauseous, and it was starting to rain again, so I decided to shelter in the arcade.

It was hot inside, blasts of warm air coming from vents to ruffle the leaves of plastic pot plants. The carpet was sticky underfoot. I blinked as I entered, first at the darkness, then at the lights flashing everywhere, inviting punters to come and play, to win money piled up high on the penny falls or grab a stuffed meerkat in military uniform.

The noise was even worse: banging music, the whizz-zoom of Formula One, machine-gun fire, explosions. Men stood, legs apart, clutching plastic guns, shooting at screens where virtual opponents ran through jungles and swung across ravines. I leant against one of the slot machines, watching a teenage boy play a game called *The Terminator* in a chair that lit up, spun him round and catapulted him into a war zone. He gave it his full attention, dodging snipers, shooting from the machine gun attached between his legs to the chair. He was utterly focused: shoulders hunched, mouth tight, eyes narrow.

I recognized the look on his face, complete concentration combined with a pleasure that was almost sexual. That was what threw me. Suddenly the clinking and beeping and explosions, the flashing lights, the heat were too much. I began to twitch, first my head, then my shoulders and the rest of my body. Sweat ran down my face and my back, and I felt my heart pound hard in my chest. I closed my eyes, trying to block out the noise and the lights and the smell, but then saw bodies lying at broken angles in dark rivers, and myself trying to make my way through it but being dragged down until I was gasping for breath, gulping, choking, almost drowned. I tried to scream but could only hear the tak-tak-tak of machine guns.

Then I was sitting in a glass cubicle that smelt of floral air freshener, a middle-aged man kneeling at my feet.

'Get her some water,' he said, and a girl with a blond ponytail went quickly out of the door.

The man put his hand on my arm. I flinched.

'Are you OK?' he asked.

He looked anxious. I wondered what had happened.

'Yes,' I said. 'I think so.'

'You had us worried,' he said. 'At first I thought you were drunk, but then it looked like some sort of fit. Then you passed out, so we brought you into the office. Heather's done a first-aid course. She said it was OK to move you.'

I looked at his round, concerned face, the face of a man who had never done anything bad in his life.

'Thank you,' I said. 'I've been a bit ill. I'm sorry for bothering you.'

'Should we get someone? A doctor or something?'

I stood up. 'No, no, it's all right. I'm sorry. Thank you.'

I left the cubicle just as the blonde girl came back with a beaker of water.

'You all right?' she asked.

'Yes,' I said, and stumbled out.

I know I should go to the doctor to see if I've caught something. I wouldn't be surprised – I've lost count of the times I've caught giardia from bad water, scabies from dirty sheets, malaria from when the mosquitoes managed to get through the layers of repellent and socks and nets.

Do you remember when I came back from the Congo with it – malaria, I mean, the bad sort, cerebral? How you came to get me at the airport and I walked straight past because I didn't recognize you? I was so hot, even though it was December. You just grabbed me and hugged me and took me to the taxi. I remember sitting in the back, leaning into you and smelling your Italian perfume – what was it? *Acqua di Parma*, I think – and knowing that I didn't have to do anything any more, just let you take me home and put me into bed, where there'd be fresh sheets and a glass of cool water on the nightstand. There isn't anyone to do that now, Susie. This time I'm on my own.

CHAPTER 20

ELIZABETH WILLOUGHBY'S DIARY

14th February 1915

Robert listened to what I said about writing more often. This morning was Valentine's Day, and a postcard was waiting for me on the hallway table: hand-stitched embroidery on fine muslin, bright silks, red and yellow, spelling out the words 'Thinking of you' against a background of flowers and birds and a single butterfly, its wing a Union Jack. On the back were four short words:

I AM, I DO.

It brought a tear to my eye, meaning just as much as the most passionate of letters, because I knew that Robert must have seen it somewhere in France just as he arrived back from his leave, thought of me and bought it then, and so what he had written was true.

As luck would have it, when I arrived at the

119

Pavilion, I was met by more postcards: a box of the ones made from Mr Fry's photographs had been delivered. We passed them around, excited. The Pavilion was splendid, the patients beautifully turned out, with not a whisker out of place.

The one of the banqueting room was the best, I thought. He had taken it in a clever way so that the lotus chandeliers fitted into the picture and light streamed into the room through the long windows, shining onto the patients. I was in the middle of the picture, lit by a sunbeam, like some sort of angel of mercy in an Italian painting, which was flattering, if somewhat far from the truth.

I sent one to Robert, tucked inside an envelope.

'Spot your Florence Nightingale!' I wrote on the back.

It seemed a little odd to be sending a postcard to the Front, although not perhaps as odd as receiving one. It's as if we're all trying to pretend that nothing very bad is happening. But the list of the dead in the *Gazette* gets longer every week, and it is just as bad for those who have survived.

This afternoon, just after I had written my post-card to Robert, Lal Bahadur had another of his terrible fits. I happened to be passing by his bed when I noticed him staring ahead of him. His eyes widened, fixed on whatever it was that he saw, then he started to shake. I knew after the last time that I wasn't supposed to help, but I couldn't stop

120

myself. I went to him and took hold of his shoulders, trying to bring him back to reality. It didn't work: he began to howl, like before, but worse: an eerie, terrible noise that wasn't human.

It was Hari who managed to calm him, sitting on the bed, holding both his hands and murmuring something, words that I didn't understand but seemed to reach him. I watched in fascination as he spoke, looking into Lal Bahadur's eyes, his voice soft and reassuring. He was gentle, his manner so different to the rather brusque way in which the British doctors treat the men. I felt a strange swelling in my chest, the sort of emotion one experiences at a moment of particular kindness, and I had to turn away.

After ten minutes, Lal Bahadur was soothed and lying quietly, but Colonel MacLeod has decided to send him to the Kitchener Hospital, up in the Old Workhouse, where there is a ward for the insane. I could not help wondering, after all the things that man has seen, whether the staring, the twitching and the howling are simply a reasonable reaction to the horror that he has lived through.

I hate to think of Robert being back at the Front, of being part of that, of leading his men through it all. I know that the Germans are the enemy, but in their hospitals there will be men going through the same horror as Lal Bahadur. I only hope they have the good fortune to be treated by someone like Hari.

CHAPTER 21

I don't know how to say this, Suze. I'm pregnant.

CHAPTER 22

19th February 1915

I am feeling rather bad about Robert. Despite my promise to write often, I have found myself taken up with events at the Pavilion, with scarcely a moment for anything else. A programme of entertainments for the troops has been devised: there are so many people from the town who want to do their bit. Yesterday it was a special matinée put on for the patients and public at the Palace Pier Theatre.

Mrs Hamilton, a rather imposing lady dressed in flowing robes and a golden turban, introduced me to one of the organizers, a Mr Das Gupta; in his own words the 'life and soul' of the Indian Art and Dramatic Society. I told him all about Robert's Indian past and how excited I am about going to live there once we are married. Mr Das Gupta clapped his hands, equally excited.

'Are you by any chance familiar with the works of Rabindranath Tagore?' he asked.

123

When I said that I wasn't, he fumbled in a bag and brought out a little book. Mr Tagore, he said, had recently won the Nobel Prize for Literature and had actually lived in Brighton for a while, sent by his father to a public school on Ship Street.

'Keep it,' said Mr Das Gupta. 'I think you will find it most interesting. Now I must excuse myself to prepare for the performance.'

A few minutes later, a hush fell over the theatre, and then Mr Das Gupta came onto the stage.

'Pandit Shyama Shankar will now perform some invocations to the divine triad: Brahma the creator, Vishnu the protector and Shiva the destroyer,' he said, and the curtain rose to reveal a man sitting cross-legged on the floor, dressed in robes of red and gold.

The man sat perfectly still for a moment, until there were no more rustlings or coughs or throats being cleared, and then began to chant. As he sang, some of the men closed their eyes, seeming quite transported by the sound. I did the same for a moment, feeling carried to the East by the music.

This opening prayer was followed by a British magician, much appreciated by the patients, then an exquisite musical performance on instruments the likes of which I had never seen before, and finally an Indian play adapted and translated into English by Mr Das Gupta himself. Although it was entertaining in its way, I found myself distracted, my eyes drifting away from the stage, seeking something out. Scanning dozens of dark heads in the audience, I found what I was looking for: Hari, sitting across the aisle, three rows in front of me, his face lifted to the stage.

As he shifted in his seat, the light fell on him and I saw that his cheeks were wet with tears. Once again I was struck by his focus, his ability to give all his attention to one thing, like when he persuaded Mohan Ram to have his operation or calmed Lal Bahadur out of his fit of nerves – and for a brief moment I wondered what it might be like to be the object of such attention. It would, I thought, make one feel rather special.

Later, at home, I looked at the book that Mr Das Gupta had given me. It was called *Gitanjali*, and was a collection of songs translated into prose from the original Bengali, with an introduction by the Irish poet W.B. Yeats. A photograph was tucked into it of a man aged around fifty, his head turned to the side, his hair curling halfway down his neck, his beard long and mostly white, with a fine nose and intelligent eyes. He wore white robes folded over his shoulder and what I now know from our patients was a Brahminical thread.

At the bottom of the page was the publisher's name and, under it, a list of cities.

Macmillan and Co., Limited
Calcutta · Bombay · Madras · London

I whispered the names to myself, thrilled at the thought of one day seeing those places for myself.

I did not find the poems terribly easy to read: there was a lot about nature – lotuses and rivers and monsoon rains, dust-stained travellers and so on. It was difficult to see what Mr Tagore meant by them. Once again, I thought of Hari. He would be able to explain them, I was sure.

'I've been reading the poems of Rabindranath Tagore,' I said the next day.

He looked at me in surprise, then nodded, with more enthusiasm than I have ever seen him express, and said that Tagore was one of India's greatest writers, that his writing was extraordinary, 'beautifully modern'. He had, he said, changed Bengali literature for ever.

I hesitated for a moment, then confessed that I had found the poems difficult to read, at which he looked rather pained, then said that perhaps it was because I had read them in translation, and that in the original they were extraordinary.

His skin was slightly flushed as he spoke, his eyes bright. I saw that I had discovered something that made Hari Mitra come alive.

He went on talking, saying that Rabindranath, as he called him, was not simply a poet: he was a thinker on the subject of the world and its workings, in particular on India and its future. Hari himself had been to an ashram owned by him, a place where people could stay and think and pray, just outside Calcutta, with an enormous prayer hall with a marble floor and beautiful gardens and an experimental school. Rabindranath, he said, disapproved of Western education, because he thought children should not be forced to learn facts.

'I'll second that!' I said, remembering the great chunks of Tennyson I had to learn by rote at school.

Smiling, he said that although Rabindranath's thoughts on Independence were inspiring, he was more swayed by the arguments of Mr Gandhi. Feeling rather ignorant, I asked if Mr Gandhi was another writer, a question that Hari seemed not to mind at all: he explained that he was another thinker, a lawyer who had just returned to India after many years in South Africa and who wanted Independence for India too, but only by non-violent means. Mr Gandhi also believed that Indians should reject all forms of Western civilization and go back to something more traditional. Hari thought that this was going a little too far, but he did agree that India could not keep modelling itself on England.

'You don't seem very—' I said without thinking.

'Grateful?' His voice was suddenly cold.

I stammered that even if England wasn't exactly as he'd expected, there must be some things about it that were to his liking, and that he must have benefitted from being at Oxford at least.

He sighed. 'There are some good parts to it, of course. But we need our independence. Look at our patients. They can't go on like this, facing death for a country to whom in the end they mean so little.'

'They want to fight, though, don't they?' I argued. 'What about *izzat*?'

To my great surprise, he began to quote Shakespeare:

'Can honour set to a leg? No. Or an arm? No. Or take away the grief of a wound? No . . . Honour is a mere scutcheon.'

I remembered the play very well, as it happened. It was another of the things I had to learn by heart.

'That's Falstaff speaking. He may have saved his life in that particular battle, but by the end of the play he loses everything.'

There was a pause – and then Hari began to laugh, saying I was quite right: he had been using Shakespeare to make a point, but it was a weak attempt.

'It's very Oxford thing to do,' he said. 'I apologize.'

I smiled and told him that Robert has a terrible habit of speaking in Latin when he wants to put an end to a conversation, and that it was probably an Oxford thing as well.

'Perhaps we have more in common than I thought.'

The Pavilion reminded him of being there, he said. The architecture was similar, with its porticoes and domes, and the stone looked like very pale English limestone, although it wasn't really: just stucco painted to look like it. There was also the sense of living in a place where everyone knew one's business. Living in college had been like being at his father's house, he said: the porters had been like the chowkidars, who knew everything that was going on. The scouts who cleaned rooms and made beds and brought coal for the fires knew as much from the contents of one's waste-paper baskets as the sweepers at home.

'Although they were to be treated with more respect, as I soon found out,' he said.

Hari had thought he had left all that 'surveillance', as he called it, behind him the day he had packed his bags for England. He had believed that here one kept oneself to oneself, that one's business was one's own, but he had come to realize that it wasn't really true.

'Surely that doesn't matter if one has nothing to hide,' I said.

'That isn't the point.'

I have never really thought about it. People have always known what I'm doing: Papa and Mamma, of course, when I was a girl, then the mistresses at school, Sister and Matron when I was learning to nurse, and now there is always someone keeping watch to make sure I don't – Heaven forbid – get too friendly with the patients. Perhaps Hari is right: why should someone always know where I go and what I do, and with whom?

Once we are married, I suppose Robert will know everything about me: my hopes, my dreams, my fears. But that is different. We'll be man and wife.

I must write to him now, must keep to my

129

promise. But for the first time I am not sure what I should say. Would he be interested in the matinée? He is always slightly impatient at concerts. As for poetry, I know he doesn't like that. My conversations with Hari always make me think about things in a different way, or bring up new things that I know nothing about. Our conversation about Shakespeare had not made me anxious, as I sometimes am when I discuss things with Robert, but instead excited, somehow alive. I know these conversations are not something I should put in my letters. Besides, there is something that makes me want to keep them for myself.

CHAPTER 23

Shit, Suze, getting pregnant wasn't meant to be part of the story. That was your thing, the thing you wanted more than anything, the thing that finally finished us, not the affairs or the arguments or the broken promises. A child was something I couldn't get my head around, couldn't even start to imagine.

I told you it wouldn't fit with my career, that you'd be left to look after it each time I went away, but it wasn't for any of those reasons, really, and you knew it. It was fear. When you began those conversations about children, a small knot appeared in my stomach, my mouth went dry – and I knew, although I would never have admitted it, that I was terrified.

Of what? Of losing you to a baby, of feeling guilty when I left for work and, I guess, underneath it all, of the things I've seen in the eyes of mothers – mothers pleading for food for their starving children, mothers gripping the bodies of their dead babies, mothers wailing as tiny coffins are lowered into the ground. Having children means the possibility of losing them, the worst vulnerability of all.

I've no idea how to be a mother. I'm frightened by neediness. You knew that, and you were clever, always managing to hide your own, putting on a front when I went away, absorbing yourself in your own life, knowing it was the only way to keep me. A child couldn't do that, I know.

After what happened on the pier, I knew I had to see a doctor. I couldn't face going back to my GP – *our* GP – in London, and so this morning I went to a surgery I'd noticed around the corner from the flat, with an old-fashioned brass plaque above the doorbell.

There was no receptionist, just a waiting room with a couple of battered armchairs. A handwritten sign propped up on the mantelpiece said: 'Please wait here until GP is available'.

After a while, someone came into the room.

'Jo?'

I blinked. It was Florence, the girl I'd met in the bar.

'Oh,' I said. 'Are you a doctor?'

'Yes, I'm covering for Dr Webster. Have you come to see her?'

I shook my head. 'I haven't got an appointment. My doctor's in London. I'm here in Brighton for . . . a while, I don't know how long. I wondered if I could be seen as a visitor. It's quite urgent.'

'We'll have to fill in some forms, but that's fine. I haven't got another patient for a bit. Come in.'

I followed her into what must have been the

132

original parlour of the house, with a desk in the bay window, shaded by grubby net curtains. Every surface was piled with papers, books, a mass of travel mementoes, everything from Russian dolls to a fraying Mexican hat. I wondered if it was where Edith had come for her medical appointments – she would have liked all that.

'So how can I help you?' Florence asked.

At the bar, I'd been in too much of a state to notice anything other than her hair. She was striking, not exactly pretty – what's that phrase the French use? *Jolie laide* – with eyes the colour of that cashmere scarf you once bought from Portobello Market one freezing December afternoon.

'It's a nice grey,' I said when we went to the pub to warm up.

'Oyster,' you said, and we were off.

'Lead.'

'Pewter.'

'Platinum.'

'Taupe.'

'Taupe? That's not grey, that's brown. Hotel-room brown. Leather-trousers-in-Chelsea brown. Drink!'

'I think you'll find I'm right. I'm the artist. I know about colour.'

'And I'm the photographer. I don't just shoot in black and white.'

You raised your eyebrows. 'Elephant's breath.'

'Pinot Grigio.'

'Éminence grise.'

We went on and on, getting sillier and sillier until I said: 'You win!'

We clinked glasses and I looked at you, your face pink from the whisky and the fire burning in the grate, and at that moment I truly thought that perhaps I could stay in London for good, and we could get married and have a child, and grow old together playing word games by the fireplace.

Sorry, I'm digressing, but I want to remember the good times, before it all went bad.

Florence's eyes were grey – or pewter, or whatever – and they were focused on me. I wondered what I looked like to her, hunched in the chair, dressed in clothes I'd pulled on without looking.

'Are you all right?' she said.

I realized that my arms were clutched tight around myself, and that I was probably staring. I untangled myself and took a breath.

'No,' I said. 'I don't think I am.'

'Tell me what's wrong.'

'I'm a war photographer. A photo journalist. Just back from Afghanistan. I think I might have picked something up there. I've been feeling pretty weird.'

'In what way?'

'Well, I feel sick a lot of the time.'

I saw a flicker in her eyes, and was embarrassed again. 'That night, at the bar, that's what was up. I was only on my first drink. I didn't want you to think—'

She nodded. 'I didn't. Anything else?'

'Well, nightmares – but that's normal for me. Oh, and I'm bloated, even though I run most days. And I'm tired, really tired. I keep having to go to bed in the afternoons.'

She made a note on the pad in front of her.

'I came here because yesterday I fainted. I was in the arcade on the pier and there was this man playing a war game, and suddenly it all became too much, and then I woke up in the office with someone asking if I was OK.'

She frowned. 'Has this happened before?'

'No.' Then I remembered the supermarket. 'Well, once, a few weeks ago. I was shopping and suddenly I couldn't stand it. I had to run out. I was almost sick then too.'

'Have you been experiencing anything else? Sweating? Shaking? Any pains in the chest? Are you feeling particularly anxious?'

'Sometimes,' I said. 'A bit.'

'You're a war photographer,' she said. 'I guess you've seen a lot of dead bodies.'

'Of course. It's part of the job.'

'Have you heard of PTSD? Post-traumatic stress disorder?'

I felt a prickle of annoyance. 'Yes,' I said. 'And I haven't got it.'

'Do you know that? How can you be sure?'

I looked at her concerned face, her grey eyes, her glossy, well-conditioned, well-looked-after hair, and the remembrance poppy she'd pinned to her jacket. I thought of Elizabeth's patients screaming with the pain of their battlefield memories, of heroin addicts lying almost dead in a Kabul drug den.

'It's not me who's got PTSD,' I said, suddenly furious. 'It's the ones who've lost their families, the people with no legs, the ones who were there when the suicide bombers hit.'

Tears welled in my eyes and started to roll down my cheeks.

She said nothing, but slid a box of tissues across the desk, then waited. When at last I had taken one of them and blown my nose, she said, 'All right, let's not talk about that for now. One more question. Is there any chance at all that you could be pregnant?'

'God, no,' I said.

She must have noticed something in my face. 'I'd like you to do a sample,' she said, handing me a jar. 'The loo's over there.'

I blundered out, through the waiting room, into the cramped toilet. When I came back a few minutes later, I gave her the jar and sat down. I watched while she took a strip of paper and dipped it in.

Please, no, I thought – but I knew the result already.

'It's positive,' she said.

I watched her behind the messy desk, trying to figure me out.

'Is there anyone you want to call?' she said.

I shook my head. 'I'm on my own.'

'I can see it's a shock. You need to go away and have a think. Decide what you want to do, then come back and we'll talk.'

'I want an abortion,' I said.

'You need to think about it first.' She scribbled on a piece of paper. 'Here's my number. Call me when you're ready. If you want a termination, we can arrange it. But I want to talk more about your other symptoms too.'

On my way back to the flat, I passed a playground full of kids: little streaks of colour running, climbing, sliding, their high-pitched voices spilling through the railings and onto the street. Women stood with prams in groups of two or three, calling to their children, wiping noses, dusting down knees, doling out water and snacks.

I can't become one of those women in the park, Suze. I'd go mad. I get my groceries from airport supermarkets. I chain-smoke on balconies in dark and dangerous places. I'm not – I can't be – a mother. I wouldn't know how.

My mother didn't know how either. She never really liked children – or perhaps it was the way we pulled her away from her work. She'd fought hard for it: a doctorate in biology against her parents' wishes, insisting on marrying Dad despite him having no money, then taking us all to the forests of Uganda to carry on her research. She and Dad were happy. They kept my little sister Emmeline in a basket nearby, and she was happy too. I liked being able to play outside all day with no one telling me what to do, but I didn't like it that Mum was never there if I fell over or got spooked by the forest and wanted a cuddle. She'd look at me over her glasses and tut – or, worse, not even notice I was there.

I remember lying in my tent at night, feeling the air on my skin, heavy with night-time damp, smelling of old earth and new shoots, and the embers of our campfire. The sounds of the forest went on long after dark: there was always an animal or an insect busy hunting food or just going about its business – bats shifting, night flies flitting. I grew up unafraid.

I never told you what happened next, when I was eight, how Idi Amin had insisted on foreigners leaving, how my parents had ignored it, sure they'd be overlooked, and how I ran back to our camp one day with a monkey skull that I'd found under a tree, so excited, and discovered the bodies, two big and one small, on the ground, each with a slash to the throat.

It was chance and luck and a lot of determined walking that got me to the nearest village. I was taken by kind people to a convent, and eventually put on a plane to London. Then it was boarding schools and holidays with Aunt Jane and Uncle Edward, who became my guardians but never really knew what to do with me. Edith was my favourite relative, the one who took me to interesting places, who'd spent her life all over the world, just like Mum and Dad.

Sometimes I lay in bed at night and wanted to cry, but I couldn't. Still can't.

So you see, Suze, I don't think I'd know how to be a mother. I never really had one myself.

The obvious thing is to get rid of it, have an abortion, as soon as I can. It'd be crazy to try to combine my work with a child. There isn't space for both.

But you know what, Suze? I'm tired. Tired of lugging around my cameras, of my sensible packing, my Swiss Army penknife, my head torch, my universal sink plug. I'm tired of eating functional food and wearing functional clothes. I'm tired of airports, of fighting for visas and working out bribes. I'm tired of sleazy hotels and taking pills to help me sleep at night. I'm tired of men with guns.

Could I really give it up? Could I swap leaping over ditches and running through jungles and hard drinking and plain talking for changing nappies and puréeing vegetables and going for walks in the park? Because here's that guilty little secret, the one I've never liked to admit to, the one you always suspected: my work's bloody good fun. I know what Robert meant when he told Elizabeth that he missed the trenches, that it was where he felt alive. That surge of adrenalin that you get when you're in a tricky situation, the thing that keeps you up and going, it's addictive. Being at war makes everything extreme, I feel things more. Everything matters. You see it in the eyes of a killer with a Kalashnikov. You see it in the eyes of a photographer running towards a mob. Normal life just doesn't compare.

Maybe it's time to stop the highs and lows. Perhaps it's time to wean myself off this, my drug of choice.

But by having a baby? Is that my happy ending?

Jesus, Susie, I don't know.

CHAPTER 24

25th February 1915

Another letter from Robert:

Dear Elizabeth,

Here I am, writing to you on yet another dark Flanders day. I suppose that soon the afternoons will start getting lighter, and spring will arrive, but not yet. It looks like perpetual autumn here: it's the barbed wire, which is everywhere, rolls and rolls of it, rusted brown like October woods.

I am worried for my men. They are excellent soldiers, but they are trained for Frontier fighting, not this. They know how to keep watch for snipers' bullets, how to look out for an ambush on a lonely mountain pass or a sudden charge of tribesmen with their knives at the ready. Here it's shells, machine guns and mortars. They are used to mountain cold, night desert cold, but not this dreary, everlasting damp, in trenches that are knee-deep in water. They can go without food and drink for longer than I would have thought possible, but their food at home is sheets of warm bread dipped into mutton stew, not cold rations they get from a tin.

They say very little. I never hear them grumble. At night I go up and down the line trying to keep their spirits up. Their suffering is evident without them having to say a word: they sit there, hunched, silent and miserable, wrapped in whatever rags they can find in an attempt to keep warm. I find that somehow worse than if they complained.

Yesterday, I saw poor Fateh Ali Shah lying dead, trampled into the mud. I thought of him in his village in the hills of northern India – an only son, the pride of his parents. I moved him myself and was amazed at how little he weighed. But there is no time here for thinking too hard about these things: I left his body to be dealt with by the sepoys and went to help a lad who'd been hit in the head by a piece of shrapnel. He'd been lying on the battlefield for a long time and was almost dead from exposure. I called for some hot rum and water, and fed it to him. We chafed his limbs for what seemed like an eternity, and slowly he came to.

I debated whether or not to send him to the first-aid post so the orderlies could have a look at him. First-aid post! I thought of your

Pavilion with its order and calm, how clean it is kept. Starched sheets, clean floors, tea at four o'clock. Here it's two medical orderlies crouched in some shell hole or behind a wall of sandbags with a stretcher and a pile of bloody bandages.

There's not much point in trying to tell you: I haven't got the words. I don't know if there are the words. When I came back on leave, I know you wanted to ask me about it, but I couldn't have answered your questions. Sometimes it's difficult: at home one is with people who don't understand, can't understand, what it's all about. One feels an odd mix of anger, because things at home are so easy and unchanged, combined with something close to pity, because it all seems a little dull. Does that sound odd? I can't think of how better to explain.

I should go now. I think I've said enough. But please know that you are very much in my thoughts.

Yours affectionately,
Robert

I felt rather sad after reading the letter. I wish he had not said that he finds things dull at home: I cannot help but feel that includes me. I wish that he could truly confide in me. He says he can't explain, but if we have a lifetime of marriage ahead of us, would it not be better to try?

His men know more about his life than I do. I have often thought that if only I could speak Urdu or Hindustani or Punjabi, I might be able to ask them about the reality of it, without always having to go through an interpreter. Today I almost managed. I was in the old Music Room, bringing an extra blanket to Lakshman Khan, one of Robert's Pathans, a stern-looking fellow, very tall, whose one remaining leg stretched almost to the end of the bed. As I smoothed the blanket, tucking it in around the mattress, his face remained impassive, but when I straightened up again, he suddenly smiled.

'*Merci mademoiselle,*' he said.

I tried to remember my schoolgirl vocabulary.

'*Vous parlez français?*' I stumbled.

'*Un peu.*'

'*Moi aussi, je parle français un peu.*'

We beamed at each other. There was a pause, then:

'*Je voudrais une bouteille de vin rouge.*'

Despite myself, I giggled.

'*Non?*' he said, pulling a sad face.

'*Non,*' I said. '*Je suis désolée.*'

Feeling rather delighted with myself, I immediately went to tell Hari. He said Lakshman Khan probably learnt to speak French when he was billeted at the Front. Lots of the men had picked up a bit, he said, at least enough to buy drinks.

I rather liked to think of the stern old Pathan going to a café and ordering a bottle of red wine.

I wondered, out loud, what the barmaid would have thought.

'She was probably surprised—' Hari said.

'Of course.'

'—that he wasn't ordering cognac. That's what I'd expect a Pathan to drink, something stronger than wine.'

He had a twinkle in his eye as he said it, and I giggled, realizing that serious Hari had made a joke. The next moment, I felt sad again. I cannot remember the last time Robert and I shared a joke together, or found the same thing amusing.

I mustn't make comparisons: lately I have found myself doing that too much.

I remarked that I was impressed that the men had picked up French so quickly. Hari said they are good at languages and that they all speak two or three as a matter of course. I asked how many he could speak, and he said five: Bengali, English, Hindustani and Urdu plus, like the Pathan, French, because his mother's family was originally from Pondicherry, a small town on the eastern coast of India ruled by the French.

'It's a little like Brighton,' he said, 'with white buildings along the seafront, all rotting in the heat and humidity. Every time my family went there, my mother insisted that we speak French. But my favourite language is Bengali, because it reminds me of Calcutta, of home.'

'Tell me about it,' I begged. 'Calcutta, I mean.'

'When I think of Calcutta, I think of small things:

the clack of rickshaw bells in the lane by the side of our house; lying in bed listening to the monkey wallah's drum; the smell of samosas frying at the side of the road, washing spread out to dry on roofs.'

I nodded eagerly, transported to India by his words.

'My family lived in north Calcutta, in what used to be known as the "Black Town"' – he raised an eyebrow – 'just off somewhere called the Chitpur Road.'

The road itself, he said, was rather busy and crowded, but his family's house was spacious, set in gardens behind a high wall and built around a courtyard with an inner balcony running around the first floor. Green shutters kept out the sun, and he smiled as he remembered how he used to get into trouble as a boy for wiping his fingers along the dust that used to settle thick on the slats.

'Outside it was always busy,' he went on. 'As soon as one leaves the gates one is surrounded by the crowds. But there are quieter places too, like College Street, just around the corner from our house, full of bookstalls, or the Maidan, which is as big as London's Hyde Park. On Saturday after-noons we'd go to the Botanical Gardens to visit the biggest banyan tree in the world and walk along avenues of palms.'

'It sounds wonderful,' I said.

He smiled, and said that there were plenty of bad things about Calcutta too, and that I'd prob-ably heard all about them.

'The Black Hole, that sort of thing.'

That reminded me of Robert, whose great-grandfather or great-great-grandfather, I couldn't remember which, was supposed to have died in the Black Hole.

'Robert says that Diwali is the happiest time of year there.'

'In that case he isn't a true Calcuttan. For us it's the Durga Puja.'

I repeated the name, rolling the words around in my mouth. Hari said that it was the city's most important festival, and that Durga was the supreme mother goddess, married to Shiva.

'The destroyer,' I said, remembering it from the concert.

He nodded. The puja, he said, marked her annual visit to her father's home, and her victory over a terrible demon. Each neighbourhood would build a house – a pandal – for the goddess to live in. Meanwhile, in a special place in the north of the city, potters took clay from the river to make each goddess: a complicated process, full of rules such as fasting for a day before they painted their eyes, in order for them to be pure.

'When the goddesses are ready,' Hari said, 'they are put in their pandals and people make offerings to them of flowers, money and food. They burn incense, beat drums and sing. Then, at the end of the puja fortnight, the idols are cast into the river to symbolize Durga's return to her husband in the mountains of the Himalayas.'

I liked the thought of seeing the puja, but Hari said that the British tended to stay away, disliking all the incense and noise.

I told him about going to my schoolfriend Violet's grand country house, which had a chapel in the grounds with a statue of the Virgin and incense burning near the altar. When we had gone to mass on Sunday there had been all manner of chanting in Latin.

'Not so very different to your puja,' I said.

He smiled and said that most of the Raj British were Protestant, and wouldn't go in for such things.

'We still have the crib in church at Christmas with all those little figures of Mary and Joseph and shepherds and kings.'

He looked at me for a moment, and we both burst out laughing. Then I asked if he would go back after the war.

'Of course,' he said. 'I want to work in one of the Calcutta hospitals, to make it the best in the city, perhaps in the whole of India.'

'Maybe we'll meet,' I said. 'I hope we do.' And I meant it.

CHAPTER 25

I guess I'm going to have to tell you everything, the whole messy truth, how I ended up here pregnant and alone. It was part of the Kabul story I'd decided to edit out – I thought you didn't need to know – but I guess that's not an option any more. It's a long story, Suze, so here goes.

I went to Faisal's house, in a nice neighbourhood near the university. Sonia, his wife, was beautiful, and his children, Farida and Farrukh, very cute. I handed over a box of pastries and the presents that I'd brought from London: toys for the children, face cream for Sonia and, for Faisal, a DVD of *Titanic*.

We sat together on cushions around a tablecloth spread on the floor. Sonia brought out a feast: rice with a dark, meaty stew, enormous naan breads, little side dishes of aubergine and carrot, a yoghurty sauce.

I was gobbling it down, happy to be eating with my hands again, glad to be back with Faisal, when I sensed a movement at the doorway. I looked up. No one said anything, so I went back to my food.

But after a while I saw something out of the corner of my eye, a flash of blue.

Faisal's forehead creased into a frown. The rest of the family stopped eating.

'Faisal,' I said. 'Who's that?'

He bowed his head a little, his features suddenly tight. 'It's Leila.'

'Your sister?'

'Yes.'

'I didn't know she was here. Why isn't she eating with us?'

'She's not hungry.'

'I'd still like to see her.'

He let out a long, exhausted sigh.

'Leila,' he called.

There was a pause, then a pale-blue figure came into the room. Faisal said something in Pashto. The hunched shape lifted the cloth.

It was hard not to gasp at what I saw. Beautiful, laughing Leila, who ten years before had told me off for my ragged nails, now had a face that was tight and pulled over to one side, the skin puckered, raw and pink. Her right eye was closed, her eyelashes and eyebrows had disappeared.

'What happened?' I blurted out.

Everyone was silent.

'Faisal?'

'It was very bad,' he said. 'I'm ashamed to tell it.'

'Please,' I said, 'I want to know.'

'I can't . . .'

'Faisal, it's me.'

'All right. But it is not a pleasant story.' He sighed again. 'Soon after you were last here, Leila was married. Her husband was from a good family, and we were pleased with the match. The family was not from Kabul but Herat, four hundred miles away, and so after the marriage Leila went to live there. She was sad to leave us behind, of course, but happy to be with her new husband.' He cleared his throat. 'At first things went well, and soon she was expecting her first child. The pregnancy was uncomplicated, and she gave birth to a baby daughter. A year later she gave birth again, to another daughter. This was when things turned bad.'

I glanced over at Leila, who sat very still, her face turned away.

'The family blamed Leila for giving birth only to daughters. They began to abuse her, especially her mother-in-law, at first with words, but then they began to beat her. Everything she did was criticized, and she was given more and more housework to do, which she could never finish, and so she was beaten even harder. Her husband, who before had been a kind man, listened to his mother and turned against her too. He began to beat her as well, in the cruellest ways he could think of. When she became pregnant again, the beatings stopped, and for a while she found some hope, and prayed for a boy.' Faisal cast a look at his sister. 'It was another girl, and the family was very angry. Two days after the birth, her husband beat her so badly that she thought she would die.'

'Did you know about any of this?'

Faisal shook his head. 'She didn't want to tell us. She was too ashamed. One day her mother-in-law came to her and said that they wanted to bring up the baby as a boy, to restore the family's honour.'

'What?'

'It happens more often than you might think. For poor families it means that the child can go out to earn money, but rich families do it too. Some people believe that it can help them conceive a real boy. We call them *bacha posh*. They wear their hair short like boys and dress in trousers, and do all the things that boys do, like go to school and to the mosque and out on the streets.'

'And what happens when they get older?'

'Usually the parents decide that she will go back to being a girl. She is dressed in girls' clothes again and grows her hair and stays at home.'

'Isn't that a terrible shock for her?'

He nodded. 'That's what Leila thought. You saw our household when you first came to Kabul. Our parents were modern in the way they treated us. Leila didn't want to put her daughter through this. Especially not to please a family that had treated her so badly. So she refused.' He gave his sister a look. 'After that, everything was terrible. The beatings became worse and happened more often, whenever the baby cried. Her husband threatened to take another wife, one who could give him sons. Leila grew very miserable. She had no one to talk to, and still couldn't admit it to us. She couldn't run away either, because she didn't want to leave her daughters. So one day, when the baby had been crying and she'd been beaten by her mother-in-law again, she took some cooking fuel and a box of matches, went to the kitchen and poured the fuel over herself, then lit a match.'

'But . . . why?'

'She says she wanted her husband to see how bad she felt, to understand so that the beatings would stop, and he would go back to being as he was when they first married. I think perhaps, though, she wanted to kill herself. She says that if she had died she would not have cared.'

'What happened then?'

'She was badly burnt. Thirty per cent of her body. She ended up in the hospital – she was lucky: they have a burns centre there. It's needed – this kind of thing happens a lot.'

'And did her husband understand why she had done it?'

Faisal shook his head. 'The family refused to visit, apart from once, when her husband went to tell her that she couldn't come back to the house: she had brought more shame on the family and she would be even less use than she had been before. That was when she asked a nurse to telephone us. I went that day, and stayed until she was well enough to leave the hospital. Then I brought her back to Kabul to live with us.'

'Poor, poor Leila.'

'The worst of it is that she has lost her daughters. She'll never see them again. She worries about what will happen to them, knowing how the family treated her.'

I felt a choking sadness – for Leila, for her children, for Faisal.

'Will you tell her I'm very sorry?' I asked him.

As he told her what I'd said, Leila looked over at me and made an attempt at a smile, then said something to Faisal, who looked surprised.

'She wants to ask you something.'

'Of course.'

She began to speak, looking not at me, but down at the floor. Faisal listened, then said something back to her, frowning. When she replied, her voice was raised. They were clearly having some sort of disagreement.

After a while, Faisal turned to me. 'She wants you to take photographs of her, to show people what has happened.'

I was surprised – if Leila was ashamed enough of her injuries to wear a burqa at home, why would she want to show her picture to the rest of the world?

'And you think it's a bad idea?' I asked.

'I'm just worried,' he said. 'I wouldn't want her husband's family to see them. They would say we have shamed them.'

'They're the ones who should be ashamed.'

'You're right, but that doesn't mean that we should shame ourselves too.'

'Why does Leila want me to take pictures?'

'She says that when she was in the hospital she met lots of girls like her. She wants people to know what is happening. She knows your photographs are shown in newspapers in the UK. People will see and understand, and perhaps thcy can do something to make it stop.'

And here's the problem, Suze – I immediately thought of the *Time* magazine cover that came out a year or so ago, with the picture of an eighteen-year-old Afghan girl who'd had her nose cut off by her husband for running away from the abuse that she suffered from his family. The caption next to it said: 'What happens if we leave Afghanistan'. No question mark.

The picture stirred up massive debate and publicity. Some people called it emotional black-mail, others saw it as an appeal to the American conscience to reconsider leaving. It was a Taliban commander who'd ordered the punishment, to make an example. The woman, Aisha Bibi, said she wanted the world to see what would happen to Afghan women if the Taliban came back into power.

So the *Time* cover came out and the photographer won awards, and Aisha Bibi went to the US and got a prosthetic nose, and people talked about women in Afghanistan for a bit – but now?

155

Her husband has been released from prison, probably after a bribe. And despite that caption, despite all that debate, America's pulling out.

But that's not even the point. The point is that, because of that *Time* cover, I knew what the editors on the big magazines would say: 'It's been done before.'

Could I say to Leila: 'Sorry, love, you're an Afghan woman with a messed-up face because of what your husband did to you, but I'm afraid you're not news'?

So instead I nodded and said: 'It would be an honour.'

CHAPTER 26

ELIZABETH WILLOUGHBY'S DIARY

3rd March 1915

Something quite ghastly has happened at the Kitchener Hospital: one of the sub-assistant surgeons has tried to shoot Colonel Seton, the hospital commander. Thankfully the gun was wrested from him and no one was hurt, but everyone is shocked.

The news began as a rumour from the ambulance drivers, but this afternoon it was confirmed by Colonel MacLeod himself. When Major Williams asked what had led to it, the Colonel looked uncomfortable and said that it was apparently a protest against levels of discipline. The sub-assistant surgeon objected, it seems, to having to obtain a pass to leave the hospital after dark.

I have never been to the Kitchener: ladies are not allowed there, not even officers' wives, but I know the rules are much more strict than at the Pavilion. I heard Colonel Seton once in

Colonel MacLeod's office complaining about his Indian staff, calling them 'the sweepings of Bombay'. He had decided that the only way to prevent them drinking and chasing women was to ban them from leaving the grounds and to establish a military guard. Officers – both patients and staff – were to be allowed out in daylight, but the other ranks would be escorted for exercise on route marches. It was the only way, he said, and he advised Colonel MacLeod to do the same.

I am very glad Colonel MacLeod decided differently. He is, I think, a gentler man, despite his evident mistrust of me. If he were as strict as Colonel Seton, I wouldn't be allowed to work at the hospital at all.

It was Hari, of course, who asked what had happened to the sub-assistant surgeon. The answer was swift: the surgeon would be court-martialled.

There was a pause, then Colonel MacLeod said that he was particularly concerned that the patients and attendants should not hear the news, and asked us to be discreet, as rumours might lead to insubordination.

I couldn't help but feel sorry for the sub-assistant surgeon. He must have been so frustrated to have attempted something so extreme. Being cooped up in that old workhouse all the time would be tedious for anyone. When I said so to Hari he agreed, saying that it was an outrage to lock up one's employees.

'Do you go out much?' I asked.

'Sometimes.'

'Where do you go?'

He muttered something about being late for an appointment and all but ran out of the door. I was left feeling a curious combination of intrigue and irritation. I cannot imagine him like Colonel Seton's 'sweepings of Bombay', chasing women in town. I hope that isn't the case. I don't know why that should matter to me, but it does.

This is not the only bad news. Yesterday brought a very sad occasion: the death of one of our patients, Mohan Lal. He was in a poor state when he came to us, with both legs amputated and a suppurating head wound. The journey to England must have been agony: I'm surprised that he survived it. He is the first patient that we have lost, and I feel so very sad about it. It wasn't the head wound that killed him, but a type of influenza. His body just could not cope with a Western disease on top of everything else. We are taking precautions now so that nobody else contracts it. Luckily, he was an officer and had his own room, so we hope it can be contained. The room has been disinfected and his bedding destroyed. We are being very vigilant: our patients are simply not used to this type of illness, and who knows what might happen if there is an epidemic.

Like everything else here, death is divided.

Mohammedans are taken to their special cemetery in Woking; Hindus and Sikhs have their bodies burnt. I got special permission from Colonel McLeod to attend the cremation at the place built for such occasions, up on the Downs.

Before we set off for the funeral, a photographer came to take a picture for Mohan Lal's relatives in India. His body lay on a bier in a little anteroom to the side of the entrance hall. Over it was draped a piece of heavy cloth, printed with a beautiful design of orange flowers against a background of dark blue. White chrysanthemums were strewn all over it.

Mohan Lal lay under his flowers, the folds of the plain white cloth in which he was wrapped turned out to show his face: very peaceful, very young. The photographer spent a long time over his picture, wanting to make sure he got the best likeness, confessing to me that he had never taken a picture of a dead man.

It struck me when he said it that I hadn't seen a dead body before either. This was the first death at the hospital, and before the Pavilion my nursing duties had never been with the terminally ill. Grandmother and Grandfather died when I was small, and besides, I don't think they would have been put on show.

A small crowd had gathered in the entrance hall: patients and staff, everyone from the sweepers, who hung at the corners of the room, to Colonel MacLeod and Colonel Campbell, who is in

160

command of all the military hospitals. When the photographer had finished, Mohan Lal's face was covered, and the bier was carried to the big black motor-hearse that waited outside the arches of the main entrance.

Mohan Lal was a Brahmin, and the other Brahmins at the Pavilion wanted to attend the funeral. Hari came too, to say goodbye to a fellow Bengali, as well as the subahdar-major and those with the knowledge and caste to carry out proceedings, plus a journalist from *The Times*, very smart in a three-piece suit. We all clambered into two of the big motor-ambulances and set off to the Downs.

Taking the road out of town, we made our way through the village of Patcham, past the church and the duck pond, then continued out of the village, the road becoming a steep track through the grass. After a while, over the brow of a hill, we saw our destination: the burning ghat. It looked more like a shepherd's hut, set amongst the gorse bushes and hawthorn trees. It was a wild, blustery day and I feared that there was too much wind for a fire, but I did not have long to wonder, because the hearse and the ambulance stopped and we all climbed out.

I had expected everything to take place in silence, but there was much discussion between the mourners and those in charge as the body was taken from the hearse. After a while, we began to climb the hill. The mourners chanted Indian verses

161

as they went, and their voices echoed around the Downs.

'*Ram Nam Satya Hai. Om Ka Nam Satya Hai.*'

The journalist asked Hari what it meant.

'The name of Ram is truth,' he said. 'They are saying that the body no longer contains the breath of Ram – the truth – and so is of no importance.'

'Right,' said the journalist, scribbling something in his notebook.

The gates to the ghat were unlocked, and we went inside a small enclosure in which stood three platforms made out of cement. One of them was carefully swept with a small brush, sprinkled with water and then heaped with blocks of wood. Outside, on the grass, the body waited on its bier, and when the preparations had been made we gathered around it, the Indian mourners closest, the journalist and me standing at a respectful distance. Then Mohan Lal's face was uncovered, and his body sprinkled with purifying water, then honey and ghee – that strange-smelling butter that the cooks use in the Pavilion kitchens – and other ritual things were passed between his lips. The mourners gathered around him, squatting down with folded hands and lowered eyes, and began to chant.

While this was happening, the other members of the party had been busy melting more ghee and preparing platters of raisins, almonds and other foods. At a certain point, when everything was ready, Mohal Lal was laid on his funeral pyre. Carefully, the mourners laid on more wood and some straw, and then a white substance held in a spoon was lit and poured on the centre of the pyre. A flame leapt and a torch was lit from it, then held to the four corners. Some of the melted ghee was poured on top, and soon all of it was on fire.

A strange, unearthly smell came towards us, lifted on the breeze, of woodsmoke and singed hair and something else: the sweetish animal smell of burning flesh. I covered my nose and mouth with my handkerchief, and forced myself to look on as the mourners threw on little pinches of ghee mixed with grains of wheat and fruits and spices.

We stood for half an hour, maybe more, and then word was given to return to the Pavilion, while some of the official mourners stayed on to supervise the fire.

Hari had been silent during the ceremony, staring into the flames with particular intensity, as if to discourage the journalist from asking more questions. When I asked what would happen next, he said that the fire would burn for many hours, and then by the next day all there would just be left a few fragments of bone and a mound of ashes: some would be scattered on the sea and the rest taken back to the Pavilion, where they would be put in a coffer and sent back to Mohan Lal's family.

I tried to imagine his family gathered together, trying to understand what had happened to their husband, their father, their son. All I could be sure of was that they would never be able to picture the scene at that strange place on the Downs.

CHAPTER 27

After my visit to Faisal, I went back to the guest house, where I spent the night sitting on my bed, chain-smoking, trying to think.

In the morning I met Rashida at the café.

'It was awful,' I said. 'She must have been so desperate. The last time I saw her she was a different person. To see someone changed so much – well, it's just—'

My eyes filled with tears.

Rashida looked startled.

'I'm sorry,' I muttered, trying to hold them back. 'I don't usually . . .'

She hesitated for a moment, then slowly slid her hand across the table and patted my arm, lightly, just once.

After a minute or two, I managed to pull myself together. 'OK,' I said. 'Let's get to work. Last night I had an idea. In every war I've ever covered, doing awful things to women is a way of getting to the men.'

Rashida inclined her head a little, so I went on.

'So, in Bosnia, rape was part of ethnic cleansing.

In the Congo, it's a deliberate means of spreading terror.'

Rashida flinched.

'I'm sorry,' I said, worried that I was being too explicit. 'It's not a nice subject, I know.'

She bit her lip. 'It's all right.'

'You're sure?'

She nodded.

'Now, in Afghanistan, as far as I can see, it's slightly different. These things happen, but it's opportunistic, not part of a strategy.'

'You want to do a story about' – she hesitated – 'rape?'

'Not exactly. I've been thinking about what happened when the Taliban were in power. The Ministry for the Promotion Of Virtue and Prevention of Vice, the public stonings, the executions in that Kabul football stadium. All that.'

'Ghazi Stadium,' she said quietly. 'I was just a teenager then. My parents tried to keep it from me, but we knew. We all knew. It was horrible.'

'And it would be horrible again if the Taliban came back. But you know, life's pretty bad for women without them too. Look at what happened to Leila.'

'It was worse when they were here.'

'Absolutely. But they got away with it because enough people let them.'

I paused.

'Go on.'

'As far I can see, most of the violence, or a

lot of it anyway, comes from men towards their wives. Remember those women we met in that compound, with the midwife: we asked them about their husbands and what they did for them, and they said "They beat us and they fuck us"?'

She nodded.

'And then there's what happened to Leila, at the hands of her husband's family. I was thinking about those men in the café, having that conversation about Afghans loving war. I still don't think most Afghans love war, but I do think that being at war for so long has had a terrible effect. People have become so used to brutality that it feels almost normal. And a lot of men feel powerless, then they take it out on their women. That's our story. That's what I think we should look at.'

Rashida frowned. I wondered if I'd pushed it too far, but then she nodded.

'You know, it won't be easy. It isn't something people talk about. It's too shaming.'

'Are there any shelters for women who've run away from violence?'

'I don't know. But I can find out.'

'Great.'

'We could also try Badam Bagh prison: it's for women only.'

'What's the connection?'

'Well, some of them are in for moral crimes.'

'Moral crimes?'

'Being found alone with a man who is not from your family. Running away from home. You were talking about being beaten. If you are beaten by your husband and you leave him, you can be sent to prison.'

'That's crazy.'

'That's how it is.'

'Well then, that's where we'll go.'

As we started the long process of getting access to Badam Bagh, Rashida got in touch with the women's shelters. Most were too scared to allow a journalist anywhere near them, but eventually Rashida managed to fix a meeting with a woman called Gulshan.

'I've worked at the shelter for ten years, since it was opened,' she said. 'By a British lady. It was the first one – before it there was nothing.'

'And would it be possible for me to talk to the women there?'

As Rashida translated, she shook her head. 'It would have been all right before,' she said. 'When it was managed by the charity. But the government is in control now.'

'Has it changed a lot?'

She nodded. 'Now each woman has to go in front of a panel that decides if she can be at the shelter. All men, of course. If they want, they can send her home. Or they can send her to jail if they think she has dishonoured her family. And if you are not married, you have to have a medical examination to prove you are still a virgin, which is a very difficult thing to go through, especially if you've been raped.'

'What?'

'They don't want women to think they can just come to the shelters because they don't want to live at home. They don't want to encourage that.'

'Do *you* think that's why they come?'

She shook her head. 'No. They come because they have no other choice.'

'And do you think I could take their photographs?'

'It would be difficult. The women might not want it, and the government wants to protect our country's reputation. The last time a photographer approached us, a few months ago, they were very unhappy.'

When Gulshan had gone, Rashida and I sat there, thinking.

'We could pay a bribe,' I said. 'That would probably change their minds. But I don't want to do that. It'd feel like paying to get to the women. Like buying your way into a brothel.'

Rashida gave a weary smile. 'Many people believe that's what those places are.'

'The shelters?'

'They think that since these women are living without men, they must be prostitutes.'

'But that's absurd.'

'My brothers would be the same. I haven't told

169

them what we are trying to do. They wouldn't like it.'

'Listen, Rashida. I don't want you to get into trouble because of me.'

She lifted her chin. 'I want to be a journalist. I studied hard for it. This is my chance, Jo-jan. At the moment it's OK. They say you are like a man but not a man, and so I can work with you.'

'Like a man?'

'Yes. You move around on your own like a man. You live alone like a man. You are free like a man. But you are not a man, and so I can be with you. If you were a man, they would never have allowed it.'

I thought, not for the first time, how glad I was that Rashida's brothers didn't know everything about me.

'All right, you decide. But if things gets too much, you tell me, OK?'

CHAPTER 28

ELIZABETH WILLOUGHBY'S DIARY

14th March 1915

The newspapers are filled with stories of success in France. Our troops have captured a village called Neuve-Chapelle and with it more than a thousand German prisoners. The news is all of the soldiers' pluck, and how far we managed to advance, but I am not convinced. The 'Eyewitness' column in the *Gazette* said that it was a 'brilliant victory', but I find it difficult to know what 'victory' means any more. They say nothing about the wounded that have begun to pour in on crowded trains.

I suspected that something was afoot. I have noticed a pattern: when a battle is about to start, the French hospitals empty their beds to make space for the newly injured. Ninety-nine patients arrived from France last week, and many more went up to the Kitchener. I wrote to Robert to ask what was happening, and if he were involved, although I knew he wouldn't be able to tell me much. When he didn't reply, I scoured the newspapers for information, but they weren't especially useful. *The Times*'s war correspondent doesn't exactly give news, just his impressions of the state of things, and the 'Eyewitness' column has plenty about the weather but not much about what is actually happening.

Anyway, now I know. The men arrive dazed from the fight, their hands clenched as if still clutching their guns. Some of them are from Robert's regiment and are badly wounded, which makes me even more anxious for news of him.

I don't know how long our new patients spent in the French hospitals, but they haven't been cleaned up very well. Yesterday a group of Sikhs arrived and were sent off for the usual bath. I never enter the bathrooms, of course, but when the patients come out washed and dressed in their hospital uniforms, I am in charge of seeing that each is given a bed and settled in. While I was waiting for this group to bathe, I heard a commotion, and then one of the orderlies came running out.

When I asked what was the matter, he said that it was the Sikhs' hair, which was full of lice and other things too: nits' eggs, dead flies, droppings – probably from mice or rats. I told him that in that case it must be thoroughly washed and deloused as usual, and that I failed to see the difficulty, but he shook his head and said that this was worse than anything else he had seen. The best thing would be to shave it, so that the problem would be got rid of straight away and they could disinfect the men's scalps. But the men, he said, were refusing point-blank.

'Cutting their hair is out of the question,' I said. 'It's a matter of religion to them.'

'But Nurse, it's disgusting.'

'I'm sorry, but someone will have to wash it, then comb it through, take out the lice and apply the disinfectant.'

He grimaced. 'I don't know if anyone will want to.'

'Well,' I said, remembering Hari's theory, 'if you don't, we might find ourselves with a mutiny on our hands.'

He was still hesitating when Colonel MacLeod approached, frowning, and asked what the disturbance was about.

I explained the situation, adding that of course I hadn't seen the patients myself, as they were in a state of undress. Colonel MacLeod looked closely at me, trying to detect any hint of insubordination, and said that he would go and see for himself. In a few minutes he was back out again, saying that I was quite right, and that he had instructed the orderlies on how to get it clean without cutting it.

Not long ago, I wouldn't have known what it meant to the men to have their hair cut off. I felt a certain satisfaction at how much more I know now.

★   ★   ★

173

This afternoon I accompanied some of our patients on a walk along the seafront. Each day a small group goes out to take the air, and today we had five patients, one in a bath chair, the others able to walk with the aid of sticks. The group was headed by Colonel Coats, a nice man who used to be in the 25th Punjab Infantry and who takes a great deal of care with the patients, often leading them around the town to show them places of interest.

We went down the Old Steine and turned left along the promenade. It was a bright and breezy day, a relief after weeks of dismal rain. The patients were in good spirits, paying close attention to Colonel Coats's commentary on what is to be found on the seafront. They were very interested in the Volk's Electric Railway, which runs from the Aquarium for a mile or so until it reaches Black Rock. The railway is so small as to be almost like a toy and is always busy with day-trippers enjoying the novelty. One of the patients said he had seen a similar train in Darjeeling, but was shouted down by the others and forced to concede that, unlike Volk's, it was powered by steam.

We walked to Black Rock, then stood for a while looking out to sea. One of the men pointed to the horizon and said something to Colonel Coats, who nodded and replied. I guessed that he was asking if that was the way to France, because after that the men stood still, looking very serious, remembering, I suppose, what happened across the waves and thinking perhaps of their friends and fellow soldiers still in the trenches. I thought of Robert too, hoping that he was all right, but also of what was behind that 'brilliant victory', and what terrible things he and his men had done to achieve it.

We made our way back through the streets of Kemptown, somewhat shielded from the wind, although it still managed to whip up the little side streets that run up from the promenade. As always, when we go out on these trips, our group attracted a certain amount of attention. On our way down St James's Street, a woman sidled up to me.

Her hair was piled messily under her hat, which was fighting a battle against the wind. She had rouged cheeks and glittering black eyes that were looking with interest at the patients.

'Good afternoon,' I said, rather unwillingly, hoping that Colonel Coats, who was up at the front of the group, wouldn't notice.

'Taking the air?' she asked.

As she spoke, I caught a whiff of something – beer, perhaps.

'Yes. It helps the men's convalescence.'

She gave a low chuckle full of suggestion, and said that she knew of other ways to make them feel better.

'All the girls are dying to help,' she said. 'They'd kill for your job.'

I was beginning to feel agitated and hot. 'It's not like that at all!'

'Isn't there a way you could get me into the

hospital? When the powers that be aren't looking? You could slip my name to some of the men. It's Rose, by the way.'

Some of the men were beginning to notice her. She smiled and thrust out her chest.

'I think you should leave,' I said.

'Why? The men don't mind.'

'Colonel Coats would. You'll get me into trouble. Please.'

The St John Ambulance man in charge of the bath chair came closer. I thought he was coming to help, but instead he said that he would be happy to take her out for a drink, at which she put on a haughty face and said that she wasn't interested in his sort. Just then, Colonel Coats looked around. One glimpse of his military whiskers was enough to convince her, and she vanished down an alleyway in a flurry of skirts.

I wonder if this is the kind of woman that Colonel MacLeod and Colonel Seton are so scared of. Judging from the spark of interest in their eyes, the soldiers had seemed to like her. I could not help thinking of Hari and his vagueness about where he goes at night, and wondering if he would like her too.

CHAPTER 29

I spent a long time looking at the images of Aisha Bibi, the girl with no nose, trying to plan my photo shoot with Leila. I used to love the speed of frontline photography, the rawness of it, the lack of time to set it up. When a situation explodes in front of you, you start to shoot, and keep going until the violence has stopped or it's too dangerous to continue. You're shooting under the influence of adrenalin, not sure of what you're going to get. Portraiture is the opposite: constructed, considered and slow, and for a long time I didn't want to do it. I've had to work out how to do it truthfully, but in a way that makes it interesting. I knew the shoot with Leila would be a tricky one, partly because of how to make it different from the pictures of Aisha Bibi, but also because I didn't know how to square it ethically in my head.

On the day of the shoot, Faisal had a meeting at the hospital and couldn't stay.

'I trust you, Jo,' he said as he left. 'Look after her.'

When he had gone, Sonia brought tea. As we sat drinking it, I looked around the room. There was one window, shielded by a piece of muslin that filtered the harsh sun.

'We need light,' I said, going over to it and lifting a corner of the cloth. 'Perhaps we could take away the curtain.'

Leila blinked and said something, her voice urgent.

'She doesn't want you to do that,' Rashida said. 'She doesn't want people to see her.'

'Of course,' I said quickly. 'We'll work with the light we have.'

'Leila's asking if she should stand or sit,' Rashida said.

I'd been wondering the same thing. There wasn't much in the room apart from a few cushions to sit on and, on the walls, the photographs that I'd taken when I first met the family in 2001. I knew that everything in the shot would mean something later on – a cooking pot could become a cliché, a hairbrush might take on too much significance.

Do you remember that book, put together by a German photographer, of those pictures of Taliban soldiers taken in backstreet Kandahar photo studios? They posed, the warriors, hand in hand – extraordinary, dreamy, holding flowers, guns, mobile phones – in front of posters of Swiss chalets, riverboats, suburban American houses, wearing thick black eye make-up. The soldiers on the front line in Khoje Bahauddin had worn mascara too, to ward off the evil eye. I'd tried to sell my photographs of them to the newspapers, but no one took them. I guessed they didn't want the troops we were backing to look effeminate. These soldiers seemed not to care. They knew that photography was banned. They knew that homosexuality was forbidden and what could happen if they were discovered, that they could end up standing in front of a wall while a bulldozer pushed down stones to crush them to death. Yet, they still had these photographs taken as they wanted, paying attention to their outfits, looking as camp as the boys who parade down Old Compton Street on Friday nights.

We looked at those photos together, didn't we, giggling at an old Afghan joke that I'd found in some book: 'In Kandahar, homosexuality is so common that crows fly above the city with one wing clamped to their bums, just in case.'

Now it was Leila who wanted to be photographed. I thought she should choose her pose.

'What would you prefer?'

'She says she doesn't know,' Rashida said.

'I want you to be comfortable, to look how you want to look.'

I realized, as soon as I said it, that she never could.

'We could try both, if you like,' I said. 'I'll take some close-ups of your head and shoulders, then some from farther away.'

Leila gestured to her pale-blue shalwar kameez.

'She's asking if what she's wearing is all right,' Rashida said.

'Of course,' I said. 'You look very nice.'

She smiled, then whispered something to Rashida, who nodded.

'What is it?'

'She says that she hasn't painted her nails since it happened, because it hasn't seemed important, but now she wants to do it. If she's to be seen with a face like this, she wants to have nice nails at least.'

I looked at her hands, their surface blotched and twisted from skin grafts. Her nails were the only part still intact.

'Absolutely,' I said. 'Take your time.'

Sonia brought nail polish and began to paint Leila's nails. I pulled out my camera and took a few shots to check the light, hoping I wouldn't have to change the lens, always a nightmare in Kabul because of the dust.

While I worked, I thought of your hands – painters' hands, strong and square with short, blunt nails, the skin rough from scrubbing to get the paint off at the end of each day. You'd stand with a nail brush at the big old Belfast sink in your studio, slightly scummy from years of use, the wooden draining board covered with water stains, while you looked out of the window. I'd watch you there, those five minutes when you were coming back down to earth from work, and I knew to leave you alone until you turned, ready to be part of us again. When we got home, you'd wash your hands again, a little ritual, pushing up sandalwood bubbles between your palms, rinsing, then drying them on the old grey towel that hung by the sink.

Later, I loved to feel your hands on my body, the skim of them over my skin.

When Leila's nails were done, she nodded. 'I'm ready.'

'OK,' I said. 'Let's try a shot with you standing against the wall, in that patch of light.'

She went over to the wall and adjusted her headscarf, then pushed back her shoulders and lifted her chin.

'OK,' Rashida said. 'She's ready. You can begin.'

Through the lens of my camera, I saw Leila's burns properly. Her skin, magnified by the zoom, was rubbery, a patchwork of colours crossed with an etching of scars. Her mouth was a shock, with no lips to buffer it – a hole, like on a Halloween mummy. One eye was closed, the other half-shut. Her eyelashes had gone – her eyebrows too. Despite her headscarf, I could see patches of scalp at the front, where her hair hadn't grown back.

She stood awkwardly, pressed against the wall, and muttered something.

'What was that, Rashida?' I asked.

'She says that no one's taken her picture since her wedding day.'

'Please ask her how she would usually hold her hands.'

As Leila folded her arms across her chest, her shoulders relaxed.

'Wonderful. Now, can you just move over towards the window? Not too far, don't worry, just a tiny bit.'

The light fell over the side of her face with the half-shut eye.

'Could you turn your head slightly?'

As she turned, a small triangle of light fell onto the shadowed side of her face, lighting up her closed eye, a classic chiaroscuro. I thought of you again, and our Sunday gallery expeditions to see the Dutch masters. Do you remember that January morning when we took our hangovers to the Wallace Collection and you rushed me past all those French pictures of bare-bottomed nymphs to the solid Dutch portraits?

After that visit you began your own series of portraits, playing with the light that poured through the windows of your studio and bounced back up from the canal. They were naked portraits, all shadows and skin, the only splash of colour a red scarf, a nod to the hat worn by Rembrandt's son Titus in the painting we'd seen in the gallery.

It was when I refused to pose that you found Lara, sitting in a coffee shop around the corner from your studio. Lovely Lara, all pale skin and red hair, and young enough not to mind taking off her clothes in front of a stranger in the daytime. Lovely Lara, the politics student, who was lying naked on the couch when I turned up one afternoon with apologies and flowers, and who in no hurry put on a wrap and drank coffee, then later the rough red wine from a bottle you were given in payment for a job, and argued for hours about what she called the 'industry of war'. Lovely Lara, who, the next time I was away, graduated from your studio sofa to our bed.

I'd always put up with your affairs, taking them as payback for my absence, for missing your openings, not being there on birthdays. I knew when you were in the midst of one: our own sex was different, closer, more intimate, as if we were making up for all that passion spent elsewhere, reassuring ourselves that we'd be all right in the end. Lara felt different, dangerous, right from the start.

As the camera shutter clicked, Leila flinched.

'I'm sorry,' I said, and lowered my camera.

'No,' she said. 'Sorry. My fault.' Rashida's eyes grew wide as she translated. 'It was that noise when you pressed the button. And the camera focused just on me. Once my husband made me stand against a wall while aiming a gun at me. I thought I was going to die, so I closed my eyes and began to pray. When the click came, I thought he had shot me. He laughed and said, "The trigger is ready: I can shoot you whenever I like."'

I put my camera down. 'Leila, I'm so sorry. I would never have asked you to stand like that if I'd known. We can stop if you want.'

She shook her head. 'No.'

I looked at her, trembling but defiant.

'All right,' I said. 'But let's try something else. Why don't you sit on those cushions and I'll start by taking some pictures of your hands, so you can get used to the camera. OK?'

As I played around with focus and light, Leila relaxed. We worked for the rest of the afternoon, the sounds of Kabul drifting through the window – children's laughter, hawkers' voices, the call to prayer – underlaid with the constant noise of roadworks. Despite the noise, our little room was calm. Leila was determined, ready to hold her poses for as long as I needed. Rashida translated and I took my photographs, trying to distance myself from what I felt, concentrating on composition, framing, light.

I focused on the contrast between the dark red of the rug that Leila was sitting on and the blue of her shalwar kameez against the whitewashed walls. Her damaged skin faded from brown to pink and back again in different parts. I wanted to show Leila as she was now, but I also wanted to hint at how she'd been before, to give a sense of what she'd lost.

I took profile shots, face-on shots and in-between shots, some with objects in the background, others without. I decided not to worry about making the photographs so very different to the one on the cover of *Time*, but just to concentrate on Leila and see what we came up with. And after an hour or two of changing poses and angles, something happened, the thing that I'd been waiting for. Suddenly the pictures came right – and I knew we had our shot.

CHAPTER 30

19th March 1915

Robert is back. He turned up at the Pavilion without warning yesterday afternoon. It was a great surprise after the postcard I'd received from him on Monday – very different to his last one: army-issue, printed on cheap grey paper, with statements that one could cross out as applicable about being admitted to hospital or sent to the base or promising to write soon.

He had crossed them all out apart from one: 'I am quite well.'

If Robert's signature hadn't been there underneath, I would not have believed it was from him. And of course the postcard had the opposite effect to what was intended, because I immediately started to think that he wasn't well at all. All week, that one short sentence preyed on my mind. I kept the card in the pocket of my apron, bringing it out when no one was looking to study it again, as if I could squeeze out another interpretation. The words stayed stubbornly the same: 'I am quite well', nothing more, nothing less.

As the week wore on, my thoughts became darker. What would happen if he never came back? What would become of the future that we have been planning together? What would become of me? I am ashamed to admit it, but my feelings were more complicated than I might have expected. For so long I have been certain of how my life would unfold, but now I am not quite so sure. My conversations with Hari, his stories of other places, of political preoccupations, have given me glimpses of other possibilities.

And then, just as I was starting to believe that I might never see Robert again, I was told I had a visitor – and there he was, standing in the entrance hall.

'I thought you were dead,' I blurted out.

He looked at me, rather appalled. 'Dead?'

I tried to explain that it was because of his postcard, then faltered as I realized how stupid that sounded.

He frowned. 'What postcard? Anyway, here I am. Shall we have tea?'

We went to the Palace Pier. I had thought we might sit in the Winter Gardens, because it was blustery outside, and I worried that the wind might whip my hair into a mess, but when we arrived Robert asked if I would mind going up to the rooftop gardens, saying that he would rather not be closed in, and so I agreed to it.

We took the little lift to the café, with its elegant archways and domes. I said to Robert that I felt as if we were in India already, but he seemed not to hear me, staring out instead at something on the horizon. When I repeated it, he turned sharply and said: 'What?' His voice was oddly loud, so I told him it didn't matter, aware that the few other customers who'd braved the winds were looking.

We ordered tea with sandwiches and cake.

'Was it ghastly?' I asked, after a while.

He looked at me for what seemed like a long time, then nodded.

'Yes, it was.'

'Will you tell me?' I said.

He gave a small, sad smile. 'I'm not sure where to begin. The noise, I suppose.'

That was the worst part of it, he said, the shells exploding, the wailing, whistling sound as they came close, then the terrible, roaring crunch, the blast of falling rocks and earth, like solid rain. Sometimes he found it hard to believe that it would ever be quiet again. He tilted his head on one side, as if he were listening for something.

'There's a sort of rumble in my ears that never goes.'

'Like the sea?'

'Not really. More sinister than that.'

As the waitress arrived with the tea and laid it out on the table, I listened to the waves swishing onto the shingle and the murmur of conversation around us, and I realized that no matter how hard I tried to understand and how much Robert tried to explain, I would never know what had really happened to him.

I sipped my tea, waiting for him to carry on, but he just kept eating his sandwich as if neither caring nor noticing how it tasted.

'I read about it in *The Times*,' I said. 'They said it was a marvellous victory.'

He lowered his eyes and broke into a soft laughter.

'Our *victory*,' he said, wrapping his hands around his teacup. 'Well, if that's what you can call moving forward a few hundred yards, then I suppose it was.' He looked up and stared into my eyes. 'But the truth is, we lost twelve thousand soldiers.'

I put down my cake fork, speechless.

'The night before, we almost froze to death. Our men just sat there, saying nothing, not even shivering, waiting for the signal to attack. When we did, they fought as if they were possessed. It took less than two hours to capture the village. The shelling was so heavy that it opened up old graves in the cemetery. The church was gone, apart from one crucifix, an enormous one about eight feet tall, with Christ looking down from his cross as if he'd seen everything they'd done and wasn't the least bit pleased.'

He shook his head, as if he were trying to rid himself of the memory.

'One of my Gurkhas came running out of the woods making a terrible noise, a sort of whoop. He was carrying a face that he'd sliced clean off with his *kukhri*. He was so pleased with himself, and I had to look at the horrible thing too and seem pleased, because my troops were there to win, and I was there to lead them.

'On the last night, when it was all over, all I could do was stand there, watching the stretcher-bearers moving through the fog, looking for the wounded, trying not to trip over the bodies that lay wherever one looked. The air smelt of blood and death, and rum from the extra rations we gave the men to help them fight. I just stood and smoked and asked myself if it was worth it.'

He gave a little hopeless shrug and looked out to sea.

I felt slightly nauseous: I had no appetite for the sandwiches now, and when the waitress came I told her to take them away.

CHAPTER 31

'There's someone I'd like you to meet,' said Rashida one morning as we sat with our coffee in the Flower Street Café.

I was intrigued. Apart from the facts on her CV – twenty-two with a BA in journalism, fluent in English, Pashto and Dari – I didn't know much about Rashida. She knew more about me from her Google searches, but I'd avoided any more personal conversations. I still hadn't got the measure of what was acceptable to ask and what wasn't. But if she wanted to tell me more, I was up for it.

'Great,' I said. 'Just tell me where and when.'

That night she sent me a text. 'Will come to guest house tomorrow 3 p.m.'

There was a party going on at Henrik's flat, but I decided not to risk a hangover. I went to bed early instead with my computer and a DVD of *Annie Hall*, but my dreams were filled with scenes from a Bollywood romance that featured a dance routine in the Panjshir Valley, with a couple serenaded by grinning Taliban using their Kalashnikovs as microphones, and I woke up blinking and confused.

★　★　★

191

At three o'clock exactly, Rashida came up the path, dressed in a silk shalwar kameez and a chiffon headscarf edged with little silver discs.

'You look great,' I said. I was wearing my usual uniform of trousers and long shirt. 'Should I change? Are we going somewhere special?'

She laughed. 'It's special to me,' she said. 'But it doesn't matter what you wear. I'm dressed up because it's Friday – and because he likes it. I was wondering . . .'

She paused.

'What?'

'Could you bring your camera? I'd like you to take a picture of us.'

'Of course,' I said, even more intrigued.

Bazir drove deep into the city, south of the river, where the streets were narrow and dark. After a while he stopped the car and said something to Rashida.

'We'll have to walk from here,' she said. 'The car can't go any farther. But we're nearly there. It's not far. Bazir will wait for us.'

She led me down a little lane, quiet in the afternoon heat and deserted apart from a small boy rolling a bicycle wheel along with a stick. As we passed him he stopped and stared, his mouth open.

Rashida smiled. 'I love this part of the city. It reminds me of being a child like him.'

It reminded me of backstreets in Naples, houses so close they almost touched, strung with washing lines between them. Here, though, there was no laundry strung out for people to see: clothes far too intimate a thing to be exposed.

At the end of the lane, the road widened. A high wall stretched around a corner, and we followed it, staying in the shade. Eventually we came to a gate with a man asleep on a stool.

'Ghulam,' said Rashida.

The man twitched and jerked awake, launching into what sounded like an apology, but Rashida quickly stopped him, and he opened the gate.

It was like stepping into another world – a secret garden spread out around an old, crumbling house. Terraces folded down from it, leading to a sunken lawn surrounded by flower beds filled with roses. Fruit trees stood in a little orchard to one side of the house.

'It's beautiful,' I said to Rashida.

She smiled. 'This is where I come to think.'

I could see why. The clamour of Kabul had magically vanished: the only sound was the cooing of turtle doves that flitted around a dovecote in a corner.

'Come,' she said. 'He'll be waiting.'

I expected her to take me up to the house, but instead she led me through the garden, past more flowers, to a pergola that again reminded me of Italy, dripping with white grapes. There, sitting in a fraying wicker chair, was not the boyfriend I'd expected, but an old man. His face was aristocratic, angular, with the same green eyes as Rashida, his hair the same white as the prayer cap perched on top of it.

'This is my grandfather, Amanullah Rahmani,' said Rashida. 'Grandfather, this is Jo.'

'How do you do?' he said in perfect English. He gestured towards another chair. 'Please, sit.'

It was wonderfully shady under the pergola, a relief to be surrounded by green leaves, the harsh sunlight filtered and tamed.

'Would you like something to drink?' he asked. 'Some coffee, perhaps?'

It was the first time I'd been offered coffee in Kabul instead of tea.

'Yes, please.'

'I'll get it,' said Rashida, and began to walk towards the house. Her grandfather watched her go with soft eyes.

'Your garden is beautiful,' I said.

'We Afghans are very particular about our gardens,' he said, smiling.

I thought of the dustiness of Kabul, the harsh winds, dirt packed hard underfoot. 'Really? Isn't it very difficult to garden here?'

'Precisely. That's why we need them. We've been very good at it, ever since the days of Babur.'

'Babur?'

He looked at me over his spectacles. 'The great conqueror, descendant of Tamerlane and Genghis Khan?'

'Please, tell me,' I said, feeling rather ignorant.

'Well,' he said. 'Where to start? He came from the Fergana Valley, in what is now Uzbekistan, arriving in Kabul in 1504. At first he killed so many people that he made towers out of their heads, but he came to love the city so much he stayed for more than twenty years. One of the reasons he loved it was the flowers that grew on the hillsides – the vineyards, the orchards. He called it "paradise on earth". Eventually he went to India and founded the Mughal dynasty, but he never loved India like he loved Afghanistan. His body was brought back here to be buried. You should go to Bagh-e Babur in the south of the city to see his grave, in the gardens he built. They're worth a look. They inspired the rest of Asia.'

'Ah,' I said, remembering. 'I went, I think, ten years ago.' Faisal had taken me to a broken place, filled with smashed terraces and uprooted trees, weeping as he told me how he used to go there for picnics as a child.

'Well then you didn't see it at its best. Gardens don't flourish in war. Ask Rashida to take you. They've been rebuilt. They're beautiful again.'

He looked around with satisfaction at his own terraces.

'This garden was planted by my grandfather, more than a hundred years ago. Your country was trying to invade us at the time, I believe.'

I flushed. 'I'm sorry—'

He made a gesture with his hand. 'My dear, this house is a survivor. It has seen so many wars, resisted so many invasions. The British, the Russians, the Americans. The mujahidin, the Taliban. There will undoubtedly be more.'

I looked up at the low white villa, an ageing beauty of a house, its windows shaded against the afternoon sun.

'You see that one there?' Amanullah pointed to a pillar on the veranda, split in two. 'That was the Russians in 1979. And that missing corner, on the left? The mujahidin, five years later. But they never got the garden.'

'I'm glad.'

'So am I.'

Rashida returned and sat on the remaining chair. 'Akram is on his way.'

Sure enough, a minute or so later another man, almost as old as Amanullah, came across the garden with a tray. None of us spoke as he laid things out on the table: a slightly chipped white porcelain teapot with a pattern of yellow roses, three matching teacups, a little silver jug, a sugar bowl with tongs and two bowls, one filled with almonds, the other with shiny red mulberries.

'These are from the garden,' said Amanullah. 'The first of the season. I hope they're to your liking.'

'I saw your trees,' I said. 'I thought they were apple.'

'Some of them are,' he said. 'We also have pomegranate and quince. And mulberry bushes in their own special corner.'

He leant over, picked up the teapot and poured steaming coffee into the cups.

'Milk?' he said.

I nodded.

'Sugar?'

'No thanks.'

He put three lumps into his coffee and two into Rashida's.

'My wife loved the gardens too. She liked to fill the house with fresh flowers. Do you see that room with all the windows – there at the end towards the orchard? That was her *gulkhana*, her flower room, where she used to sit in winter to take the sun. Would you like to see some photographs of the gardens as they were?'

'Yes please.'

'I'll fetch them,' said Rashida, getting to her feet again.

'I am very fond of photography,' said Amanullah. 'I bought myself a Leica camera on a business trip to Islamabad in the '60s. It became quite a hobby of mine.'

'What were your subjects?'

'Oh, family, friends, the usual things. But also landscapes. I travelled a lot for my work, and I wanted to show my wife where I had been.'

Rashida came back with Akram, carrying a stack of photograph albums, which he put down on a chair. As he cleared away the tea things, Rashida passed one of the albums to Amanullah. He sat for a moment with the book on his knees, his eyes half-closed, as if remembering what was inside, then brushed off a layer of dust and opened it.

The first picture was of the house, still intact and glistening white, with two servants standing at the entrance. A sports car was parked in the driveway and in the foreground a peacock picked its way over a perfectly clipped lawn.

'The house was lovely then,' sighed Amanullah. 'And the gardens. We had five gardeners, always busy.'

I looked at the other photographs, stuck into gummed corners: the fruit trees in blossom, hundreds of roses spread around a fountain, box hedges trimmed into fantastical shapes. In one of the pictures a woman, laughing, held a chubby baby up to smell the roses. She was very beautiful, and wore a tea dress printed with little flowers.

'That is my wife, Alima,' Amanullah said. 'With Khadija, Rashida's mother, our first child.'

As we were looking at the pictures of the Blue Mosque in Herat, the call to prayer came drifting over the high walls. For a moment we were silent, allowing it to fill the garden with its melancholy sound.

'We'll leave you, Baba,' said Rashida. 'I know it's time for you to pray. But first, do you mind if Jo takes a photograph of us together?'

He sat up straight in the old wicker chair, and Rashida squatted next to him, her cheek next to his, her arm around his shoulder – two ends of a century in the garden of a house that had seen it all. Mindful of the old man's prayers, I worked quickly, firing off a series of shots, hoping they'd be good.

'We'll bring you a copy of the best one,' Rashida said.

He smiled. 'I'd like that very much.'

CHAPTER 32

27th March 1915

I had hoped that Robert and Hari might become friends, but their first meeting was a disaster. I thought they had found something in common, when Hari told Robert he was from Calcutta. Robert loves the city, he has always said so, but now for some reason he said, in an unpleasant, scoffing sort of way, that the old capital was fading fast and that Delhi was a much better place to live.

I pretended to busy myself with some dressings, secretly pleased to hear Hari say that all the same he would be going back to Calcutta, to his family, and not to Delhi.

'I'm a Bengali,' he said, with a smile. 'I can't go anywhere else.'

'Well,' Robert said. 'I'll be interested to see what will happen to Bengal.'

'I hope there won't be another attempt at partition. The last time was a fiasco.'

'Partition was ten years ago, and it didn't work because of the people's sheer stubbornness. It makes perfect sense to have separate Hindu and Muslim states: Bengal is far too big to administer on its own.'

I didn't know what they were talking about, but they both seemed to be getting rather cross.

'Dividing us up creates trouble,' said Hari, with an edge to his voice.

'It won't be for you to decide,' said Robert.

Giving an awkward bow, Hari excused himself and left the room.

As soon as I was sure he was out of earshot, I turned to Robert and told him he had been horribly rude. It was as if he had chosen his words on purpose to provoke.

He shrugged and lit a cigarette.

'I don't understand why you've said those things about Calcutta when I know that you adore it,' I said. 'You were born there, it's home to you.'

But all he could do was shrug again and say that now that Delhi was the capital, Calcutta was unimportant.

'That isn't the point,' I said. 'You have insulted Hari.'

He inhaled, sucking on his cigarette until his cheeks became hollow, held the smoke for a moment, then exhaled for a very long time and said, 'I would prefer you to call Hari by his proper name, Mr—'

'Mitra,' I said.

'Aha!' he said. 'That explains it.'

'What?'

'His attitude, studying at Oxford, that Bengali pride.'

Drawing on his cigarette again, he said that the Mitras were one of Calcutta's oldest families – in his words: 'arrogant and rich'. Most of them were lawyers; he was surprised that 'young Hari' had been allowed to study medicine. It was no surprise on the other hand, that Hari was 'rather above himself'.

'I don't know what you mean,' I said.

There was a pause while Robert carried on smoking.

'What did Hari mean by "partition"?' I asked.

Robert made a careless gesture and said that it had been back in 1905, when Bengal was divided into East and West.

'And what did he mean when he said it didn't work?' I persisted.

'Well,' Robert said, 'people didn't like it. They thought we were setting Hindus against Muslims, and so there was some unrest: boycotts of British goods, terrorist acts, bombs in the streets, that sort of thing. And so after a while the two halves were reunited.'

'So Hari was right: it wasn't a good idea.'

'I don't care to discuss it any further.'

I was left feeling a little confused. Why had Robert been so unpleasant to Hari? It is not the first time I have noticed this kind of attitude towards him. The orderlies are always courteous to our patients, but several times when Hari or another of the medical students have tried to give them instructions, they pretend not to hear or drift away.

I went to find Hari. He was sitting on a bench in the garden, taking short puffs on a cigarette.

I asked if I could sit next to him, and he nodded, not looking me in the eye. I perched on the bench, trying to think of what to say, and then on an impulse asked him for a cigarette. I wanted to do something bad for once, something of which Robert and Colonel MacLeod and all of the rest of them would disapprove.

'You won't like it,' he said, but fumbled in his pocket and gave me a cigarette anyway, then looked on as I fumbled myself, unsure of what to do. When it was lit, I coughed and choked, my eyes streaming from the smoke.

Hari gave a thin smile. 'Let me take that,' he said, removing the cigarette from my fingers.

I tried to say sorry for Robert's behaviour, but my words were inadequate.

'I don't know what has come over him: he isn't always like that.'

'No need to apologize.'

'But I must. I am his fiancée and I feel responsible.'

Hari turned to me, his cheeks flushed, looking as if he were about to say something important, then gave a short shake of his head and asked how long we had been engaged.

'He asked me to marry him two years ago, but I've known him much longer than that. I first met him at a dance when I was just eighteen and out of school.'

He had already been an officer, eight years older and handsome in his uniform. I smiled at the thought of it, then frowned.

'I really can't understand why he was so difficult.'

Hari sighed, and asked if he could tell me a story.

'Before I arrived at Oxford,' he said, 'my cousin, who'd gone up a few years before, told me that the thing to do was to join some societies, where I could make friends. I'd often taken the lead in plays at school, and so I decided to audition for the amateur dramatics society at my college, which was putting on *Oedipus Rex*. I didn't get a leading role, but was happy with my part in the chorus. At the first rehearsal I was confident, but as we went on I realized that the others were trying to stifle their laughter. At the end of the rehearsal, the director asked me to stay behind. He told me that a chorus had to speak in unison, as one voice. I didn't understand at first, and he looked rather awkward then said, "Well, it's your accent, you know. It just won't work." Until then I hadn't known I had one.'

'Oh,' I said, not knowing what else to say.

'Yes,' he said. 'And that was the end of my career as an actor.'

He said that going to Oxford had made him realize the truth: that in the eyes of the British he would always be seen as second-best.

I protested, but he gave me a weary look and said that Indians were tolerated at the university, sometimes even liked, but always kept at a distance.

'It's true,' he said. 'You're the first friend I've had here. I feel as if . . .'

And then he stopped abruptly. The flush in his cheeks had grown darker.

CHAPTER 33

There's a grand mirror that hangs in Edith's hallway, a huge Venetian looking glass with twirls and swirls and crests, humming birds and flowers etched around the border. Last night I took off my clothes and stood in front of it, dressed in just my underwear – an old black bra that had seen better days and an ancient pair of knickers, grey from the wash.

It was always you who wore the nice things, wisps of lace from fancy shops that you hand-washed on Sunday afternoons. You tried to buy me nice lingerie, to make me feel better about what I had to wear on top of it, my everyday uniform of trousers and sturdy shoes, padded jackets, loose shirts. Everything practical: deliberately androgynous, unflattering.

The night before I went to Iraq you gave me a tissue-wrapped package of lace and silk. I said nothing, loving you for trying, sad at how little you knew. I took it with me knowing I'd never wear it, that the hand-washing I'd be doing wasn't the sort to keep it pretty, that it wasn't the kind of thing to hang out to dry in front of the troops.

When I took off my underwear I saw how I'd changed: my hips are curved, a little wobble of fat on either side. My thighs are filling out. For the first time in my life I've got breasts, Suze, breasts! I don't feel quite connected to my body: it's as if it's making this baby without me, while my mind works out if it was something I want.

I'm crossing back over that line from honorary man to woman. I wish you were here to help.

The last time I saw myself naked like that was in Kabul, after a trip to the Bagh-e Babur gardens. Inspired by Amanullah's reminiscences, the next week Rashida and I got Bazir to take us there. I saw the gardens from a long way off, a patch of hopeful green in the Kabul brown, brightening the side of a hill. As we drew closer I was surprised to see crowds.

'Is it always so busy?' I asked.

Rashida smiled. 'It's Friday.'

Ten years before, when I was there with Faisal, it had been a wasteland, all the trees chopped down for firewood by the families who lived among the ruins. Now orchard terraces rose around a central watercourse, all the way up to an elegant white pavilion.

We climbed through rose gardens, past gurgling fountains, children splashing in pools, couples sitting in the shade of trees. Families were spreading picnics out on the grass, three generations together. There was a holiday atmosphere of a sort that I'd never seen before in Kabul, a sense that everyone was there to have a good time.

By the time we got to the top, we were out of breath and giggling, giddy from the exertion and thin air.

'Turn around,' said Rashida.

The gardens spread out before us, surrounded by enormous walls. The river curled past, then came the city, sprawling across to the foot of snow-topped mountains, a vast range, ridged and creased, as if it were made of folded cardboard. I imagined Babur standing with his advisors, looking out onto what was then countryside, deciding that this was the place for his gardens, his last resting place – and then I thought of Edith's favourite Mughal miniatures. This is where it had all begun.

'Where's the grave?' I asked.

Rashida led me behind the pavilion to more terraces, where a little marble mosque stood, three sides open to the elements, next to a dark-green water reservoir.

'The mosque was built by Shah Jahan,' Rashida said. 'The man who built the Taj Mahal.'

Babur's tomb stood behind the mosque, a little farther up the hill, surrounded by a delicate enclosure carved from more marble, with latticed archways allowing a glimpse inside. We stood for a while, listening to birds singing in the fruit trees. Behind the tomb was an inscription.

'What does it say?' I asked.

'If there is a paradise on earth, it is this! It is this! It is this!'

We went back to one of the terraces and sat in the shade of a tree, unpacking our own picnic – fruit and bread we'd bought from a stall at the side of the road. I kicked my sandals off and sat cross-legged, looking out at the gardens below. As the lilting sound of a flute drifted along the terrace, I thought back to that trip to Spain, after Madrid, when we went to the palace of the Alhambra, drifting through Moorish courtyards, listening to the sound of running water, standing hand in hand at the top of the Generalife gardens, looking over at more mountains capped with snow.

'This is lovely,' I said.

Under the next tree a couple sat, murmuring to each other, laughing at private jokes.

'Have you got a boyfriend?' I asked Rashida, without thinking.

She looked a little flustered.

'No,' she said, after a pause.

'Would you like one?'

A little bird flew down next to us. I watched it hop closer, hesitant at first, then bolder, pecking for crumbs in the grass.

'No,' she said. 'Not yet. There's a lot I want to do, Jo-jan. I want a career, like you.'

'Of course,' I said.

'What about you?' she asked.

You always used to challenge me on this one, ask me how the world would ever change if people like me stayed in the closet. And I'd argue that coming out would get in the way of my work. One of the best things about being a woman photographer in a war zone is the access you get that men can't. I'm hardly going to be welcomed in the women's quarters if they think I'm there to seduce them.

Don't assume things, I thought. Rashida's a friend. Give her credit for understanding.

'Well,' I began.

Just then the call to prayer floated through the gardens, carried on the wind. All around us men began to ready themselves, facing towards the top of the gardens, to Mecca. I decided not to risk it.

'I like my career too,' I said. 'And it's meant sacrifices. It's hard to keep a relationship going when you spend most of your time away.'

It wasn't a lie, but it wasn't the truth either. Rashida nodded and I changed the subject. After lunch we went back to town. The gardens were beautiful, but I had work to do.

That afternoon, at the guest house, I downloaded the images from Leila's shoot onto my computer. They were good – we'd been right to keep the curtain: the light was soft, diffused by it. The ones I liked best were of Leila's hands, still elegant despite her scars, her crimson fingertips resting in the folds of her shalwar kameez. But it was the ones of her face that would sell, the ones that editors might put on covers.

I chose six to give to Leila, and went to a photo studio around the corner, which doubled as an internet café. As I waited for the prints, I logged on to a computer to check my email. Immediately, a picture of a woman flashed up: blond hair, pale skin, on her back, her legs spread, fake breasts pointing straight to the ceiling.

A quick check at the browser history showed that the last user wasn't unusual. Apart from email, nearly all the sites last viewed were porn: a woman, sometimes two, on their backs or knees, lips parted, eyes half-closed, looking back at the viewer. I thought of the stares I got from the men on the street, despite my headscarf and careful clothes, and shuddered.

I closed down the computer and waited at the front desk. When the man came back with the prints, I paid him quickly and left.

That night, in my room, I locked the door and put a towel over the window, then stripped off my clothes and stood naked, feeling the air against my skin. The mirror in the bathroom was small and placed high up, as if to discourage vanity. Instead, I set up my tripod, focusing it on the bedroom wall, and then stood, looking into the camera. I thought of Leila, trembling as she posed for me, and of the women on the internet, posing for a living – and then Lara, naked on your sofa, looking back at me, coolly confident, challenging, young.

I pressed the remote shutter release a few times, then took my camera over to the bed and looked at the snaps. My face stared back at me – I'd tried to look neutral, but there was anger in my eyes that I hadn't been able to hide. I'd lost weight, and with it any hint of hips. I went straight up and down, like a boy. I was pleased about that – I didn't want to look like the women in the porn shots. I deleted the pictures from my camera and quickly fell asleep.

The next day I met Rashida and showed her the prints. She was quiet as she studied them closely, then nodded slowly, once.

When Leila opened the package, later that afternoon, she said nothing for a while, and I was worried that they were too much for her to handle. The only mirror in Faisal's house was old and blotched: these were high-definition close-ups.

Eventually, she turned to me, her good eye clouded with tears. Rashida translated as she spoke.

'They're what I wanted. I'm not beautiful, but you've made me into something that people will look at.'

CHAPTER 34

15th April 1915

I am in a dull mood, preoccupied by thoughts of Robert. Something very bad happened to him in France: that is obvious from his manner, from small things, like the way he reaches for a cigarette without realizing that he already has one between his fingers.

This morning we went for a walk along the seafront, an attempt on my part to get him away from the Pavilion and all its reminders of the Front. It was a blustery day, and so we turned away from the sea, out of the wind. It was lovely to walk along the smaller streets, the tiny twittens flanked with flint-fronted cottages. Men pushed handbarrows piled high with fish, calling to housewives to buy the last herrings of the season, a shilling for twenty-four. On the corner stood an organ grinder, cranking out his tunes while a little monkey in a red coat held out a tin for coins. He was very sweet, and I asked Robert for a penny to give to him. When he didn't reply, I looked around and saw that he was clutching at his chest.

There was a little garden in front of us, and I pulled him into it. Gradually his breathing calmed, and the colour came back to his cheeks. I took his hand and asked if he was all right, to which he said: 'I thought I was back in Piccadilly Circus.'

'What?'

'Not that one. We used to name different parts of the trenches after London streets so we knew where to meet each other: Hyde Park, Oxford Street, that sort of thing.'

When I asked what on earth had made him think of that, he said it was the streets, that their narrowness reminded him of the trenches. 'It was as if they were closing in on me. I couldn't see the sky.'

I waited, wanting to hear more, trying to understand.

'It's nothing,' he said eventually. 'Just one of those things one must put up with.'

It didn't seem like nothing to me, but I sensed there was no point in saying so, and we walked back to the Pavilion in silence.

After lunch, I was going about my duties when I noticed someone sitting with two of the patients, talking intently: an older man, well-dressed, with a large moustache and small, wire-rimmed spectacles. Plenty of retired military men come to visit the patients, but this one didn't have the air of a colonel or a brigadier, and I was immediately curious.

I approached the little group and introduced myself. I was astounded when he got to his feet and said: 'Rudyard Kipling, at your service.'

For a moment I faltered, then said: 'Rudyard Kipling? The writer?'

His eyes twinkled behind his spectacles. 'Indeed.'

I immediately told him that I was going to live in India soon, and how much I enjoyed his books, that they were really all I knew of the place.

'Oh, don't believe in everything you read,' he said, with a smile.

I laughed, and asked him what he was doing at the Pavilion, and he replied that he had enormous admiration for the way that our patients were prepared to lay down their lives for Britain. It had been, he said, both his duty and a privilege to talk to them. His son was the same age as some of the men, and about to enlist. He hoped that he would acquit himself as well as they had done. I was amazed to hear that Mr Kipling lived not far away from Brighton, in Burwash. I had imagined him in a bungalow in the foothills of the Himalayas.

On my way back to the Pavilion, I bumped into Robert, who was helping some patients with their letters. I thought the news of our special visitor might cheer him up, and indeed he was impressed to hear about Mr Kipling and asked me all about it, seeming very interested in what I had to say. Encouraged by his reaction, I asked him about his men's progress, and what they had said in their letters.

'They talk about the things that one would expect,' he said. 'How their wounds are healing, how well they are treated at the Pavilion, the battles that have brought them there, that sort of thing. They are rather prone to exaggeration on some fronts. One of them put in a cigarette card with his letter, a copy of a portrait by Joshua Reynolds, saying to his friend that he can procure the lady easily and send her to his village if he wants! Another said – I remember it exactly – "The ladies here are very nice and bestow their favours freely. But contrary to the custom in our country, they do not put their legs over the shoulders when they go with a man." Priceless, isn't it?'

He let out a hearty laugh, then saw my face.

'Do you know what you've just said?' I snapped. 'Or who you're talking to?'

'What?' He blinked, as if I had surprised him.

'I'm not going to repeat it, but Robert, I am worried about you.'

He lit a cigarette.

'I'm perfectly well,' he said, and turned away.

I was angry with Robert after that, as I seem so often to be these days. Since his rudeness to Hari, I had wanted to invite Hari to tea to make up for it, but resisted, knowing that Robert wouldn't like it. Now I went to seek him out.

Hari looked rather taken aback when I asked him, but I carried on regardless. We could go to the Winter Gardens, I said, but he said he had a better idea: he knew of a tearoom in Kemptown that served Indian food.

'Would you like to try it?' he said.

Entirely aware that no one I knew would approve and, in my new, cross mood, not caring a bit, I said that I would.

The tearoom was set back a little way behind St George's Road. I liked it as soon as I set foot inside. It was just one room, simply furnished, rather dark. At first glance it was thoroughly English, with chequered half-curtains up at the windows and prints of Sussex views on the walls, but there was something different about it, which after puzzling for a minute I realized was the smell – a warm, exotic sort of smell, like the one that comes from the Pavilion kitchens, of spices and frying and India.

We took a table at the window, and soon a waitress came to take our order. I told Hari to decide for both of us, and he asked the waitress for a string of things that I had never heard of.

Our tea arrived quickly, accompanied by three plates, one piled with some triangular pastries, another with puffed rice topped with crispy vegetables and the last one with some white, spongy-looking dumplings.

'Try the pastries first,' he said. 'They are called samosas.'

'I recognize the name,' I said. 'You told me about them before.'

Cautiously, I bit into one, trying not to drop crumbs, which was not easy. It was delicious, stuffed with vegetables and spices, but with an aftertaste so hot it made me cough. I tried to hide behind my napkin, as Hari called for a glass of water.

The puffed rice, which he said was a Bombay speciality, was much easier to stomach, tasting slightly of fruit. He told me that they sold them at the beach, in paper cones, so one could eat them as one walked along the sand.

The best, Hari said, he had saved until last: the white balls, called *roshogolla*.

'They're made from cheese and semolina, cooked in syrup. Close your eyes and drop one into your mouth.'

His description did not sound particularly appetizing, but I did as he said. Immediately, sweet juice ran down my throat: a heavenly, sticky mess. When I opened my eyes, Hari was looking at me, smiling.

'Did you like it?' he asked.

I nodded, dabbing at the corners of my mouth with my napkin.

'Delicious,' I said. 'Quite unlike anything I've tasted before.'

His smile grew, and he said he was glad, and he hoped that I approved of his choice.

'It's marvellous,' I said. 'And being here is

marvellous too.' I hesitated for a moment, but then decided to say it. 'It means a great deal to me that you see me as your friend.'

Looking pleased, he said that it meant a great deal to him too, but added that he didn't want to cause any trouble.

'Trouble?'

He nodded, and said quietly, 'Your reputation.'

Suddenly I noticed that sitting at the other tables were other Indians, some of them with their friends, but others with the sort of Brighton ladies that Colonel MacLeod had been so keen to discourage. I remembered how Robert had agreed with him, and felt a flash of defiance.

'Don't worry about that,' I said, taking a sip of tea. 'Now, tell me, how did you come across this tearoom?'

He lit a cigarette and said that someone from the Kitchener had told him: a fellow Bengali, Gautam Dath, a sub-assistant surgeon.

'Not the one who tried to shoot Colonel Seton,' he added with a smile.

One day Gautam Dath had gone into the tearoom and struck up a conversation with the owner, Mr Johnson. Business had slowed down since the war began, and Gautam Dath, who was the son of a successful Calcuttan businessman, had suggested that Mr Johnson might try selling Indian snacks. There were plenty of officers at the Kitchener and the Pavilion who would come there to eat. Gautam Dath had sent down a cook from the Kitchener to teach Mr Johnson how to make them. Word had quickly spread, and business was soon thriving.

'It must have been a blow when Colonel Seton decided to keep his staff locked up in the Kitchener,' I said.

Hari nodded, but then added rather mysteriously: 'Yes, but there are ways of getting out.'

We did not stay at the tearoom much longer, as Mamma was expecting me home, but what little time we had there was delightful. It had been a world away from the formality of the Winter Gardens, and all the better for that. I could not help comparing it to the time that Robert and I had sat on the rooftop, eating sandwiches and discussing the horrors of Neuve-Chapelle. Sitting in the tearoom with Hari had, instead, been fun.

CHAPTER 35

After weeks spent following up my letter to the Ministry of Justice, I found out that the Ministry of the Interior had taken over responsibility for Badam Bagh and that I needed to write to them instead. I wrote. I pleaded. I chased again and again, and eventually they gave me the precious signature at the bottom of my letter.

After that, I had to make my way to the Central Prisons Department, to sweet-talk someone called General Jamshid into counter-signing. The first time I went he wasn't there. The second time he was too busy to see me. But the third time he was there, and signed the grubby piece of paper.

A few days later, Rashida and I went to the prison.

'Do you know what Badam Bagh means?' Rashida asked on the way.

I thought about it. 'Something about gardens? Like the Bagh-e Babur?'

'Jo-jan, you're learning our language!'

'Not sure about that,' I said, smiling. 'Anyway, what does it mean?'

'The Almond Orchard.'

'Wow! In England we usually just call prisons after the place where they're built. Wormwood Scrubs. Pentonville. Holloway. Not quite as poetic.'

'We're a very poetic people,' she said, smiling back.

The car drew up outside a wall topped with rolls of razor wire. We got out and approached the makeshift guardhouse that leant against the prison wall. Around it stood men in uniforms smoking, their guns slung over their shoulders. We showed our papers to one of them, who nodded and led us through a door in the flat metal gate.

There, behind a fence, stood a white three-storey building. Washing hung from every window, bleaching in the sun. As we walked over to yet another gate, I saw that the fence, too, was stuffed with pieces of clothing, tucked in there to dry. Beyond the fence were children playing in the scrubby grass and women hanging more laundry on makeshift lines.

Inside, the corridors echoed with chatter, bursts of laughter, slamming doors. We were shown to the office of the prison commander, who was sitting behind a desk piled with documents held down by paperweights.

I showed him the letter.

'I'd like to talk to some of your prisoners – and, if they're willing, take some photographs.'

'It's not possible today. They are busy.'

'Busy?'

'Yes. Come back another time.'

'But—'

Rashida coughed. I had come to know Rashida's coughs and their different meanings. This one was to tell me to shut up.

'All right,' I said. 'We'll come again tomorrow.'

By the end of the week, I had got to know the commander's office well, particularly his paper-weights, a collection of snow globes from around the world. Just as I was starting to wonder if they were bribes from previous journalists, and if I should go to the bazaar to buy one, his mood suddenly changed and he said we could go in.

We were shown around the prison by the head guard, dressed in a grey prison-issue trouser suit and – to my surprise – no headscarf.

'We are proud of our prison,' she said. 'Many journalists have visited, even the BBC.'

'How many prisoners do you have?' I asked.

'A hundred and twenty-five. Plus their children – there's about forty of them.'

'Why their children?'

'They were born here. There's nowhere else for them to go.'

'And what are the women's crimes? Why are they here?'

'Some of them are in for smuggling drugs, murder, attempted suicide-bombing. Others for moral crimes. Come. See.'

We walked along the corridor, passing through a series of gates that she unlocked with a key hanging from a huge, old-fashioned loop. Small children loitered in doorways, watching us with big, kohl-rimmed eyes, clutching stuffed toys.

The head guard left us in one of the cells, instructing another guard to keep an eye on us. The women were having a beauty session, threading eyebrows, painting each other's toenails.

I looked around the room. An empty bookshelf stood against one of the walls. Four bunk beds were squeezed in at right angles; the women had attached scraps of material across the lower bunks as makeshift curtains.

I'd expected the women to be shy, but they weren't.

'Hi,' I said to the woman doing the threading. 'I'm Jo. What's your name?'

Rashida began to translate.

'Shahzada.'

'And can I ask you why you're here?'

She looked up and grimaced. 'I ran away from home.'

'Why?'

'My husband liked young boys more than me and brought them to the house. When I complained, he beat me. My neighbour helped me escape to my sister's house. My husband called the police and told them I'd committed adultery. I was four months pregnant and he said the baby was the neighbour's. They gave me fifteen years.'

'Do you think he really thought the baby wasn't his?'

She shrugged. 'I don't know. It doesn't matter: it's what he said. My neighbour ended up in prison too. I feel very bad for his wife and children.'

'What happened to the baby?'

She pushed forward a small boy holding a toy giraffe. 'I had him here. It was a difficult birth. I almost died.'

'Has your husband been to visit you?'

She laughed. 'No! But I prefer it that way. I don't want to see him ever again. I'll stay here with my boy—'

The guard interrupted. 'They have a bad attitude,' she said. 'All of them.'

The women turned on her, their voices angry.

'It's true,' she said. 'Ask that one what she did – go on.' She pointed to a sweet-looking girl, very young. 'Gulpari, tell her!'

'What did you do?' I said.

She sighed. 'I killed my husband.'

Although I did my best to hide it, I was shocked. 'What happened?'

'When we first married, he was always kind, but after a long while we were still not blessed with children. We prayed, we even went to the Band-e Amir Lakes in Bamyan Province so I could let the water heal me. But nothing worked. My husband changed. He said he was ashamed to be married to a sterile woman, and he started to beat me. Afterwards he would go out and not come back for hours. I only asked him about it once – he broke my arm. Soon after that, he kicked me in

225

the stomach. The day after, I started to bleed. I had been pregnant, but I lost the baby.

'One night, when he had gone out, I took a poker back to where we slept and kept it next to me. When he came back and fell asleep, I took it and smashed it down on the back of his head – once, twice, I can't remember how many times.

'I slept well that night, because I knew the next day he wouldn't hurt me. When morning came, I ate some food and drank some tea, then waited for someone to come. At the trial they said I was mad, but I wasn't. I just wanted him to stop.' She gave a little shrug. 'So here I am.'

'And now?'

'Now, nothing. Prison's not so different. Here I have to ask permission to do some things, but I had to ask my husband permission for everything. And I couldn't leave the house, either, not without him—'

She stopped abruptly. I felt someone behind me – someone, from the look on the other women's faces, to be reckoned with. I turned to see a large woman with piercing blue eyes. Her arms were covered in rough-looking tattoos. She said something to Rashida.

'She's asking why we're here.'

'Tell her it's to take their pictures.'

The woman said something else, moving her hips suggestively. The others laughed.

'She wants to know if you're going to make them into movie stars,' Rashida said.

'Sorry,' I said. 'Not this time.'

The woman said something else.

'She wants you to take her photograph.'

'What's her story?'

'She killed her husband too.'

'And what had he done to her?'

Rashida asked the woman, who laughed.

'Nothing. She just didn't like him. They had an argument and she stabbed him.'

'Is she sorry?'

When Rashida asked her, the woman snorted, and I knew the answer.

I realized I had no idea what I was going to do with these women or their photographs. Leila had wanted me to use her to show the world what was going on. I doubted they would feel the same.

One of the others spoke, smiling. 'She's asking where your husband is,' said Rashida.

'I haven't got one,' I said.

The woman said something that made them laugh and clap their hands. Even Rashida smiled. 'They said that you are like them.'

I smiled too, feeling as if the shoot might go well after all.

Blue Eyes flicked her eyes towards me and asked Rashida another question.

'She wants to know if you have any cigarettes.'

I'd never smoked in front of Rashida – it seemed somehow unladylike. Don't laugh, Suze, it's true. It's just not done for women to smoke in Kabul, unless they're very poor or very rich or a prostitute, just like it wasn't for Elizabeth. On the other hand, I wanted them to like me. If I could gain their trust, the photos would be better.

I pulled out a packet and handed it over. Blue Eyes threw cigarettes to a couple of the others and lit up. She took a long drag.

'So why do you want to take our pictures? Why us?'

For a moment I hesitated, then came out with it. 'I'm taking photographs of women who've suffered violence from their husbands or their families.'

There was a flurry of discussion between the women.

'Hah!' said one of them, very beautiful except for a jagged scar that stretched the length of her face. 'That could be any woman in here.'

'Any woman in Kabul,' another said.

'Don't you know the saying: "Women belong in the house or in the grave"? If you want more you pay the price.'

'Who would want to see such photographs?' the beautiful woman asked.

'I don't know,' I said. 'I don't know if anyone will. But I think it's worth a try.'

'And then?'

'I don't know that either.'

'You don't know much!'

They laughed again, then talked among themselves.

'All right,' said Blue Eyes. 'You can take our photographs. But make us look good.'

'Great,' I said. 'Just try to act normally. I'll work around you.'

The beauty session began again, and I moved around the room taking a few shots, trying to figure out the light. It was very bright, the sun streaming in through the windows, pooling on the floor.

I wondered about a sequence, starting with Sonia painting Leila's fingernails, her graceful hands with their careful manicure, then more shots of the women in prison, their beauty routines, their nails. It might work, I thought, and so for an hour or so I took as many pictures as I could: close-ups of eyebrows threaded into solid shapes, hair combed smooth, fingernails filed and painted.

At noon the women spread an oilcloth across the floor and set large bowls of rice and meat in the middle. We sat cross-legged around the cloth and ate, forming balls of rice and meat with our fingers. The meat was gristly, the gravy thin and sour.

Afterwards some of the children were taken to the bathroom at the end of the corridor, then put, two to a bunk, to sleep. The women sprawled on the upper bunks or on the floor, staring out of the windows, drowsy in the heavy heat of the afternoon. I took some pictures of them, and then of the yard outside the window, its scrubby grass parched and yellow from the summer sun.

I decided to try a series of portraits, like police mug shots, two views of each woman, front and side, to put together with the women's stories. I spent the rest of the afternoon getting the shots, while Rashida spoke to the women, getting them to tell her what had happened to them. Some showed me their own collections of photographs: wedding snaps, pictures of their children, themselves in happier times, and I took some other, gentler portraits to give to them.

By five o'clock the guards were getting twitchy and I knew it was time to leave. As we left, the stairwells echoed again with the sound of women and children. We passed through the layers of gates and security and finally were back outside the perimeter wall. Bazir was waiting, his car a welcome streak of silver in the dust.

CHAPTER 36

1st May 1915

A terrible day, which has left me more convinced than ever that something is very wrong with Robert.

It began with shocking news: a story in the *Gazette* of an alleged assault on a fifteen-year-old girl by yet another sub-assistant surgeon from the Kitchener. There was great debate in the courtroom over whether she should be believed. She failed to pick him out of a suspects' parade, and her own stepmother gave evidence that she was 'out of control' and prone to 'wandering'. In the end, the surgeon was acquitted. As a medical man and an officer, his word held more weight than that of a girl whose story seemed somewhat fantastical.

Hugo was sent away from the breakfast table, and then Mamma and Papa asked if there was anything they needed to worry about. I reassured them that the Pavilion is very different from the Kitchener. Mamma said that the Kitchener is

231

clearly not a very pleasant place, and Papa harrumphed and said that it is badly run. I tried to point out that the suspect was acquitted, but I could see they were thinking the same as Colonel MacLeod and all the others in charge: that Indians are not to be trusted.

This afternoon, I asked Hari if he thought that the sub-assistant surgeon had done it or that the girl was lying.

'I think,' he said, 'that today is not a good day for you to be seen talking to me.'

I was about to protest when I sensed someone behind me and turned to see Robert, stumbling in my direction, his face flushed, clearly drunk.

'What are you doing here?' I asked.

'I've come to see my men.'

I was at a loss as to what to do, but one thing was certain: it would be a disaster if he were to be seen by Major Williams, or worse, Colonel MacLeod.

'Would you like to take a seat, Sahib?' said Hari. 'Let me get you a chair.'

As Robert faltered, Hari took his arm, at which point Robert jerked away, shouting that he should take his filthy hands off him.

'Sit down,' I said. 'Now.'

He fell into a chair, then sat, staring at us with an expression that had something dark and dangerous behind it.

'We have to get him out,' Hari said in a low voice. 'Do you know where he's lodging? If we can get him into bed he may be able to sleep it off.'

'A boarding house,' I said. 'Not far away, in Kemptown.'

'I'll take him.'

'I'll come too,' I said, frightened of what Robert might do or say without me.

I put my arm through Robert's as if we were going for an afternoon stroll and escorted him through the gardens. It was teatime, and so most of the patients and staff were inside the Pavilion, leaving our path clear, but the drivers were standing next to their vehicles, smoking. When they saw Robert approach, they threw away their cigarettes and stood to attention.

'Sir!'

Robert said nothing, simply swaying from side to side. I explained that he was feeling unwell.

'We're escorting him to his lodgings,' Hari said. 'Perhaps you could help?'

'Of course, Nurse,' said one of the drivers to me.

The drivers sat chattering to each other in the front of the ambulance, while we sat in silence in the back, Robert looking greener by the minute. As we bumped over the potholes, I was frightened that Robert might be sick, but soon we arrived safely at his street.

It was too narrow for the ambulance, and so I told the drivers to wait while we escorted him to the boarding house. As we manoeuvred him along the pavement, a woman came towards us. She looked somewhat bedraggled: her skirts were trailing, her hat askew. When she saw us she broke into a smile.

'Hello dearie,' she said. 'I didn't think I'd be seeing you again so soon – not after last night.'

Robert looked down at her and gave a little groan.

I felt the buildings loom above me, closing in, until I could hardly see the sky, like Robert in the Lanes.

'Madam! I think you are mistaken,' said Hari, and we pulled Robert off the street and into the boarding-house vestibule.

Hari and I said nothing more to each other about it, but I was filled with shame. I may not be very worldly, but I know what sort of woman she was, and that she very clearly knew Robert.

Tonight, as I write, I feel many things. I am still angry, very angry with Robert. I keep thinking of that letter in which he complained of his life here being dull. It seems that he has found a way of making things more interesting, one that does not include me. I am angry at the way he treated Hari, but I am angry with Hari too, for calling him Sahib, for treating him as a master. That isn't fair of me, of course: he was simply trying to help, just as he has done from the very start.

CHAPTER 37

'That prison was hard work,' I said to Rashida the day after our visit to Badam Bagh. 'Let's give ourselves some time off, do something fun.'

'What sort of thing?'

'Is there anywhere else like Bagh-e Babur, somewhere we can relax?'

She thought for a second. 'There's the Qargha Lake. It's a – how do you say? A place where water's kept for people to drink.'

'A reservoir?'

'Yes. That's it. I've been there with my family a few times. The air is clean and there are lots of trees. I think you would like it. But we can't go around there on our own. Bazir would have to come with us.'

'Where is it?'

'About half an hour away, north of the city.'

I hadn't been out of Kabul since I'd arrived three months before. 'Let's go!' I said.

To enter the town we passed under an archway saying 'Welcome to Qargha', in English and Dari.

As we went through the inevitable checkpoint, I felt a sudden sense of space and calm. In contrast to the dusty mountains that surrounded it, the water of the lake was a startling green, speckled with little dots of yellow and red. As we came closer, I realized they were plastic pedalos in the shape of swans, pedalled by couples, wobbling slightly on the waves.

Rashida had been right, the air was definitely cleaner than in Kabul. I breathed it in, filling my lungs, soaking up the holiday atmosphere. Families gathered on the shores, brewing tea and roasting meat on portable gas cookers. Boys hawked balloons from enormous, bobbing bunches, and there was even a stall selling fluffy whirls of candyfloss.

'This is great,' I said.

'I'm glad you like it.'

'What shall we do?'

She pointed to a Ferris wheel by the side of the lake. 'Shall we try out the fairground?'

I tried to hide my shudder. I've always been embarrassed at how scared fairgrounds make me, but I wanted Rashida to have a good time. 'Sure,' I said.

Up close, the Ferris wheel looked pretty rickety.

'Have you been on this before?' I asked.

'Oh yes,' Rashida said.

'Come on then.' I swallowed nervously.

As the wheel turned and we rose higher, my stomach began to churn. The only way to cope with it, I decided, was to take some snaps and try to forget where I was. The views were great, and so were the colours: not just the pedalo swans and the green water of the lake, but the fairground rides and the holiday clothes of the girls who rode on them. I fired off a series of shots, hoping they'd come out well, then turned back to Rashida. She was the happiest I'd ever seen her – eyes bright, cheeks flushed with excitement, her headscarf coming loose in the breeze. I pointed the camera at her and took some snaps.

I was pleased to be back on the ground. Bazir, who had stayed behind, gave me a look as if he understood how I felt.

'Let's get some lunch,' I said. 'Where's good? How about that place over there, right by the water?'

'Do you mind if we go somewhere else?'

'Sure,' I said. 'But why?'

'That's the Spozhmai Hotel. It's a very nice place, I've been there with my family. But . . .'

She hesitated.

'What?'

'Last time we went, there were groups of men drinking beer. The restaurant sells it openly, the waiters carry it on their trays. My father disapproved. I don't think he would like me to go there without him.'

'How about that place next door instead?'

'That looks better.'

We had our own tent at the restaurant, a little

pavilion complete with a red carpet and flowered curtains.

'You have to try the *sheer yakh*,' said Rashida.

'What's that?'

'Ice cream, made by hand. It's famous here.'

And so, after a kebab lunch we did, while Bazir puffed away on a hookah.

'This is fantastic,' I said. 'What's in it?'

'Pistachios,' said Rashida. 'And rose water.'

'What's the spice?'

'Cardamom.'

I felt pretty happy, lying back on the cushions, looking out onto the lake. 'Thanks, Rashida,' I said.

'What for?'

'For everything you've done. For today. We make a good team.'

She blushed. 'Jo-jan—'

'What?'

'I . . . oh, it doesn't matter. Look at that boy, there, on the horse.'

She pointed down to the beach. 'My brothers always like to take out horses when we come here. They ride them through the water.'

Her voice was wistful.

'I always wondered what it would be like to ride one too.'

On our way back to town, Rashida was quiet, staring out of the window.

'Are you all right?' I said.

She inclined her head in a way that could have meant anything.

I waited, looking out of the window too, watching street after street of brown houses and dirt road pass by. The neighbourhood we were passing through wasn't like Qala-e Fatullah or Wazir Akbar Khan. There were more donkeys than cars, carrying bundles of firewood or stacks of grubby plastic containers filled with water. It reminded me of Khoje Bahauddin.

'I have a problem,' Rashida said eventually.

'Tell me.'

'My brothers . . .'

She paused.

I knew that Rashida had three elder brothers: Ahmed, whom I'd met, and two others, one a teacher and another who was in import-export, whatever that meant.

'What is it?'

'They're unhappy.' She stopped again.

'Why?'

'They've been asking questions about our work. What you photograph. Where we go.'

'And?'

'And, well . . . they're unhappy.'

We had arrived at the wedding-hall district. A bride posed for pictures outside one of them next to a stretch limousine. A beggar lay on the ground outside the gates, his trouser legs roughly chopped off to accommodate his stumps, reaching up to guests as they arrived.

Rashida turned to look at me.

'They don't approve of our project. They didn't like that we went to the prison. They said the women in there have done bad things and I shouldn't be mixing with them.'

'But Rashida, you know they're not all criminals. Most of them are in for things like running away from a violent husband.'

She shrugged. 'It doesn't matter to my brothers. Those women have dishonoured their families. They're worried that by mixing with them I'll dishonour myself too, because people will think the worst. That's enough.'

'Even if it's not true?'

'Yes.'

There was a pause.

'There's something else,' she said.

'What's that?'

'My brothers are worried about what will happen after you've gone. When everyone's left.'

'Everyone?'

'The ISAF forces, the NGOs, the journalists. They think the Taliban will start all over again. First they'll punish the people who worked with the foreigners – the drivers, the interpreters, security guards. They'll close down the guest houses where the foreigners stayed. And then they'll move on to the people who spoke on television or wrote for newspapers or took photographs.'

'How would they know about you?'

'They find things out. People talk, they betray each other. That's what happened last time, and it will happen again. There are enough people who would think that these photos are shaming for our country, that Westerners will look at them and say what a terrible place Afghanistan must be if things like this can happen.'

'It *is* terrible that these things happen, though, isn't it?'

There was a pause. '*I* think so, yes. That's why I'm working with you. I think that people should know the truth, but my brothers are right about one thing. The Taliban will come back – and when they do, there will be trouble.'

I didn't know what to say. I could have argued about the importance of bearing witness, of letting the world know what's happening – it's what I've based my whole career on. But I couldn't argue about the Taliban.

'I'm so sorry, Rashida. I love working with you, but I don't want to put you at risk.'

She smiled.

'What do you want to do?' I said.

'I don't know. I need to think about it.'

I went back to the guest house, wondering what to do. Working in Kabul without Rashida would be pretty much impossible, but I didn't want to push her. It was becoming clear to me that there wasn't all that much between a brother's disapproval and ending up in Badam Bagh.

★   ★   ★

241

That night I looked at my pictures of Leila and the prison. They were good – with one more shoot I'd have enough to put together as a feature. I spent the night trying to figure out what that final shoot might be, but came up with nothing. My dreams were filled with visions of barred windows and slammed doors and I was glad when I woke at dawn.

Rashida called soon after breakfast. She sounded odd, her voice strained.

'Are you OK?' I asked.

'Last night I had a call from Gulshan.'

'Gulshan?'

'From the women's refuge, remember? She's spoken to the director and he's agreed to talk to us, today at two o'clock. Perhaps you'll be able to persuade him to let you take some photographs.'

'That's brilliant. Shall we meet outside, five minutes before?'

There was a pause. 'Last night I promised my brothers to stop working with you. I had no choice: they insisted.'

'Ah.'

'I'm so sorry.'

'It's fine. I understand. Don't worry, I'll manage.'

I couldn't keep the disappointment from my voice.

There was another pause.

'I'll come with you one last time, Jo-jan. I want to finish the job.'

'Really? That would be great.'
A small hesitation, then: 'Of course.'
'Thank you, Rashida, thank you so much.'
'I'll see you there.'

CHAPTER 38

ELIZABETH WILLOUGHBY'S DIARY

6th May 1915

A new battle is raging, this time in Ypres. The Germans have a new weapon, poison gas, which is carried on the wind and fills the trenches, forcing the men to climb out into enemy fire or killing them by suffocation. The newspapers are filled with stories of men blinded, wracked by coughing, spitting up blood before a long and painful death.

This morning I came across Hari cleaning his instruments and looking morose. My heart swelled. Since that afternoon with Robert things have been awkward. In part there is a sense of complicity, a secret shared, but it embarrasses us both so much that when we do meet we find it difficult to talk. I miss our conversations. I miss him. And so, when I saw him standing there, frowning as he disinfected a pile of scalpels, I swallowed hard and went to him.

'Are you all right?' I said.

He turned, looking sombre. 'I'm thinking of what we've done with these scalpels. We've cut out the bad bits, made the patients well enough to go back to the Front, but it's even worse for them than before, because now they know what to expect.'

'But don't they want to go?' I asked, cautiously. 'I thought they wanted to die in battle, that it was an honour.'

He sighed and said that it was more complicated than that.

'When the men first go into the army, *izzat* obliges them to fight and to die if required, but once they have fought, their duty is done. If they've been wounded honourably, they don't need to fight again.'

There wasn't much I could think of to say to that.

'They don't want to get well, especially since they heard about the gas. I hate to see the men sitting in their beds or on the garden benches, impressing the visitors by how much they've improved, when what they are really thinking about is what happens next. They're sick with worry: it consumes them day and night. I don't know if I can carry on making them better just so they can be torn apart again.' He shook his head. 'That's not my idea of medicine.'

I was struck by a terrible thought. 'You're not going to leave?'

'Why should I not?'

'The men would miss you dreadfully. It must

be so reassuring for them to be looked after by someone who can talk to them, properly, in their own language. If I were ill abroad, I'd much rather be treated by a doctor who was British.'

He smiled. 'They'd much rather be seen by a British doctor, because the British are in charge.'

'But . . . what else would you do? Where could you go? A field hospital?'

'Too dangerous. It's not very gallant of me, perhaps, but this isn't my war. I've no sense of *izzat* any more, not since working here.'

I couldn't help it. 'Don't go,' I said, in a rush. 'I would miss you very much.'

An odd look came into his eyes.

'Elizabeth,' he said. 'I must speak to you. I care very deeply—'

'Go on,' I said, feeling a little prickle travel up my spine.

'It's about what happened the other day. I haven't been able to put it out of my mind.'

'I wanted to talk about it too. I'm so sorry, I've felt so—'

'Please, Elizabeth. This isn't an easy thing for me to say.'

'Yes?'

Speaking slowly and deliberately, he said that, in his medical opinion, what had happened at the Front had had a terrible effect on Robert. He was suffering, he thought, from something that he had read about in a medical journal called shell shock. If that were the case, I should be careful.

'Careful?'

He nodded and said that marrying a man in that condition would be – he thought for a moment, trying to find the right word – 'unwise'.

I shivered, as if I had caught a sudden chill.

'Don't be ridiculous,' I said. 'You don't know Robert like I do. Besides, you're not fully qualified. You . . . you just don't know.'

Hari looked shocked, as if I had struck him. Quickly, he excused himself and left.

I stood, shaking, unsure as to what had just happened. Why had I reacted that way? After all, I have thought about consulting a doctor on Robert's behalf. He is not Lal Bahadur, with his jolting legs and staring eyes, but something has taken hold of him, that much is certain.

And now I have treated Hari badly, which I bitterly regret. He is the only person I talk to about things that really matter. My work takes up so much time, and my childhood friends have married or moved away. I must confess as well that I have neglected some of those friendships, because it has been clear to me that I was going to leave them anyway, when I married Robert and went to India.

For years I have been waiting for that marriage for my life to truly begin.

But now? What am I waiting for now?

CHAPTER 39

I was lost in thought as Bazir made his way through Kabul's perpetual gridlock – cars pushing through the bumpy streets, claiming every last inch of space, navigating around hawkers, bullock carts, small boys riding bicycles piled high with stacks of bread. I knew that without Rashida I had no hope of ever understanding the place. There wasn't much point in staying without her.

Looking out at the jumble of little stalls and roadside shacks, I realized I'd miss it. I liked the anarchy, the little gestures of refusal, of resistance that kept popping up through the cracks, like the Banksy-style graffiti on the government building that we were passing – a sea of sharp-shouldered women in burqas surrounded by helicopters, dollar signs and poppies.

Getting closer to the refuge, I began to worry that Rashida wouldn't turn up, that her brothers had stopped her from coming. As we crawled through the traffic, I checked my phone constantly, expecting a text to tell me she wouldn't be there. But as we turned the corner onto the road where the refuge was, I saw her, a slight figure in a green shalwar kameez, looking around for me.

Just then, a battered car drove up fast behind her, swerving wildly. As it reached the gates of the refuge, it exploded – a sudden, awful blast of noise and light. The gates blew in: a fireball hurtled towards the building.

I flung open the door and ran to where she had been standing.

'Rashida!' I shouted, but there was nothing left apart from the blackened shell of the car, the driver burnt to death inside.

I skittered about, looking for any trace of her. Then I found it: a hand, with a little gold ring on its index finger.

Everyone in this game has a tipping point, a moment when something changes inside, when you just can't face it any more. That was mine, Suze: I hit it then. For once I didn't pick up my cameras. This was a story I couldn't bear to record.

Soon there were police and officials and onlookers everywhere, shouting, waving their hands, taking pictures on their mobile phones. I was in shock, clutching myself, unable to move, until I noticed a man filming me.

'Fuck off,' I shouted. 'Go away.'

Women from the refuge were led out, their faces blackened with soot, wisps of hair escaping from their headscarves. Some of them held children who were wailing in confusion.

The police began to gather body parts and scraps

of clothing, putting them into transparent plastic bags labelled 'Evidence'. Tears began to slide down my face.

By the time I got back to the guest house, news of the attack had spread around the world. I watched the BBC report on my computer, showing the remains of the car, the blackened porch of the refuge, soldiers with guns keeping guard, groups of men standing about, giving their opinions, or just staring at the camera. The headline kept to the facts:

> Kabul, Afghanistan: Suicide attack on women's refuge claimed by Taliban. Five dead, sixteen injured.

I sat on the bed with my head in my hands. Five dead: Rashida, the refuge guards, the bomber himself. I imagined him driving towards the refuge, negotiating the traffic, inching forward, knowing he wouldn't be driving back. Had he really believed it was a brothel? Did he have a wife he liked to beat who'd left him? Or was he simply following orders? I remembered what Orla had said about feeling safe until something happened. I'd been lulled into a false sense of security. Now it was well and truly gone.

Bazir drove me to the Gandamack Lodge in Wazir Akbar Khan. It was a Thursday night, and that meant a barbecue in the garden and an expat piss-up. The checkpoints and guards and heavy steel doors didn't feel like the usual hassle. I wanted to be safely behind them, away from the rules, to behave as badly as I liked, to forget where I was.

The Gandamack was its usual refined self: a low, white villa with wicker chairs on the veranda and lanterns lighting up the garden. Milling about the barbecue were the people with the money to stay there – mercenaries, spooks, the odd journalist with an expense account – mingling with aid workers, UN staff and diplomats, all young, free and single.

I got myself a beer and lit a cigarette, then wandered around the garden. Pretty soon, I'd finished the beer – a weak import from Dubai – and went to get another.

I'd hoped that Orla would be there, but I couldn't see her. Instead, I bumped into François, a journalist working for *Le Monde*.

'Are you all right, Joséphine?' he asked.

'Not really.'

'That doesn't sound good.' He led me over to the cluster of wicker chairs and muttered something to the men sitting in them. They were happily drunk and got to their feet, making their way back over to the barbecue.

We sat down close enough to put people off joining us.

'What happened?' he said.

251

I told him about Rashida, trying to fight back tears.

François put his hand on my knee. 'Joséphine – this will sound heartless, but it isn't meant that way, OK?'

I nodded.

'We've all lost people. Our job brings trouble. Remember when we were all here together, back in 2001 at the Intercon?'

I nodded again.

'And that noticeboard, covered with tributes to our colleagues who'd been killed?'

'I remember,' I said.

'What I mean is – it happens. Journalists understand the risks. We all know it's part of the job.'

I took a deep drag of my cigarette, then blew the smoke out into the garden, watching it drift away.

'The thing is,' I said, 'those journalists chose to come to Kabul. They were chasing the story. They decided the risks were worth it. Rashida wasn't following a story, not her own one. She was doing it for me.'

'She still chose to do it.'

'She wasn't going to. Her brothers had made her promise to stop, but I got her to come with me, one last time. If it weren't for me, she wouldn't be dead.'

He signalled to a waiter. 'Two brandies.'

Turning back to me, he shook his head. 'Joséphine, you're in shock. But you cannot blame yourself. There's no point. War is like everything else in life: it's about being in the right place at the right time, or the wrong one at the wrong time. It's about chance, and one thing leading to another. That's just the way it is. An Austrian prince takes a wrong turn up a side street, gets shot, World War One begins, bam! See what I mean?'

The waiter brought two glasses of brandy.

'Let's make a toast to your friend,' said François.

Wearily, I raised my glass. 'To Rashida.'

François kept up with me as I drank my way down the bottle of brandy. The garden was buzzing now, full of people clustered into little groups, the conversations louder, interrupted now and then by bursts of laughter.

I looked at François. He was a good-looking man – typically French, I guess you'd say, like in those films you used to drag me to – dark, a little shaggy at the edges, lines around the eyes from laughing a lot and working in sunny places. And for the first time in all my years of leading this crazy way of life, I felt a sudden shiver of some-thing like lust. I imagined myself kissing him, pressing myself against his body, feeling his hands on my back. I felt my cheeks flush, my heart begin to race.

'François . . .' I said.

He drained the rest of his brandy and stood up. 'You must excuse me. I have a reservation for dinner at L'Atmosphère. Just a few people, you'd like them. Do you want to join us?'

I felt a stab of disappointment. There was no way I could sit in a restaurant, pretending to carry on as normal.

'No thanks,' I said. 'I think I'm going to take myself off to bed.'

He kissed me on both cheeks. I fought not to cup his chin and kiss him harder, the way I wanted.

'Goodnight Joséphine,' he said. 'I hope you feel better soon.'

I ordered another brandy and took it out into the garden, away from the lights of the veranda. What am I doing? I thought. Why am I here?

I was restless, pacing around the lawn – *prowling*, I realized suddenly, looking for trouble. My head was pounding, blood coursing through my body.

I spotted a group of men near the barbecue: broad-shouldered, with close-cropped hair. Private security. Mercenaries. Contractors, as they like to call themselves. Unconcerned by ethics, alert to opportunity. Perfect.

Pretty soon I was chatting to one of them. And no, Suze, I don't remember his name. Tall. Strong. Not bad-looking. Not the kind of man I'd ever have given a second glance to.

Not the kind of man I'd ever have given a second glance to?

What the hell am I saying? I haven't slept with a man for twenty years.

Hadn't.

More brandy made me bolder. I was properly drunk now, enough not to care about consequences, enough to make me feel invincible. The pounding was getting stronger, a pulse beat in my hand as I gripped the glass.

He was interested too. I could see it in the way he leant in close as we talked. I wasn't especially flattered – he was drunk too. At least we had that much in common.

'Did you know this isn't the original Gandamack?' he said. 'It's the second.'

'Er, no.'

'The first one was opened just after the fall of the Taliban. By a British cameraman.'

'Oh.'

'Before that it was owned by one of Osama's wives. He used to stay in what's now Room No. 1. Can you imagine?'

'Blimey.'

'I've got a room,' he said, looking at our empty glasses. 'Not Osama's, but it's pretty nice.'

'I'm a lesbian,' I said.

He smirked. 'I don't mind if you don't.'

There's not much point in giving you the details. For the first time that day, the first time since I'd arrived in Kabul, my mind switched off, and I was just a body – and that was all I wanted. Afterwards we had a cigarette but didn't talk much, and then I took a shower, pulled on my clothes and left.

On the way back to the guest house I didn't feel

anything much, apart from sober. Sleeping with him hadn't seemed like a choice, but like something I had to do, right there and then, with no time to think or question or worry about anything else. I'd never felt like that before. I knew it was dangerous.

CHAPTER 40

17th May 1915

I have something very strange and very difficult to admit: I am in love with Hari Mitra.

Just writing it gives me at once a thrill and a pang of regret. Perhaps regret is not the right word. Perhaps it is fear. Perhaps it is anticipation.

Whatever the word, it is something that I know is true and will not go away. It is something that is not new, but which I did not want to see before. This morning, however, it became clear to me.

There has been another battle at Neuve-Chapelle, another slaughter. The Germans were much better prepared than last time, and thousands of our soldiers perished. So many were wounded that it took days to get them to the field ambulances waiting on the second line.

We have been tremendously busy with new patients – so busy that the surgeons have begun to allow their assistants to carry out operations. This morning I entered the theatre and saw Hari treating a patient with horrific wounds, cleaning them out with his fine fingers. The look on his face was one of utter absorption and tenderness. His brows were knitted in concentration, his movements were deliberate, precise, but also fluid, as he worked with absolute confidence. I watched his hands, marvelling at their light precision. I saw that this was a doctor who truly loved his patients, and suddenly I knew that I loved him.

But I am not free to be in love with anyone except Robert. Robert, my whole reason for wanting to work in the Pavilion, the person who first made me excited about India and living somewhere different.

Robert, who is now so very changed.

He is still as handsome, blue-eyed, square-jawed, the very model of a military man. His uniform is impeccable, his boots always shined. He is the perfect product of Wellington College and Sandhurst: a man of honour, valour, grit. He was a fearless leader of his men in the trenches, and remains devoted to them now.

But I have realized the true meaning of the feeling that came over me when Hari told me that marriage to Robert would be unwise. It was the chill of recognition that he was right. There has been a cracking, like a glass that chips, then, at the slightest pressure, one day shatters. Robert has come back damaged from the Front. It is a damage that was imperceptible at first, but then became more evident in his small twitches and odd reactions, and then those horrible stories of what the men had put in their letters home, followed by the final affront, the woman on the street outside his boarding house.

There is a sickness in him, if not in his body, in his mind. This war has broken him: it has got to his very core, and is still there, bubbling away like the gangrene that the surgeons cut from their patients. Robert has become like a patient too, of the worst kind, the sort that will not admit to being ill and refuses the treatment that would save them. As a patient is how I now see him: a patient for whom I feel much tenderness, wanting him to get well. But I no longer see him as a man, as a future husband with whom to spend the rest of my life.

Over the past weeks, the pictures in my head of our life together in India – the touring honeymoon of the great sights, a moonlit walk by the Taj Mahal, summers in the foothills of the Himalayas, children, a boy and a girl, the two of us sitting on a veranda together when we are sixty, watching the sun go down – all those pictures, as clear to me as slides on a magic lantern, have faded one by one and disappeared.

I grieve for those old imaginings as if they had been memories, as if all of that had happened and was then lost. But as those dreams have vanished, new ones have taken their place.

Six months ago Hari would have been part of the background: a nameless Indian. I remember the group of soldiers coming down the station platform and thinking how foreign they looked. I never thought I might have a conversation with one of them, let alone be enchanted by his stories. How foolish I was, how naive.

If Colonel MacLeod or Colonel Campbell were to find out, they would clear their throats and be gruff and pained, and we would both be sent away. They would think I was no better than the women who climbed on the railings to catch a glimpse of the patients.

Perhaps I *am* no better. I no longer care.

Mamma and Papa would care. Papa may well be a matter-of-fact man who talks about all people being the same on the operating table, but I know enough to be sure that such thoughts would disappear were he to be faced with the prospect of an Indian son-in-law.

Son-in-law? What I am thinking, to speak of marriage? I must confess that I have indulged in daydreams, replacing my previous imaginings of Robert and me with ones of Hari and me, disembarking from the boat at Bombay arm in arm, then travelling on the overnight train to Calcutta, the train pushing through the darkness, over the Indian plains, while we sit in our compartment talking tales of Bengal and beyond.

These are wicked thoughts. A week ago, I was preparing to commit myself to Robert for life. I would have stood in a church and made my wedding vows, promising to be with him for better for worse, for richer for poorer, in sickness and in health. Instead, at the first hint of sickness, I am ready to leave.

I may very well be wicked, terribly wicked, to transfer my affections from one man to another with such seeming ease. It is not with ease. I mourn and grieve the one I leave behind. But this war has taught me something: that happiness cannot be counted on: it is fleeting and must be grabbed and held on to.

CHAPTER 41

When I woke up it took me a moment to remember, then I felt an awful, crushing sadness. I lay for a while on the hard bed, my head thudding, sweating out the alcohol, then got up and checked the news on my computer. There wasn't much more, except a confirmation that the bombing had been ordered by the Taliban. An updated body count was given, but no names. I thought of Molly, a decade before, talking to victims' relatives, scribbling furiously in her notebook.

'I always take down names,' she'd said. 'Give a person a name in a news report and they're important. They mean something. That's what you'd want for your family.'

I knew Rashida would have been buried already, following Islamic custom, but I didn't know where. After a while, I phoned Faisal.

It was a difficult conversation. Both of us were close to tears.

'If I hadn't persuaded her to help me that one last time, she'd be alive.'

There was a pause.

'Jo,' he said. 'In that case, I could say that I am guilty too. I recommended Rashida to you. Who can say where anything starts? We just know where it ends.'

'Her brothers won't think like that. Should I contact them? Should I speak to her father?'

There was another pause.

'I don't think that would be wise.'

'Please Faisal, I want to see her grave.'

'I'll find out where it is.'

As I was leaving the guest house to go to the cemetery, I saw that there was a voicemail waiting on my phone.

'Hello Josephine. David Holmes here, a friend of your great-aunt Edith, the executor to her will. I'm afraid I have some bad news. Edith died three days ago, on Monday. The cancer spread very quickly at the end. I'm not quite sure where you are – I know you often work abroad, but the funeral will be on Friday, at the Lawn Memorial Cemetery in Brighton. I do hope you'll be able to come. My telephone number is—'

I cut him off, unable to believe what I was hearing. Edith had never mentioned being ill. When I saw her last, before I left, she'd seemed frail, but no more than usual. I'd brought her a bottle of whisky and we'd sat together, sipping it from crystal tumblers. Had she held me tighter than usual when she'd said goodbye? Had she known it was the last time she'd see me?

Edith. The last one that I could call family. Gone.
The chowkidar beckoned to me.

'Taxi,' he said.

I made my way over to the car. Faisal looked at me and said nothing, probably thinking my tears were for Rashida. I didn't know whom my tears were for any more – they weren't something that could be divided, assigned to an individual.

I pulled my headscarf over my face. 'Come on, Faisal,' I said. 'Let's go.'

The cemetery, in the west of the city, was one of the bleakest places I've ever seen, a wasteland of brown dirt heaped into mounds. No gate, no fence, nothing to show that this was a place to honour the dead. No headstones, no flowers, just pieces of rock, a few poles hung with tattered rags. The only other person there was a woman, kneeling in the earth, her burqa pushed back as she wept with her head on a rock that she gripped with tight, weathered hands.

We made our way across the cemetery, stumbling over rocks and lumps of dirt, trying to avoid the graves. Faisal seemed to know where he was going, and I followed two paces behind, my eyes screwed up against the gritty dust.

Rashida's grave stood out among the others – freshly dug, the earth soft. The mound was very small. I thought of tiny, smiling Rashida, lying there for ever and I began to cry again, for her and for everyone else who'd died: the people I'd

264

worked with, the people I'd photographed, Edith, my sister, Mum and Dad.

I can't do this any more, I thought. I've got to stop. I'm going home.

Leaving Kabul took a while. There were people to see, goodbyes to be said. I went back to the prison, to give the women prints of their photographs, hoping they wouldn't ask about Rashida. I paid a visit to Leila and the rest of Faisal's family. Faisal and I looked at each other helplessly, knowing how much there was to say and how little we would.

'Will you come back?' he asked.

'I don't know,' I said. 'Perhaps, one day, in a while.'

'Will you write?'

'Of course. I'll let you know what happens to Leila's pictures.'

First I had to get myself back home, wherever that was. I'd been in touch with David Holmes to explain that I couldn't go to the funeral. That was when he told me about the flat. As soon as he said it, I thought about hiding out there for a bit.

'Can I do that?' I asked.

'Officially we should wait until probate is granted.'

'How long will that take?'

'It could be six months, even longer.'

'Oh.'

There was a pause. 'Edith was never a stickler for rules. And she was very fond of you. I know you have a key. Why don't you go and look after the place while we sort out the legalities?'

Which is how I ended up in Brighton. Twenty-four hours before, I'd packed up my rucksack and my camera bags, taking only what I needed, leaving books for the guest-house library next to a pile of clothes and odds and ends for the man who cleaned my room. Pulling on jeans and an old hooded top, I paid baksheesh to the sweeper and the chowkidar, then got into a cab.

I didn't go straight to the airport, but to the old city and the house with the high walls. Standing outside it, remembering the peace of that afternoon, the coffee and mulberries, the photo albums of Kabul, I realized I couldn't go in, couldn't face the old man and his grief. I shoved the envelope with the print of Amanullah and Rashida into the hands of the chowkidar together with a dollar bill, and ran back to the taxi.

As we made our way past the roadside stalls and pavement hawkers, ragged boys and stray dogs, I leant my head against the taxi window, thinking of how much and how little the city had changed since I first drove in from the Shomali Plains a decade before. I'd thought there might be hope when I'd seen the crazy wedding halls and all those new blocks of flats. Now all I felt was a heavy, miserable exhaustion.

On the plane, I took off my headscarf and put up my hood, retreating into it, staring out of the window at the mountains. I moved through Dubai airport like a ghost, then spent the flight to Gatwick drinking whisky. A train to Brighton, a cab along the seafront and, well, you know the rest.

CHAPTER 42

22nd May 1915

I have spent the past three days in a horrible state, my mind filled with hopes and their corresponding fears. It is all very well to indulge in daydreams of Hari and me together, of trains to Calcutta and boats to Bombay, but where is my proof that he feels the same?

There was another reason for my reaction when he warned me about Robert. I realize now that I had hoped he might declare his feelings. I find myself going over conversations, looking for clues as to his intentions, but all I find is a collection of incidents, of looks, like the flush in his cheeks when he had called me his friend. 'I feel as if . . .' he had said, and then stopped. What had he meant to say next?

Should I declare myself to him? Until I am certain, I must keep my feelings to myself. Each morning I spend longer than usual at my dressing table, checking my reflection in the looking glass to make sure that there is nothing out of the ordinary about me, that I look like Nurse Elizabeth Willoughby about to start her day at work, no more and no less.

This has not been easy. Each time I catch sight of Hari I have to turn away to catch my breath, to stop myself observing him with surgical scrutiny. I want to know everything about him, to get to know the angles of his face, to determine the exact colour of his eyes, to be sure of which side he parts his hair. It is as if by knowing these things I will possess him and make him properly mine. It is a strange greed, a hunger that shocks me with its intensity.

When I look at Robert now, I feel the opposite. I have spent so many hours gazing at him over afternoon tea, at dinner, at dances. In his absence, I have stared at his photograph, the very one that sits on my night table now. There is no other face that I know as well: the curve of his lip, the length and spacing of his eyelashes, the slight crookedness of his left eyebrow. I know that when he is moved the skin below his ears flushes the faintest of pinks. When he is angry a small pulse beats below his right eye, like the racing heart of a tiny animal. But now I have to force myself to look at him, because to look at him is to remember, and that is painful. I make myself do it, because I am not yet ready to tell him how my feelings have changed. And part of that, I must confess, is for a very simple reason: I am frightened. Of what? Of provoking him, of

269

bringing out the fighting man, the soldier with his head and his heart still in the battlefield. It is as if he is perpetually poised, ready to attack or be attacked.

This morning, when he came to visit the men, I greeted him as usual, careful to give nothing away. He smiled at me: it was one of those rare and special smiles that make his face light up.

'You look beautiful today, Elizabeth.'

I felt myself flush. 'Do I?'

He brought out a bunch of sweet peas from behind his back and said that he was sorry for his behaviour over the past weeks. He hadn't been himself, he knew that, and he wanted to apologize.

I couldn't think of anything to say.

'Elizabeth? Will you forgive me?'

His voice held such hope and such regret and sadness that I found myself saying, with as much sincerity as I could, 'Of course I will, Robert. Of course.'

But it is not a question of forgiveness: that would be a thousand times simpler. The truth is that that this war has changed not just him, but me too. I am not the blushing schoolgirl I was when we met. I am not the nervous fiancée having dinner at the Grand Hotel. Working at the Pavilion has changed me: I notice things; I question them. And I like my work. I like to feel as if I am part of the world, not just an observer.

Has Robert noticed those changes? He has not noticed the most important one of all. I must tell him, I know, and it will feel cruel, the final blow to a man who has suffered so much already.

I have tried to find distraction in my work, but it is proving difficult. This afternoon I arranged for the orderlies to take the patients into the gardens, where we set up the usual card tables and refreshments. It was a beautiful day, sunny and warm. The Sikhs had rolled up the sides of their temple tent, and the sound of their hymns drifted across the gardens, which are now in bloom, with even a few bluebells spread under the trees.

I was pushing a patient to a shady spot when I saw Hari walking along the path, deep in conversation with Atash Khan, one of the Pathans from Robert's regiment. A group of other Pathans was sitting on the grass and, as we passed, one of them began to sing, like an opera singer, with vast, expansive actions, making his fellow patients grin and slap their thighs in appreciation. I thought of how I would like to sit on the grass under a tree with Hari, listening to music. Perhaps he could sing me a song from India, a raga, like the ones he has told me about, different depending on the time of day it is sung.

As Hari and Atash Khan drew closer, the Pathan stopped, listened for a moment, then said something to Hari, and abruptly left him, going instead to join the others.

Hari was left looking rather lost, like a schoolboy whose friend had deserted him. I couldn't prevent myself from going to him.

'Is something wrong?' I asked.

He blinked, as if he were waking from some sort of trance.

'I'm perfectly all right,' he said. 'Thank you all the same.'

I was standing so close that I could smell his hair pomade, something very English that smelt of lavender. It took all my strength not to lean in closer. I wanted to be alone with him, for something to happen, something that would tell me whether or not he felt the same way as me.

'Will you come for a walk?' I asked, surprising myself with my boldness.

'What?' he said. 'Oh. Yes, I suppose so, if you like.'

We began to take a turn around the gardens. Neither of us said anything for a while, then Hari broke the silence by saying that he had been up to the Kitchener to visit Lal Bahadur. Eagerly, I asked how he was. Hari looked grave and said that he was unchanged: most of the time he lay in his twitching state, with occasional fits of the sort that we had seen.

'They dosed him with morphine,' he said, 'to keep him from feeling too much.'

'Sometimes I'd like some morphine for myself,' I blurted out.

Hari looked at me, shocked.

I managed to stammer that sometimes all the suffering that one sees at the Pavilion is too much to bear. I meant nothing of the sort, of course: the feelings I wanted to suppress were all to do with him. I felt an odd thrill, as if I were testing myself, skating close to the edge of a confession, but not quite tipping over.

He frowned. 'Do you know where morphine comes from?'

I thought for a moment, recalling my training. 'Opium?'

'Let me tell you a story.'

A long time ago, in Calcutta, Hari had a friend, Aditya. Their families lived nearby, and the two boys had grown up together. Hari always wanted to be a doctor; Aditya a lawyer, like his father.

The boys had dreamt of going to Oxford together, but Aditya did not pass the entrance examinations. Both of them had been awfully upset and Aditya's father was furious. One day, in the long, terrible build-up to the monsoon season, when the temperatures were at their peak, and the air heavy with damp, teasing the city with the promise of rain, Aditya and Hari had slipped out of Hari's house. Hari did not know where Aditya was taking him.

'Where did you go?' I asked.

'To Bow Bazaar, near Sealdah, one of the biggest railway stations. We were not supposed to go there: it's one of the so called "grey areas" between the

273

Black and White Towns. It's where the Anglo-Indians live, with the Portuguese and the Armenians.'

Hari thought that Aditya might take him to see the dancing girls that Bow Bazaar was famous for, but instead they went down one of the narrow lanes to a door that was painted blue. When, after a long wait, the door was opened, the face that peered from it was Chinese.

Hari had heard of the opium dens in Bow Bazaar, but he had never dreamt of visiting one. For a moment he hesitated. He and Aditya had smoked their first cigarettes together and drunk the whisky that his father kept for guests, but this was much more serious, and Hari was nervous.

'I tried to tell Aditya but all he would say was "please".'

Hari knew how terrible Aditya's disappointment was that he could not go to Oxford. In two months, he would be left behind while Hari went to England. And so, knowing he could not leave him now, he followed Aditya inside.

The room they stepped into was dimly lit. Customers lay on benches covered with thin mattresses, their heads propped up on wadded pillows.

'The heat in the room was unbearable,' Hari said. 'The air was filled with smoke, but not like from cigarettes, a sweeter smell than that. We were given a long pipe each and some little balls made out of something sticky. "It's called Black Earth," Aditya said. "Pure Bengali opium made from poppies grown in fields that the British took from Mughal princes."'

At first Hari had felt strange lying on the thin mattress, in full view of everyone else in the room. But after his first choking pulls on the pipe, he hadn't cared a bit. Instead, he said, he had felt the deepest sense of calm that he had ever known, and had drifted into a hazy bliss.

By the time they left, it was night. They had walked back to Hari's house unsure of what was real and what was not, picking their way over the lines of men who slept at the sides of the streets, seeing things in the shadows that flitted between the houses.

'I never went there again,' Hari said. 'At first Aditya tried to persuade me, but then he gave up and went alone. By the time I left for England he was there every day. He was there the day I left from the station. At the beginning I wrote to him from Oxford, but the replies I got were more and more confused, so I stopped writing.'

'I'm so sorry,' I said.

He shook his head, as if to banish the memory. 'So you see,' he said. 'Never think about taking morphine. When I see the look on some of the patients' faces I can guess what is in their minds. The pain may be taken away for a while, but the drug will bring out the things they saw on the battle-field, and those are not things that one should remember.' There was a pause. 'I would not want that to happen to you.'

I felt humbled by his story. Suddenly I knew that I had to tell him how I felt.

'Hari,' I said. 'Mr Mitra.'

I don't know why I had said Mr Mitra, as if a declaration of love required some degree of formality. I stumbled on, having no real idea of what to say.

'Hari,' I began again. 'Working at the Pavilion has meant a lot to me. In fact, I could say that it has changed everything about my life. And a great deal of that is due to you.'

I paused, wondering if I should continue, my heart thudding in my chest so hard that I almost felt sick from it. 'I really feel as if I must tell you . . .'

And then I stopped. I could not bring myself to say it – not yet.

CHAPTER 43

So there you have it, Susie, now you know. It's not a pretty story, is it? I'm not proud of myself for having sex with the guy, but that's not the point – it's what happened to Rashida, I can't get it out of my head.

I can't sleep – or when I do, the nightmares start. I go to bed wondering which instalment it's going to be, where I'm going to go: Eastern Europe or Africa, desert, jungle or some godforsaken mountain pass. Is it going to be dismemberment or a hanging? Will the soundtrack be screams or shouts, machine-gun fire or, worse, the silence after the final bullet?

The other night I thought of that dinner party we went to after I'd just come back from Liberia – at Charlie and Mo's – when their children came to say goodnight after their bath, dressed in their pyjamas, all excited because they had visitors, and I blurted out, 'Those are the first kids I've seen for months who aren't dead or carrying a gun.'

I knew I mustn't get like that again. I went back to see Florence the doctor. Her first question was pretty direct.

'Are you still considering a termination?' she said. 'If you are, you should make your mind up soon. It's much more straightforward if you do it early.'

I remembered that museum we once went to, the only visitors in a Victorian gentleman's house. The drawing room was silent apart from the ticking of the grandfather clock in the corner. On a shelf, next to the stuffed birds and badger skulls, stood a row of jars filled with clear liquid, each holding a single, floating foetus. Tiny almost-humans stared out, pale and unformed ghosts. We'd argued again the night before about having kids – you desperate, me feeling guilty but unmoved. I stared at the strange, other-worldly little shapes for a long time, trying to think of what to say. When I turned around, your face was streaked with tears.

Now I sat opposite Florence, trying to imagine something like that inside me. She was looking at me with those clever grey eyes of hers. It was making me nervous.

'How are you otherwise?' she asked.

'How do you mean?'

'The last time you were here, you were having some problems. Nightmares, panic attacks.'

'And you asked me about PTSD.' I remembered how angry I'd been.

She nodded. 'So how are you now?'

There was no point in hiding it. 'No more panic attacks. I'm still having the nightmares, but there's a lot on my mind. This is the first time I haven't worked for years. I'm remembering stuff, and a lot of it's pretty bad. But that's my job.'

'There are ways of coping with this kind of thing. I could put you in touch with people who could help.'

'I'll think about it,' I said, knowing that I wouldn't, that it would seem self-indulgent. I'm the one who's here and safe. I'm the one who's still alive.

I decided it was time to get out of Brighton, that a change of scenery might help. I've been working my way through Edith's bookshelves, rediscovering Virginia Woolf – inspired, I thought I'd go to Sissinghurst, to Vita Sackville-West's garden.

Do you remember going to see the film of *Orlando* together on the South Bank on a freezing Sunday afternoon, holding hands throughout the whole thing, loving the whole crazy, gender-bending glory of it, both of us fancying Tilda Swinton like mad? Later, in the summer, we went on a pilgrimage to Vita's gardens, with that amazing tower that made us dizzy when we looked up at it from below and saw the clouds scudding by. The gardens were busy, tourists buzzing around the herbaceous borders like bees. There was that woman, remember, with her husband, going on and on about how terrible the sandwiches were in the café. We followed her up the tower and, as she went up the stairs to look at the view, we pressed

279

our faces against the wrought-iron barrier, peeping through to Vita's writing room and her little library, just a glimpse behind. You slipped your hand into mine and nodded towards the chaise longue covered in yellow velvet corduroy and we giggled, thinking of the coy line in the exhibition we'd seen on our way in: 'Their friendship lasted until Virginia's suicide in 1941, but she never spent a night at Sissinghurst.'

'Afternoon delight,' you whispered, and pinched my bum, just as the woman came back down the stairs, still talking, her husband trailing behind.

This time I was on my own, and it was November, not July. I hired a car, made sandwiches and even filled Edith's Thermos up with coffee. It was a gusty, vicious sort of day, the wind crashing off the sea and up over the Downs, but I felt safe in my little car, tootling along the country lanes, rocking a bit from the gales but happy just to drive with the knowledge that there would be no mines or block-ades in the road. I put on some music and hummed along, thinking of Virginia Woolf driving over from her house in Rodmell, hunched over the wheel. For some reason that's how I picture her: squinting at the road, concentrating hard, although I'm sure she would have had a driver.

Virginia didn't have children. Leonard was too scared of what it might do to her health, mental or otherwise. I wonder how many books she'd have managed to write if she had. Vita had two sons and wrote more than fifty, but I bet she had a nanny. In the end, kids or no kids, Virginia killed herself anyway – oh God, Susie, I don't know. I'm no Virginia Woolf or Vita Sackville-West. I'm just Jo Sinclair, forty and pregnant, and I make a living from taking pictures of the terrible things that people do to one other. I can't even call myself an artist.

It was quite the journey from Sussex to Kent, along twisting roads, through tunnels of trees, bleak without their leaves. Twigs and branches clogged up ditches, felled by gales. As I turned off the road to the little lane that led up to the house, I saw a neatly painted sign:

HOUSE AND GARDENS CLOSED.
ESTATE AND FARM-SHOP OPEN.

I carried on to the car park anyway, cursing myself for not thinking, for not realizing the gardens might be closed. Switching off the engine I sat there, wondering what to do. There didn't seem much point in going back to Brighton, so I rummaged on the back seat for my Thermos and the sandwiches, put them into my rucksack and set off for the house.

The place was deserted – which suited me fine. No tourists in sunglasses and baseball caps, no Bloomsbury aficionados in flowery dresses and wide-brimmed hats. Just me and a nice woman in the ticket office who said I didn't need a ticket to go around the estate or to the exhibition, and that I was free to wander wherever I liked.

I pottered around, admiring the weathered bricks of the castle wall and the sturdy oast houses with their white fins. The exhibition was in one of them. Virginia's old printing press was there too, maybe even the one she used for *Orlando*.

A couple of bookshelves held thrillers and romances on sale for fifty pence, but there was nothing I wanted, so I left the oast house and went over to an archway that looked out onto more fields and vast woodlands. Perching on a bale of straw, I took out the thermos and sandwich, and sat, warming my hands on the cup of steaming coffee, staring at the view. I felt a strange nostalgia for England – an England I've never known and always slightly despised: a National Trustish sort of England, an Edwardian England of afternoon tea and well-clipped lawns, faded rugs and chintz-covered sofas, antique globes in stands. I thought of Mrs Dalloway and young men like Elizabeth's Robert going off 'to save an England which consisted almost entirely of Shakespeare's plays and Miss Isabel Pole in a green dress walking in a square'.

It was a swooping, sad sort of feeling, for something lost for ever. Then I realized. It wasn't for those things, Suze, those things I never knew and never cared about. It was for us.

It was on the way home that I became aware that something was wrong. Driving along, I felt a wetness between my thighs. Looking down I saw a dark stain on my trousers. I swerved off the road onto a verge, fumbled for my phone and dialled Florence's number. It rang four, five, six times.

'Please be there,' I muttered. 'Please, please be there.'

On the seventh ring, she answered.

'Jo!'

'I need your help.'

'What's up?'

'I'm bleeding.'

Her voice turned professional. 'When did it start?'

'Just now.'

'And is it heavy?'

'I don't know.'

'What colour?'

'Colour?'

'Bright-red or brown?'

'Sort of . . . brown. Florence, am I having a miscarriage?'

My heart pounded in my chest as I waited for her to answer. I was sweating, my breath coming in little pants. Despite all my doubts about the baby, I realized I was terrified of losing it.

'I don't know,' she said. 'It's possible. You need to have a scan to see if there's still a heartbeat.'

'Where?'

'The Royal Sussex, it's on Eastern Road, near your flat. Go to the Early Pregnancy Unit, Thomas Kemp Tower.'

'Will you . . . I mean . . . could you come with me?'

There was a pause.

'I'll come,' she said. 'But not as your doctor. As a friend.'

Florence was waiting for me outside the hospital. For a moment we were awkward, then she hugged me close.

'Don't panic,' she said. 'Plenty of women bleed when they're pregnant.'

We went through a series of corridors and stairs, past a chapel smelling of incense and polish, though some swing doors, finally arriving at a crowded waiting room. We signed in and moved towards the rows of chairs.

The afternoon ticked on. The queue moved slowly. As I waited, I thought of the future. And the funny thing was, Suze, the only one I could imagine was with the baby: holding it in my arms, taking it for walks along the seafront, rocking it to sleep. The other future, back on the front line, sweating in forty-degree heat, lugging my cameras through airports, had vanished.

At last, my name was called. Inside the consulting room, the doctor began to ask questions. The first ones were easy, confirming my name, my date of birth, address. Then they got harder.

'Is this your first pregnancy?' the doctor asked.

'Yes.'

'When was your last period?'

I hesitated.

'Mid-August,' said Florence.

The doctor looked from me to her and gave a little smile.

'And why are you here today?'

'I'm bleeding,' I said. 'I think I might be losing it.'

'Not necessarily,' the doctor said. 'Bleeding in the first trimester is quite common. Hop up on the bed and we'll take a look.'

I couldn't decide whether her calmness made me feel angry or reassured.

'Usually we'd do a vaginal scan, but you're around twelve weeks, so I'm going to try your abdomen.'

She pushed my jeans down far enough to make me blush. A dollop of cold gel slapped onto my stomach, then came the ultrasound probe. As she moved it around, pressing harder than I'd expected, a sound filled the room, like horses galloping.

'That's your baby,' she said. 'Good, strong heartbeat.'

My eyes were suddenly wet with tears. Florence squeezed my hand.

'Let's see,' said the doctor, turning the computer screen towards me.

And there it was, like all those pictures of baby scans that people send around on email or post on Facebook: a cone of light shining down on this tiny, curled-up thing, with a head and eyes and even tiny fingers. The difference was that this one was mine. I felt a flash of crazy, stupid love and I knew that I would keep it.

Florence filled out forms and made appointments and arrangements for me to see the midwife. The next six months were planned out, plotted on a calendar – blood tests, measurements, the next scan at twenty weeks. It was the most organized my life had been for years.

I rushed home, filled with sudden purpose. When I got there, I pulled my bags out of the corner and unpacked properly, opening all the pockets, taking off luggage tags, putting everything on the bed. Taking out my cameras, I brushed them off, then held my bags out of the window, shaking them, watching the last of the Kabul dust fly away on the wind.

I threw all my leftover Marlboros in the bin, all except for one. I wanted to smoke it, to say goodbye to my life as it had been. I sat in the Lloyd Loom chair taking long drags, watching the smoke as I exhaled, thinking of all those cigarettes in all those places, another part of the danger, the danger that I secretly loved. I smoked it right down to the stub, then ground it out in the ashtray and sat holding my belly, looking out to sea. All my angst had vanished, replaced by a feeling that everything would be all right.

'It's you and me, kiddo,' I said to my little Afghan bug.

So there we are, Suze. The thing that finally broke us up, that one big difference that we couldn't overcome, the problem we couldn't solve, is happening, despite my best intentions, to me. I couldn't understand your need for it, wouldn't empathize. It was only when it was almost snatched away that I understood. I'm doing this all by myself. Don't think I haven't noticed the irony.

CHAPTER 44

25th May 1915

I find myself shaking as I write this: my pen skitters and slides across the page. I do not want to write it at all, but write it I will, because when I began this diary I said it would be my true and faithful record of the war, and that is what it shall be.

Yesterday, at the end of my shift, I was in the vestibule gathering my coat and hat, when I heard a familiar voice calling my name. I stiffened: it was Hari.

I knew that I had shadows under my eyes from too many nights spent lying awake. He looked even worse: his skin was grey, his eyes bloodshot and swollen. Usually so neat and well-pressed, his clothes were crumpled, as if he had slept in them. I wondered what was wrong.

He asked if he might talk to me, and I said that I was about to go home.

'May I walk with you some of the way?' he said.

There was nothing I could reply to that without being rude, so I nodded, and together we left the Pavilion.

We wandered in silence down to the seafront, awash with afternoon sunlight. It was warm, and people were taking dips in the sea. Usually Hari and I would have walked happily together, our conversation easy and quick, but today we were caught in the sticky mud of embarrassment and floundered there. We were not helped by the curious glances thrown at us by passers-by, who had probably read about the assault on the girl by the sub-assistant surgeon and were making assumptions. If only they knew, I thought to myself, would they feel pity or would they think I was a fool?

We had almost reached Kemptown when he broke the silence.

'Elizabeth. I've been thinking about our conversation in the garden. I believe you were trying to tell me something important.'

I felt a flicker of hope. 'I was.'

'Elizabeth,' he said again, then gestured to a bench. 'Will you sit?'

We sat, looking out onto a flat sea.

'I have felt things . . .' he began, and then stopped.

How could he stop? I wanted to take him and shake him and know for myself if it was anything like what I had felt for him.

'The sea is very blue today,' he said, instead. 'In India we call it the Kala Pani. Black Water. Crossing the Kala Pani to sail to England is a taboo for Hindus. It scares us, because it's supposed to mean the end of reincarnation. After one has crossed it, one's next death will be the last.'

'Does that worry you?'

He shook his head. 'I don't believe in any of that. Even if I did, I wouldn't care: I've always wanted to get away from Calcutta, from my family, from the people who know me. I've always wanted to start again, somewhere new.'

'Why?'

'Do you remember the song the Pathans sung in the garden – the one they found so amusing?'

I nodded, remembering how I had dreamt of lying under a tree with him, listening to Indian ragas.

'The patient I was with, Atash Khan, gave me a translation. It's a famous Pathan song called "Zakhmi Dil", which means "Wounded Heart". It starts like this: "There's a boy across the river with a bottom like a peach. But alas I cannot swim."'

Hari was sweating now: little beads of perspiration glistened on his forehead. 'The Pathans were singing it on purpose. They know things about Atash Khan. They saw him with me and were making a joke about us.'

'What sort of joke?'

'One that wasn't especially funny. I . . . I don't know how to explain it.'

'Don't be like that. Tell me, Hari, please.'

The Pathans had guessed a truth about him, he said, a truth that he had always been careful to hide. It was that truth that he wanted to explain to me now.

'Go on,' I said.

'I have felt things for you . . .' My heart quickened. 'What I mean to say, Elizabeth, is that I have felt things for you that I have not felt for any other woman.'

I felt a glorious, soaring surge of joy.

'Wonderful things. I enjoy our conversations. I look forward to seeing you every day. I feel a tenderness that moves me.'

I turned to him, looking up at this complicated, difficult man, this man I had grown to love.

'But it isn't enough.'

I shrank back as if he had struck me. 'I don't understand.'

He hesitated for a moment, then his words came out in a rush. 'I cannot feel those things for women.'

The sky became suddenly heavy and close – the noise from the beach, children's shrieks, the roar of the waves filled my ears.

'I don't understand,' I whispered again.

Sitting straight-backed, staring out to sea, he asked if I remembered his story about Aditya and the opium. Aditya, he said, had been his great love, from when they were boys. That was the reason he had wanted him to come to Oxford, so that they could be together, away from their families.

That was the reason he had followed him into the opium den. He would have done anything Aditya had asked.

When he had smoked the opium, he said, he had seen things, felt things that had delighted and terrified him. He knew then that he would not be able to keep his feelings to himself for long. And so he had left Aditya to come to Oxford, where he thought he might find someone else to love. He had thought that an intellectual environment might be more – he hesitated – understanding.

'And was it?' I asked, in a voice that did not sound like my own.

'A little.'

'And did you,' I said, my voice cracking, 'find love?'

There was another pause.

'I thought so,' he muttered. 'But he wouldn't be seen with me. It was bad enough to be . . . whatever we were. It was worse to be that with an Indian.'

That was really why he had come to the Pavilion, he confessed, and he was glad he had, because that was where he had found me.

'It has been wonderful,' he said. 'Really. I truly mean it.'

'But not enough,' I said. 'I am not enough.'

I felt a sort of closing-up inside, a smothering disappointment. Getting to my feet, I set off down the promenade. The tears soon came: hot, stinging tears of humiliation as I realized that, despite all my desire to find out more about India, I knew nothing about the world.

I was attracting more glances now, of disapproval, of concern. In an effort to avoid them, I decided to get away from the seafront and make my way home through Kemptown. As I crossed the road, narrowly avoiding a charabanc full of day-trippers, I looked back to where Hari and I had sat. He was still there, still looking out to sea.

I cannot write what happened next, not yet, not now. All I want is sleep. I am horribly tired. I must sleep.

CHAPTER 45

Happy Christmas, Suze! I woke up early this morning, to a choppy sea and heavy clouds, but I didn't let that bother me. I got up, made toast and sat, eating it, watching the seagulls circle in the sky, feeling better than I have for weeks.

Florence had invited me to lunch, but before that I went to put some flowers on Edith's grave.

The taxi driver was chatty. 'You'd be surprised how many people do that at Christmas,' he said. 'Go and see the ones they've lost, make them part of the day.'

We drove past a giant bingo hall, up a hill, past rows and rows of red-brick bungalows and through the Kemptown racecourse. Suddenly we were in the countryside, passing horses munching hay.

I'd braced myself for avenging angels and Victorian cherubs, but instead the cemetery was a field with views across the South Downs, all the way to the sea. The gravestones were laid flat into the ground, but the grass was dotted with giant plastic tulips, petrol-station carnations and miniature Christmas trees, making it look like a crazy, psychedelic summer meadow. As I got closer, I saw that people had left other things to remember their dead: a bottle of Smirnoff Ice to mourn a teenager, solar-powered lanterns to light up a grave at night, a child's windmill turning in the breeze. There were flags in football colours, flapping next to little statues, the kind you find in garden centres: gnomes, mermaids, a Venus with amputated arms.

Families clustered in corners, talking quietly. A group of drag queens who looked as if they hadn't been to bed stood in their party clothes raising champagne flutes to someone called Peaches. I smiled at them as I passed by.

Edith's grave was easy to find, in the newest section of the graveyard: a plain slab of stone – French grey, as you'd have put it – simply cut.

EDITH BARCLAY

1916–2011

IN MEMORIAM

Taking out the poinsettia that I'd brought, I put it at the head of the grave and stood for a moment, remembering.

I took another taxi back to the seafront. Like the cemetery, it was busy, full of joggers and dogs and kids running around, high on Christmas excitement. For once the Pier was silent, its lights turned off, the helter-skelter and the ghost train still, but when I got out of the cab, I saw a crowd gathered on the beach. Most of them were wrapped up warm like me, but shivering on the shore was a huddle of people in swimsuits.

'What's this?' I asked the woman next to me.

'The Christmas Day swim,' she said.

Suddenly, with no announcement, the swimmers dashed into the sea, running through the waves and shrieking at the cold. Most of them ran straight back out again, but some of them dipped down, disappearing under the grey foam. There was clapping and cheering, corks popped and hooters parped. Dogs barked in solidarity, scampering in and out of the water. At that moment, I loved Brighton. Smiling to myself, I set off to Florence's flat, just off the Hove seafront, in a townhouse on the side of a garden square. People milled about on first-floor balconies, laughing and drinking, looking out at the view.

Florence came to the door, a smudge of flour on her cheek.

'Jo!' she said. 'Come in, let me take your coat.'

The room we went into was enormous, a sitting room and kitchen combined, bigger than Edith's flat. It was filled with light, despite the December darkness, the walls, ceiling, floor all painted white, the only colour coming from the spines of books that lined the whole of one wall. A fire was burning in the grate, smelling of apple logs.

A table was laid for six – white china on a red cloth, silver cutlery lined up straight.

Being pregnant was definitely having an effect,

I thought. I'd never taken notice of a table setting before in my life.

I loitered in the kitchen, waiting for Florence to come back. The fridge had photos stuck on the door, and I went close to check them out.

The doorbell buzzed, and voices came from the hallway, then the kitchen was busy with people taking off coats and scarves, pulling bottles from plastic bags.

'This is Jo, everyone,' said Florence. 'Jo, this is Theo and Anna, Lizzie and Claire.'

Theo and Anna were the sort of couple that had grown into looking like each other, sleek and blonde, dressed up for the occasion. Lizzie and Claire were jolly, scruffy, dressed like me in jeans and cosy jumpers. Theo opened a cupboard and took down glasses. Florence popped a cork.

When Theo handed me a drink, I hesitated, then said, 'I can't: I'm pregnant.' It was the first time I'd said it out loud. It felt a bit weird.

Lizzie was the first to speak. 'Wow!'

Claire held up her glass. 'To the baby.'

I felt a combination of embarrassment and strange pride.

'Did it take a long time?' asked Anna.

I didn't want to have a conversation like the ones we used to have at parties, about sperm banks and IVF and the difference in price between clinics in London and flying to Denmark. I blushed and said, 'Er, no.'

★   ★   ★

Florence, it turned out, was a great cook. I concentrated on the food, listening to the others chatter on, but eventually, as I'd known it would, the conversation turned to me.

'What about you, Jo?' asked Theo. 'Florence says you're a war photographer.'

'Yes,' I said. 'Well, so far. I'm . . . I'm trying to figure out what to do next.'

'Because of the baby?'

I nodded. 'Partly.'

'And where were you last?'

'Afghanistan.'

'Tough one. With the troops?'

'No. I've been trying to broaden out a bit.'

She took a sip of wine. 'To what?'

Anna put her arm around her girlfriend. 'Don't worry, Jo, she does this all the time. She's a barrister. She likes to interrogate.'

'It's fine,' I said and, oddly, suddenly it was. 'I was doing a project on domestic violence. There's a lot of it in Afghanistan.'

'Not just there,' said Lizzie. 'I work at the hospital. I see it every Friday night.'

Theo pulled a packet of cigarettes out of her bag.

'Girls!' said Florence. 'Jo's pregnant, remember?'

'Sorry,' said Theo. 'We'll go on the balcony.'

'It's fine,' I said. 'I like the smell. I used to smoke a lot.'

Florence brought an ashtray and they lit up. I gave the air a guilty sniff.

'Did the photos turn out well?' asked Anna.

'I think so,' I said, realizing that I hadn't looked at them since I'd come back.

'What happens now?' asked Florence. She was looking at me – a gentle look, filled with concern. I didn't want her to start going on about post-traumatic stress again.

'What do you mean?' I said, I said, a bit too quickly.

'With the photographs.'

'Mmm,' said Theo. 'I'd love to see them. Are they going to be published soon?'

'I hope so, but I didn't go to Kabul with a commission. I just went out freelance and hoped to find a story. So no one's bought the images yet.'

'Where've you tried?'

There was a pause. I was suddenly ashamed of not having got in touch with my contacts, of not having made the effort to get the pictures published. I'd made a promise to Leila. Rashida had paid with her life.

'I haven't yet,' I said.

'You're pregnant,' said Florence. 'You've had a lot on your mind.'

'I will, though,' I said, quietly, more to convince myself than anyone else.

Later, the others went off to a party. I was going to leave as well, but Florence said softly, 'Why don't you stay a bit longer?'

I sat on the opposite sofa, keeping the coffee table between us.

'They're nice, your friends,' I said.

She smiled. 'They liked you too.'

For a few moments, neither of us spoke. I listened to the rain beating against the window panes, and the wind whistling down the chimney. Inside, everything was peaceful and right, from the steady flames of the candles on the table to the music playing in the background – soft, rippling sounds, gentle strings.

'Jo,' she said quietly. 'I like you a lot.'

Her voice broke the spell.

'I'd better go,' I said. 'It's late.'

As I left, she gave me a hug goodbye. I leant into her, her hair soft against my face, breathing in musky perfume, then I pulled away.

It scares me that she likes me. It scares me that I like her too. You'd tell me to stop thinking and just go for it. Funny how I've spent years doing exactly that in my work, but never managed it in any other part of my life.

You know what I'm going to do before I go to bed? I'm going to water the plants. I've never stayed anywhere long enough to keep plants alive. First time for everything, I guess.

CHAPTER 46

26th May 1915

This is the rest of the story, the part I couldn't finish yesterday. I am going to write it quickly: perhaps that will make it less awful.

I cannot explain why, after leaving Hari, I ended up in the street outside Robert's boarding house, why I walked up the steps and rapped the knocker once, twice, three times.

The landlady was protective of her lodgers and unwilling to call Robert down from his room, but my tears persuaded her, and soon he was beside me, his new, softened self, asking what was wrong. The little sitting room that the landlady had showed us to was filled with gentlemen reading the newspapers, and so, after Robert had explained that I was his fiancée, I found myself climbing the stairs to his room.

It was a nice enough room, which probably had a sea view if you leant out of the window, but I

301

was in no state to do that. Instead, I sat in the chair that Robert steered me into. He sat opposite me; a little table was between us.

'Whatever's the matter, my darling?' Robert said.

I blinked. I had not thought about what I would say to him. I could not tell him the truth. I looked around the room, seeking inspiration.

'Things have been so difficult between us since you've come back from the Front,' I said. 'When you gave me the flowers just the other day it was lovely, but it made me terribly sad because' – here I faltered a little – 'I was sad that things were so bad that you had to apologize.'

Robert nodded, looking grave.

'We've been planning our future for so long,' I continued, 'waiting to make it a reality. When you came back and I saw how much you had changed, I was frightened.'

He looked up at me with sad eyes, like Hari had done just half an hour before. 'I'm sorry,' he said. 'Sometimes it's hard for me to remember that I'm not still at the Front. Sometimes, without a warning, I feel a surge of anger, of madness – just what you need to feel when you are about to go into battle. When it happens, I can't concentrate on anything else: it takes over my whole being.'

'I'm trying to understand,' I said. 'I'm doing my best. But sometimes, when you're back there, and not here with me, I find it so very hard.'

He reached across the table and took my hands in his.

'Let's keep trying, darling. I do care for you, very much.'

I bit my lip and nodded.

As I stood to leave, I let him take me into his arms and kiss me. It was a soft kiss, of the sort he had given me at the end of dozens of dinners or after the theatre – a kiss that did not require anything more from me. I expected then that he would break away and open the door for me to leave, but he didn't. The second kiss was harder, his lips tense. I stiffened, trying to pull away. Our faces parted for a second, and his eyes looked into mine as he whispered my name and kissed me again, harder still.

I was rigid with shock as his hands began to move over my body, caressing my back and the nape of my neck.

'Elizabeth,' he said again, pressing himself closer.

Suddenly, in one quick movement, he lifted me and took me over to the bed. His breathing was urgent now, his eyes glazed. I felt removed from myself, as if I were watching from the ceiling as he lay on top of me, still covering me with kisses, all over my face and down my throat. His hand crept up my stocking, past my garter, around my thigh.

I did not protest, did not cry out, did not resist. Not because I knew there was no point to it, because he had changed to this new, other self, but because I knew that Hari was gone, and so was my chance of getting away, and that we were engaged to be married, and this was how it would be, for ever after.

After all, I had gone to his boarding house. I had knocked on the door. I had come to him.

It hurt, as I had supposed it would on my wedding night. I stared at the picture of a woodpecker on the wall until he was finished. After he had groaned and rolled away, I peeled myself off the bed and stood unsteadily to put on my drawers.

By the time I got home it was late, and Mamma was anxious. I told her there had been an emergency at the hospital. Before supper I locked myself in my room and cleaned myself up at the washstand, then I went downstairs and made conversation with Mamma and Papa.

CHAPTER 47

Poor, poor Elizabeth. Poor Hari. Poor Robert. I feel awful for all of them. Hari forced to come out to Elizabeth; Elizabeth running in shock into the arms of the only other man she trusted; Robert so unhinged from what had happened at the Front. It's a bit too close for comfort, Suze, I don't know if I can read on.

My own news seems tame in comparison. Yesterday I went for another scan. There were measurements and the identification of organs, and reassurances that the right bits were in the right places, then suddenly the shapes and shadows came together and there was my baby, its forehead curving round into a tiny suggestion of a nose, its thumb in its mouth.

'Oh!' I said, stunned at seeing it properly, then it wriggled a bit and went out of view. The nurse laughed and said it was camera-shy, and I laughed too at the thought of that.

I'd forgotten about finding out the sex, hadn't even thought of what I wanted, but as soon as they told me I felt a surge of happiness. I'm going to have a daughter, Suze, a little girl! I'll teach her not to pay attention to any of that rubbish in the papers or on the telly about how she should look or dress or behave. I'll bring her up not to be scared, to believe that she can do anything, not like Elizabeth, thinking her future could only be to marry Robert, not like the women in Badam Bagh, trapped by so many rules and expectations. Not like me, either, who ran so far the other way. Oh I know, she'll probably love pink and want to play with dolls, but wouldn't it be fantastic if she didn't?

Leaving the hospital, I took a walk along the seafront, still smiling, all wrapped up, my belly cosy in the fake-astrakhan coat I bought the other day in a charity shop. I felt like someone out of a Russian novel – more babushka than Anna Karenina, but that was fine with me.

Brighton was even whiter than usual, little flurries of snowflakes tumbling soft out of the sky. I walked along, my boots crunching over the pebbles, hands stuffed deep into my pockets. When I reached the nudist beach, mercifully deserted, I stopped and looked out to sea, and then something wonderful happened, Suze: I felt the baby move, a fluttering, like someone stroking my belly from the inside.

'I'm here, little bug,' I said. 'Not going anywhere.'

Florence came over in the evening for dinner. It was the first time I'd had someone else in the flat, and it was nice, immediately easy. For once, I'd

306

cooked, bœuf bourguignon from Edith's old copy of Elizabeth David. The beef had braised all afternoon, filling the flat with smells that made it feel like home. I'd laid the table properly too, remembering Florence's Christmas effort, putting out napkin rings and silver cutlery. She noticed, as I'd hoped she would, tracing the initials that were etched into the napkin ring with the tip of her finger.

Afterwards she wanted to see my Afghan photos. It was the first time I'd seen the images since I'd edited them in Kabul and they were good: striking, sharp. As we went through them, I told Florence the women's stories. She listened, watching closely, saying nothing, concentrating hard.

The very last photo was a snapshot I'd forgotten about, of Rashida on the Ferris wheel at the Qargha Lake, laughing, her headscarf about to fall off. I thought of her translating at Leila's photo shoot, smiling up at her grandfather, her worry as she told me that her brothers weren't happy with her working, the green shalwar kameez she'd been wearing as I drove up to the refuge. Suddenly I was dizzy and gasping for breath.

I ended up telling Florence all of it, apart from what happened at the Gandamack – not that, not yet. She listened in silence and, when I'd finished, nodded slowly.

'Yes,' she said. 'I can see why you freaked out. But you're getting better. Now you've got to get these pictures seen.'

'It's hard to find the right place. You need the context to make sense of them, but they're more likely to sell just as separate images. But then I'd lose all control. If a magazine used them as a cover, they could put any caption they liked. A feature would be better, but that's almost impossible without a commission.'

She smiled. 'And? You don't strike me as someone who gives up that easily. You're in the second trimester. For the next couple of months you'll be invincible.'

'Invincible?'

'Yep. Trust me, I'm a doctor.'

I sat for a moment, hearing myself breathe, feeling her close to me. Something had shifted. I felt better. Not quite all right, but better. It would do as a start.

And now? Now it's New Year's Eve, the biggest night of the year in a town that loves to party. I'm in my pyjamas, sitting by the fire, a blanket tucked around my legs. I had comfort food for dinner: tinned tomato soup and crackers with cheese. Florence asked me if I wanted to come to a party, but I wanted to be alone. New Year's Eve's a time for nostalgia, even without the whisky. I've been going through Edith's old records, the ones she'd have listened to as a girl – Noël Coward, Cole Porter, the songs you used to tease me for liking. Do you remember dancing to 'Señorita Nina' at that wedding in the Cotswolds, doing a tipsy tango to music that didn't match? I listened to that tonight, and thought of us kissing in a corner of the marquee.

While the music played, I indulged myself, typing my name into Google. I wanted to see myself on Wikipedia, listed for awards, featured in agency archives. I wanted to know that Jo Sinclair still exists and has done OK, even if I'm holed up in my great-aunt's flat, accidentally pregnant and alone.

It was strange to look at my website, a carefully edited account of my life over the last two decades, a roll-call of wars. Bosnia, Chechnya, Sierra Leone. Rwanda, Kosovo, Liberia, Congo. Afghanistan, Côte d'Ivoire, Gaza, Iraq. Hundreds of pictures showing the worst of what people do to one another – or not the worst – not quite. Those are the images I never put on the website, just filed away on my computer and shielded with a password – the ones that are too brutal, the ones that have darkened my soul.

Tonight I forced myself to go through them. Afterwards I hovered over the folder with my mouse, wondering whether or not to click Delete. In the end, I didn't. It wouldn't help – they're etched into my memory for ever – and deleting them seemed somehow a desecration of the people who are in them, the ones who suffered, who died. But I don't need to look at those photos again. I don't need to go to those places again. I'm through.

★　★　★

I've been looking at another folder too, also password-protected, but for different reasons. When we broke up, I put all the photos of us in there together. Hundreds of photos taken by you and me: our holiday snaps, blurry party images, comedy close-ups. The whole glorious series I did of you naked, draped on your studio couch like a modern-day Rokeby Venus.

Tonight I added some more pictures – more naked ones – of me and the bump. I want to remember this, this odd feeling of being taken over from the inside, the little thing that's pushing out my body in weird ways. I'm not that big yet, really – not compared to the pictures I've seen online. I've discovered a whole industry that I never knew existed: women looking dreamy, holding their bellies – lots of draping, windows, shafts of light. Partners too – some looking as if they'd been forced into it, others stripping off and getting right on in there. I put the pictures of me in the folder with our other ones, because it felt as if that's where they would have belonged, if things had happened like you wanted, like they should have done. It seemed like an end to our story, the end we never had.

The last ones I've been looking at are the ones you didn't want me to take, the ones you asked me not to, of the night that we split up.

New Year's Eve 2009. You getting dressed, peering into the bathroom mirror, putting on make-up, doing your hair. Me cleaning my boots, making them shine. Us having dinner before the party.

I still find it odd that you went through the motions of dinner knowing what you were about to do. A sort of last supper, I suppose. Welsh rarebit followed by a chicken casserole you'd made that afternoon. You were beautiful, looking at me with sad, serious eyes, just like the Modigliani print that was hanging on the wall behind you. I tried to jolly you up, to make you forget the argument we'd had the day before about me going back to Iraq. You'd given me a deadline to decide about children. I said I hadn't changed my mind, would never change my mind, that I couldn't, wouldn't do it.

'Let's make our resolutions,' I said, getting down the book that we wrote them in every year.

'Jo,' you said, and it sounded like a warning, but I was so determined to make it better that I ignored you.

'Come on,' I said. 'It'll be fun.'

'I've only got one resolution,' you said.

'What's that?'

'I'm sorry. It's to end things with you.'

And that was that – well, of course it wasn't, not quite. There was silence, then tears, then explanations, recriminations, then you went off, all dolled up in your dress, to Lara, who was waiting, always there instead of leaving like me; Lara, whose mind was on you and not work; Lara, who was young enough and in love enough to talk about babies. Lara, who always listened to what you said.

I can't say I blamed you. I'd have left me too.

★   ★   ★

311

I can hear the fireworks from the Pier. They don't frighten me like before. I'm ready for the New Year, whatever it may bring. How strange finally to feel like this, after so long and after such a lot of angst.

Happy New Year, Suze. I love you. Always will.

CHAPTER 48

26th June 1915

When war begins one knows one's life will change, and that is what has happened to me. Not through the blast of a bomb or being forced to flee my home, but through chance and the vagaries of love. Today I am utterly lost.

My reason for this despair is very simple: I am expecting a child.

After what happened at the boarding house I thought that Robert would stay away from the Pavilion, but instead he has continued to visit every day, talking easily to the patients and behaving as if nothing has happened, so convincingly that I have almost begun to question it myself.

I have sought refuge in work, both from Robert and from Hari. It has been painful for me to look at Hari. I harbour no illusions: his confession was clear enough, but my love for him is not a logical

313

force. I still feel a thrill when he is near; the rest of the time I feel a strange, dull sadness.

It soon became clear that there would be repercussions from the other events of that afternoon. A week ago I began to experience a terrible itch. I knew it was not a thing to take to Dr Findlay, who has known me since I was born, and so I went to a place that I had heard of before the war, when I was working at the hospital, the private practice of a lady doctor.

No matter how often a doctor may say that they are there to treat the failings of a body, it is rare that there is no moral judgement attached; I know that from conversations between my father and his colleagues when they think no one is listening. And so I was nervous in the waiting room. But Dr Martindale was a kindly woman of learned appearance, with her grey hair tied up neatly in a bun and small spectacles perched on the end of her nose. Her rooms were inviting, lined with books and furnished simply with a screen for changing one's clothes, an examination table and a large mahogany desk, like Papa's. It was rather fine to see her, a woman, sit behind it.

The examination was quick. Afterwards, when I had dressed and she was back behind her desk, she looked at me over her spectacles and said that I had contracted a venereal disease.

'Do you know what that means?' she asked.

'I'm a nurse,' I said, trying to hide my horror. 'I do.'

She went to a dispensing cabinet, unlocked it and took out a small bottle, then told me to apply the antiseptic lotion to the affected area twice a day, morning and night, after washing thoroughly with carbolic soap. If the itching persisted or if anything changed for the worse, I was to come back. The disease was not particularly serious, she said, but she wanted to take some blood to rule out the possibility of anything else.

I immediately imagined syphilis: lesions, tremors, daily injections of mercury or arsenic. Was that what she meant? I asked, and she nodded and said that she had taken a sample to test for gonorrhoea too.

I submitted to the blood test, a feeling of terrible shame creeping over me for what I had allowed to happen in the boarding house, combined with burning anger at Robert for what he had done.

As I stood to leave, the doctor cleared her throat and asked if the incident that had led to this might have had other consequences. I did not understand at first, until she asked directly if I might be with child.

'Oh!' I said faintly, and for a while was unable to say much else.

The doctor waited for a moment, looking at me, then asked when the incident had taken place.

I sighed, not wanting to remember, but of course I could: every detail of that afternoon is burnt into my memory.

'The twenty-fifth of May,' I said.

'You are not married?'

'No,' I said, because although a fiancé would have made it better, I did not want to claim Robert as mine.

'You should pay attention to how you feel. If you experience nausea or soreness in your breasts and do not bleed for another month, then it is likely.'

'Is there anything you can do to tell me for certain?'

'I'm sorry: the only way to find out is to wait.'

The next day the sickness came, and with it the realization that my future was set, that no matter how I feel about Hari, no matter how I feel about Robert, no matter how he has changed, my life will be with him and with our child.

I sat in the lavatory in the Pavilion, thinking it all over, looking for answers and finding none. I cannot bring up a child alone. I would have no money and nowhere to live: the shame of it would be too much for Mamma and Papa to bear. After long and painful consideration, I saw that there was no way out. I would have to learn to be like our patients and to accept my fate.

This morning I asked Robert to meet me on the seafront after work. In his new, accommodating way, he agreed, but by the time we met I could see that his mood had changed. I had thought hard about how to break the news to him, but now I knew that nothing would be right, so I decided simply to say it.

'Robert,' I said. 'I have something to tell you.'

His face was dark, and he was frowning. 'I know,' he said. 'It's all so perfectly obvious. I cannot believe I didn't realize before.'

He turned to me, bringing something out of his pocket, which he thrust at me, saying that he had been stupid not to notice what was going on under his nose.

I turned over the piece of paper. It was one of Mr Fry's postcards.

'A.H. Fry, Brighton,' it said, along the bottom, 'Official Photograph.'

Seven of us stood behind the operating table, dressed in our surgical gowns. I was at the end of the line, next to Major Williams, and next to me was Hari. I felt a wave of sadness at the sight of it, and of longing for how we had been at the start of it all, how we had worked side by side and become friends. How strange to be captured for ever, to become part of the history of the Pavilion, with a photograph that says so much and yet, in reality, nothing at all.

Robert jabbed his finger at the postcard.

'You – and that Mr Mitra, who believes himself to be such a gentleman! How could you?'

'What are you talking about?'

'It's quite clear that you've been having a love affair. That's why you've been so distant. That's why you introduced him to me: to put me off the scent.'

My face was burning. 'Don't be ridiculous,' I said.

'Ridiculous? I saw you in the gardens walking together, discussing something that was clearly important.'

I knew I couldn't tell him the truth: that if I ever admitted to how I had felt, it would be the end of everything. As for the rest of it, Hari's own truth, it was not mine to tell. But he persisted, asking about the afternoon when I had come to him.

'What had happened, a lovers' quarrel?'

'Stop shouting, and listen to me! You know very well what happened that afternoon. You are the one who should be ashamed. You took advantage of me, and now there will be consequences.' For a moment I hesitated. 'I'm going to have a baby.'

An extraordinary look passed over his face, a combination of hope and fear and disbelief. Then he said, slowly: 'Is it mine?'

I was so shocked that it took me a moment to answer. When I did, my voice was bitter.

'Of course.'

He began to pace up and down, muttering to himself, occasionally pausing to grip the railings and stare out to sea. Then he turned to me and began to talk very quickly.

'It will be obvious when it's born, that's for sure. If it's mine, I can't abandon it: you're my fiancée, how would that look? It would ruin my reputation and yours.' After a long pause, he added: 'There is only one solution: we must marry, very soon. I'll talk to Colonel Groves about a transfer back to India.' He looked at me: his blue eyes were hard and cold. 'If I find that you have made a fool of me, there will be other consequences, do you understand?'

'Yes, Robert,' I said.

'And I will see to the Bengali.'

I sit here tonight in something of a daze. I don't know if I have done the right thing or not. I wish I could talk to Hari, but that would be impossible. I have made a choice, a hard choice, but one that means some chance of a future. My child will have a father and I a husband, at least of sorts. All I can do is hope that Robert will recover from whatever it is that is making him like this, and that I can forget these few short months when I felt alive in the company of Hari, when for the first time in my life I saw other possibilities. That is my only hope now: that I can try to forget.

CHAPTER 49

I started off the New Year feeling hopeful, determined to get my photographs out there. As soon as I knew people were back in the office, I got on the phone. It was hard going.

'You know, they might work,' said John from one of the big agencies. 'The press is going to want to drum up support for our boys there. The troops aren't looking too great at the moment. The Taliban beating up women would work in their favour.'

'It's not the Taliban who're beating them. It's their husbands.'

'Hmm. Not going to work.'

The magazines weren't much better. After a week of bugging everyone I could think of, all of them had said no. I was sitting in the *gulkhana* with a cup of tea, plotting my next move, when the phone rang. It was Theo.

'I've been talking to Florence. She said you're trying to get your pictures published.'

'I haven't done very well,' I said. 'It's difficult. The press isn't much into Afghan women at the moment.'

'I noticed. It's all about American soldiers pissing on dead Taliban, right?'

I'd seen the YouTube video – four soldiers in combat gear and sunglasses standing over three corpses lying in the dust, legs splayed, clothes torn, plastic sandals dangling off their feet. The soldiers were laughing, playing to the camera as they peed over the bodies, telling them to 'have a great day'.

'I've had an idea,' Theo went on. 'My chambers have handled a few domestic-violence cases. One of them last year was pretty high-profile – a celebrity was involved. I think I could get them to sponsor an exhibition in a London gallery. We've done it before. It went really well.'

'You mean it?' I said, feeling a spark of hope.

'Send them over,' she said. 'Let me have a look.'

As I waited for her to get back to me, I thought it over. It wouldn't be quite what I'd promised Leila, but it would be better than anything I'd managed so far. The only problem was that I've always found exhibitions a bit weird. It's all very well to publish this kind of image in a newspaper, so people know what's going on, but different when they're in some gallery, presented as art.

I tried to explain that to Theo when she called back. She wasn't having any of it.

'Listen,' she said. 'The images are well done. I think your use of light is beautiful. But the words next to them will tell the story, and that'll make the images into something else.'

'But—'

'And how many of the people who see your work in the press remember what they see? An exhibition is much more likely to make them think about it properly, and tell their friends. That's what you want, isn't it?'

'I guess.'

'So will you do it?'

I thought of Leila and Rashida, and the women in Badam Bagh. They wouldn't have been so precious about it, they'd have jumped straight in. She's doing you a favour, I told myself. Take it.

'Yes,' I said. 'And thanks.'

A few days later, Theo called again with details of a gallery in Clerkenwell. They'd had a cancellation for a show supposed to start in six weeks' time. It was last-minute, and I'd be pushed to get it ready, but I jumped at it.

It felt good to get back to work, a different preoccupation, something other than the baby, and I chose the pictures easily. The words were harder: a maximum of three hundred for each image didn't give me space to say much. I began with the mug shots from Badam Bagh, sticking to the facts, hoping they'd be enough to make an impact.

Shahzada, 21: accused of adultery when she ran away from her husband who brought boys to their house for sex. Pregnant at the time, had her son in jail. Sentence: 15 years.

322

Khatira, 26: attempted suicide after five years of beating and slavery inflicted by husband's family. Sentence: 10 years.

Gulpari, 19: convicted of the murder of her husband following years of violence when she couldn't get pregnant. Sentence: life.

Leila's story was harder. I puzzled over it for hours, putting the pictures in different orders, taking out words, adding others. Eventually I went back to my computer, looking through my images to see if there were others I could use. Flicking through them, I noticed the snapshot of Rashida again, the one of her laughing at the fairground. It was completely different to the others, wouldn't go with the series, but I knew I had to put it in as well: Rashida had been behind it all – the photographs wouldn't have existed without her.

Rashida, 24: journalist, fixer, producer. Killed at work in Kabul on 25th August 2011 by a suicide attack.

Today I went to London to see the gallery and visit my favourite framer, who'd said he'd manage to fit me in. It felt odd at first to leave my seaside hideout, but as the train trundled through forests and fields, then suburban allotments and gardens, I felt a rising excitement at being back in the city, the place that I'd left and come back to for twenty years, the place where I got my first commissions, the place where I first met you.

I walked from King's Cross up Gray's Inn Road, thinking of how it had changed since I first arrived at the station, fresh from university, with just a backpack and the Nikon camera that Edith had given me. Some of the old burger joints were still there, blasting out wafts of stale cooking oil, making the bug turn in my belly as I walked past.

The gallery was perfect: light and airy, unpretentious. Theo introduced me to the owner, and we walked around measuring and planning where to hang the photographs. Afterwards, Theo took me for lunch in a café near Lincoln's Inn Fields and talked about the show while I ate steak and chips. I'm always hungry now: the little bug's insatiable.

Theo soon steered the conversation to Florence.

'She likes you a lot, you know.'

I smiled. 'I know.'

'Are you going to do anything about it?'

'Are you always this direct?'

'I'm fond of Florence. And she hasn't been interested in anyone since, well . . . since she had a fling with me a few years ago.'

'With you?'

'Yes. Do you mind?'

I thought about it for a second. 'No.'

'So? What are you going to do about it?'

'Look at me. Five months up the duff. Possibly – according to Florence – suffering from some

324

form of PTSD. Jobless for the foreseeable future. I'm not exactly a catch.'

'Isn't that for her to decide?'

'She doesn't know what she'd be taking on.'

'I'd say she has a pretty good idea.'

Coffee arrived, and we sat sipping it, both of us quiet for a while.

'Do you like her?' Theo said, after a bit.

'Yes,' I said. 'I like her very much.'

'Well, think it over. She's worth it.'

On my way back to Brighton, I leant my head against the window. I don't know what I'm doing, hiding out in Edith's flat, letting the days pass, disconnected from the rest of the world. For all its glitter and razzmatazz, its drag queens and its naughty weekends, Brighton's still a small town by the sea. London feels real, a place of possibility. I've always loved that it's a city where no one cares who you are, where you can make yourself into whatever you want.

But with a child? It wouldn't be like it was before, a place to leave and come back to at will, somewhere to dip in and out of, to get the best of and move on. A child needs dependability, security, things I've never been much good at, things I'm going to have to learn.

I'm scared, Suze, all over again.

I'd brought Elizabeth's diary to read, but I couldn't face it. Instead, I thought of what François said that night at the Gandamack – about chance and circumstance, and being in the right place at the right time or the wrong place at the wrong time. At least I'm not going to be forced into marrying someone I don't love. I've got options. I'm all right.

Just past Hassocks, my phone buzzed: a text from Florence.

'Fancy a coffee?'

Tempted, I smiled, but I was tired and my head too full of thoughts, and so I texted back and said very nicely but definitely no.

CHAPTER 50

ELIZABETH WILLOUGHBY'S DIARY

28th June 1915

Robert meant what he said about 'seeing to' Hari. He has also seen to me.

When I arrived at the Pavilion this morning, I was told to report to Colonel MacLeod at once. He was waiting for me in his office, looking extremely angry.

'What do you know about this?

He pushed a copy of the *Daily Mail* across his desk, open at a page showing a photographer taking a picture of a nurse standing beside the bed of Jemadar Mir Dast, a Pathan who came to us in April after being badly wounded at Ypres. He displayed great bravery that day, leading his platoon and commanding them when no British officers were left. He will be awarded a Victoria Cross in July, which is why the newspaperman was interested in him.

The nurse, of course, was me. I had been posing for Mr Fry, who was taking a photograph of Mir

Dast and myself. Just as Mr Fry was about to take the photograph, the *Daily Mail* photographer had dashed up and taken his own of the three of us.

'It looks as if we're courting publicity,' he said. 'And it looks as if you are actively nursing the patients. You had already been warned, Miss Willoughby, and I'm afraid I have no choice but to dismiss you from your position.'

There seemed little point in further protest. I had no future at the Pavilion anyway, given my condition. I thanked him, stood up, turned and walked out of the door, trying to hold back my tears. Making my way along the corridor with my head down, I bumped into someone: the smell of hair pomade immediately told me who it was.

'Hari,' I said.

'Hello, Elizabeth.'

He looked dreadful, even worse than before, and exhausted, as if he hadn't slept for weeks. I supposed I looked just as bad: a month of worry and sickness had left me crumpled and worn.

'Can I talk to you?' he asked.

We went out into the gardens and found a bench under a tree, away from any overlooking windows. Not that it mattered any more: I no longer had to play by the rules.

'What's the matter?' I said as soon as we sat down.

'You go first.'

I told him what had happened with Colonel MacLeod.

He grimaced and said that he had also seen him this morning, with Colonel Campbell too.

'It was a difficult meeting. Apparently someone has reported that I'm having' – he hesitated – '*relations* with an Englishwoman.'

'Was it Robert who reported you?'

'I don't know,' he said. 'I expect so. They didn't mention you by name, but they made it very clear whom they meant.'

'And what is to happen now?'

'I'm to be sent to the Front.'

I felt a terrible, crushing sensation.

'What? But . . . you're not a soldier.'

'I'll be a medical officer for the Indian Corps,' he said in a shaky voice, 'setting up Regimental Aid Posts.'

'But that's terribly dangerous. You'll be shelled. You could be killed.'

He made a gesture with his hands – of acceptance or defeat, I don't know which – and said that he thought that was the whole point.

'Can they do that?' I stammered. 'Can they make you go?'

He nodded. 'I'm part of the Indian Medical Service. I was granted a temporary commission when I came to the Pavilion, and I won't be given an honourable discharge now.'

I couldn't believe what I was hearing.

'I'll talk to Robert. I'll tell him again that nothing happened between us. Or I could tell him what you told me. That would prove it once and for all.'

'Don't!' he said, urgently. 'Promise me you won't. It would only make it worse.'

'You're facing the possibility of death,' I said. 'It can't be worse than that.'

'What I am is against the law. I'd be sent to prison. Can you imagine an Indian sent to a British jail for a crime like that? I wouldn't last two minutes. At least the other way I have a chance, a small one, but still a chance.'

I suddenly saw that there was a price to be paid for my having broken the rules, for falling in love with him, and that horribly, unforgivably, it was he who would pay it.

I hung my head. He looked at me and smiled, and made that little gesture again, and I knew that I still loved him, and was filled with the most desperate regret.

I found Robert in another part of the gardens, talking to one of the patients. Marching straight up to him, I asked him loudly what he had done, not caring if I made a scene.

He took my arm and led me away.

'Elizabeth.' His voice was calm. 'What do you mean?'

I told him how I had been called to Colonel MacLeod's office that morning, and how he had dismissed me over the photograph in the *Daily Mail*. We both knew, I said, that wasn't the real reason, that the hospital had been photographed since the day it opened. Robert shrugged.

'I've been talking to Hari too,' I said. 'He told me he's being sent away to the Front.'

Robert raised his eyebrows in a way that infuriated me all the more. I felt a deep, unholy rage, wanting to run to him and beat his chest with my fists.

'It's because of you,' I said. 'You're sending him off there, knowing there's a good chance he'll never come back. You're utterly wrong to do it: nothing ever happened between us.'

'I only have your word for that,' he said.

I was outraged. 'And my word is not enough?'

'This is war, Elizabeth,' he replied. 'No one's to be trusted.'

Deciding to change tack, I took a deep breath. 'Robert,' I said gently. 'I'm going to be your wife. I'm carrying your child. Surely you can believe what I say.'

He took my hands, shaking his head. 'Can't you see that it's my duty to protect you, to protect your reputation? Whatever you do reflects on me – and I won't be made a fool. People talk: they've seen you with Hari, laughing together, walking on the seafront. You've shamed yourself, and me as well. I won't stand for it any longer.'

'But nothing ever happened.'

'It doesn't matter whether it happened or not: the question is whether it looks as if it might have done.'

There was a pause, then I tried one last time. 'How can you do this? You have been at the

Front, you have seen what it's like. How can you, in all conscience, send someone into that hell?'

There was again that flash of something awful in his eyes.

'It's what he deserves.'

CHAPTER 51

It took me a while to decide what to wear for the private view – not easy when you're as big as I am now. My belly stuck out high and proud – there was definitely no disguising it. In the end, I cobbled together a version of my usual look for these things – spike heels, black trousers and a jacket with a stretchy T-shirt underneath. The trousers had an elasticated waist and the heels had to go in my bag until I got there, but the overall effect wasn't bad at all.

I caught the train to London early: there was somewhere I wanted to go before the gallery. I took a cab to Fleet Street from the station, feeling a pang of regret as I thought of all those meetings with editors, the planning sessions before a trip.

I paid the driver and slipped into an alley. Suddenly the traffic noise was replaced by birdsong. Just outside the church was a tiny coffee van. The cheery owner smiled and gave me a little biscuit.

'For the baby,' he said.

'Thanks!' I said, touched, and popped it in my mouth.

I stood on the threshold for a moment before I went in. St Bride's Church, designed by Christopher Wren, scene of Samuel Pepys's christening. Scene of too many memorial services for friends killed in the field.

I used to go there before jobs to prepare myself, getting my head around what I was going to see. Now I sat in one of the choir stalls, looking up at the arched ceiling. The church was deserted, apart from a cleaner in a pale-pink tracksuit dusting the altar. In my belly the bug twisted and churned.

Please, I thought, let this be the right thing.

The altar to the left of the nave was covered with a white cloth. On top stood framed pictures: journalists killed in Mogadishu, shot dead in Kyrgyzstan, Somalia, the Afghan province of Uruzgan.

'And the Word was made flesh and dwelt upon us,' said the carving below.

On the wall was a list of people who'd died covering the war in Iraq – correspondents, cameramen, sound recordists, translators – and the names of the places they'd worked for: Al-Jazeera, the BBC, Reuters, *The Washington Post*, *The Boston Globe*, *El Mundo*, Channel 4.

Fumbling in my bag, I brought out the photograph I'd mounted on a piece of card, with Rashida's name below it, her dates and how she died. 'Journalist' I'd put in bold, so she'd be remembered the way she wanted. I propped the photo up with the others on the altar, took a candle from the box and lit it from the flame of another. Fitting it into a holder, I stood still for a moment, remembering.

'Goodbye, Rashida,' I said. 'I'm sorry.'

I'd dithered about inviting journalists and editors that I knew to the show, but then gritted my teeth and fired off a batch of emails. To my amazement, they all came.

The bug caused a bit of a stir. Everyone was trying to be cool, but there were raised eyebrows and confused looks all round. Friends said 'Congratulations' and 'When's it due?' and 'Let's meet up' – and I knew they were dying to know more, but oddly enough I didn't care.

And what was really great, Suze, was that they seemed to like the photographs. They weren't just there for the booze – they weren't just glancing at the pictures and moving off to chat: they were reading the words and looking – properly looking. I made a speech, just a short one, about the women in the photographs, about Leila, Badam Bagh and Rashida, tucking away a mental image of the crowd to report back to Faisal and Leila.

By the end of the evening my heels were killing me, but it didn't matter. I had a pocketful of notes scribbled on the back of business cards, with names of people asking me to call. I'd posed with Theo for the press in front of Leila's picture and given journalists the story behind it. I'd finally kept the promise I'd made to her – and it felt great.

★   ★   ★

I travelled back with the Brighton girls, all on fine form after the free drinks and excitement. As the train rumbled on through the night, one by one they fell asleep, heads resting on each other, coats over their knees against the cold from a window that kept blowing open. Soon Florence and I were the only ones awake.

'How're you doing?' she asked.

I nodded. 'Pretty good. Better than I've been in months.'

She smiled. 'You were great. And they loved your pictures.'

'I was scared. I'm glad.'

'You're pretty impressive, you know,' she said.

When we got to the station there was a discussion about taxis.

'You take it,' she said to the others. 'There isn't space for five. I'll sort myself out.'

The wind was blowing hard, straight off the sea, and funnelled up Queen's Road. I pulled my coat around me, my hands jammed into my pockets. I looked at Florence smiling at me, her hair blowing in the wind.

'Come on,' I said. 'Let's go.'

The next morning – *this* morning, I guess – I lay in bed next to Florence, looking over at Edith's Mughal miniatures on the opposite wall, and felt surprisingly good. Comfortable even, happy.

Florence woke and yawned, then smiled, propping herself on her elbow.

'Morning,' she said.

'Hello.'

She leant over to kiss me and I kissed her back, the pillows collapsing under our combined weight.

'I can do this,' I thought. 'I can be all right.'

Just then, a foot shot out and kicked me from inside. The bug was awake too.

Florence giggled. 'She's jealous!'

The bug kept kicking, churning in my belly. Florence rolled back to her side of the bed and stood up.

'I'll make coffee.'

She walked, naked, to the doorway. 'By the way,' she said. 'Do you always sleep with your passport by the bed?'

I blushed. You remember the drill: passport, wallet, phone – all together on the bedside table so I can stretch out an arm to grab them and run.

'Yes,' I said. 'You never know.'

CHAPTER 52

14th July 1915

Hari was sent to the Front on the hospital train with some of the men that he had helped to heal. I knew that Robert would be watching me in case I tried to slip to the station, and so I had met him the day before. Neither of us had known what to say.

'Will you write?' I asked.

'There's not much point. Robert would intercept any letters, if the censor didn't get me before.'

'I'm so sorry,' I said, knowing my words were not enough.

'I know.'

I kissed Hari on the cheek, and he raised his hand to where my lips had been. As I hurried away, hot tears trickled down my face.

Our miserable little marriage took place last week, in St Matthew's, where I was christened. It was a beautiful summer's day, just as I had always

338

imagined it, and I wore Mamma's veil and her wedding dress, cut down and let out. All the time, as I walked down the aisle on Papa's arm, as I stood next to Robert listening to Reverend Waters, who had held me over the font as a baby, I was thinking that this didn't have to happen, that I could stop it there and then, but when the vicar asked if anyone knew of any just impediment, Robert looked at me, and I swallowed and kept quiet, hating both of us, and said a little prayer for Hari.

Afterwards we went for lunch in a hotel, and no one seemed to notice anything odd about Robert. Later, when it was time for bed, he climbed on top of me, and I lay there thinking of India and wondering if things would be any different there.

India was the reason we gave for getting married now. I don't know how Robert managed to arrange it, just as I don't know how he got Hari sent away. Perhaps his superiors can see that he is erratic and not quite to be trusted, and think he would be less trouble there. Or perhaps they don't see that at all, and think he will be an asset. Who knows, whatever the reason, we are on our way.

I have got what I always dreamt of: a July wedding to Robert, a trunk full of trousseaux, the prospect of a family and an Indian adventure. It is almost comic how dreadful it makes me feel.

Our marriage was reported, just as I hoped all those months ago, in the *Gazette*, in 'Military Weddings'. Apparently I was 'charmingly attired

339

in white with veil to match, in keeping with the beautifully decorated sanctuary'. The presents 'were numerous and useful, including, from the Misses Jenmans and Puttick, a silver butter dish, and from Mrs Meaton silver fish knives and forks'.

It's all packed up in trunks now. I am writing this in our cabin, somewhere near the Horn of Africa. Robert has gone to smoke on deck: the smell of cigarettes makes me feel even worse than the motion of the boat. I cherish my moments without him; I will never forgive him for what he has done. If Hari is killed, Robert will be as responsible for his death as the man who fires the bullet.

I will always remember Hari, the man who brought India alive for me. In Calcutta I will seek out the places he talked of: College Street, the Maidan, the Botanical Gardens, the Oxford Book and Stationery Company. I will venture outside the European parts of town onto the Chitpur Road, and explore the alleys of Bow Bazaar. I will listen out for the monkey wallah's drum and gobble down white balls of *roshogolla*. When the Durga Puja comes, I will go and pay homage to the goddess, even if the other Europeans disapprove.

I feel such a fool to have believed what I read at the beginning of the war, those stories about the Germans' cruelty, those newspaper columns about Good versus Evil. What I have learnt since is that anyone is capable of evil, and no one is completely good.

I have one of Mr Fry's postcards, the one of

Hari and me in the operating theatre, slipped between the pages of this book. From time to time I take it out and look at it, and wonder how things could have been so very different.

CHAPTER 53

This morning I took a bus up past the university, then walked through muddy fields in drizzling rain. Set into the side of a hill were three granite slabs and steps leading to a white dome held up by elegant columns. The Chattri Memorial, built on the spot where they cremated the Sikh and Hindu soldiers, odd in the same way as the Pavilion is odd, a piece of what Edith would have called the Orient in the most English of settings. It was deserted, silent, apart from birdsong and a couple of sheep munching grass.

On the memorial was an inscription:

> To the memory of all Indian soldiers who gave their lives for their King-Emperor in the Great War, this monument, erected on the site of the funeral pyre where the Hindus and Sikhs who died in hospital at Brighton passed through the fire, is in grateful admiration and brotherly affection dedicated.

I stood, looking out at the soft curves of the South Downs, thinking of the soldiers who were burnt on these ghats, so far away from home. I thought of Elizabeth too, crossing the Black Water, the Kala Pani, pregnant with the baby who would become Edith, off to a life in India with a husband she could never love. I thought of damaged Robert and his vicious revenge. I understand him better than I'd like, but it's Hari I feel worst for.

Complicated lives, Suze – and mine's not that much simpler. Will I stay in Brighton? Can I really ignore the thrill I felt on the train to London, that feeling of excitement at being there? What about Florence, who refuses to listen to why I'm such a bad bet? She doesn't seem to care that it might not work out. Perhaps I should learn from Elizabeth's words – happiness cannot be counted on: it's fleeting and must be grabbed and held on to.

And so, my love, I'm not going to write any more. I'm finally going to do what they all said I should – let go and move on.

The call came late on New Year's Day. I was still shut up in our flat, on the sofa, staring into space, working my way down a bottle of whisky. I'd spoken to no one since you'd left, ignored all the New Year's texts, but when the phone rang and it was Charlie, I picked up.

You were hit by a car that was going too fast, the wrong way up the street, the driver still drunk from the night before. Death on impact, the coroner said later. Three short words. Such a horribly efficient way to describe the end of a life.

343

I raged for months. I raged at God and fate and all those things that I've never believed in, at the sheer, bloody unfairness of it all. I was the one who took the risks. It should have been me who ended up dead, not you. I raged at myself, too, for pushing you away, for not doing enough to keep you. Afterwards, I put myself in stupid situations because I didn't care any more if I lived or died, because if you hadn't left that night, you wouldn't have been on that street, Lara's street: you would have been with me.

That's all over now. I guess I'm becoming the person you always wanted. I'm just sorry not to be doing it with you.

Please know that I always loved you. I promise I'll always remember.

Goodnight, Susie, my love, goodnight.